READ SERIES IN

MW01268218

JUDGMENT

is Book 3 of the Angel Sagas and After Life series.

The sought-for freedom of Lumine and his followers has turned into a nightmare and mutiny is in the air. Now with the revelation they may not return only one course of action is possible to save his Kingdom. But would he dare lead them to do the unthinkable?

Welcome to the Judgment.

Part Two tells the cautionary tale of the After Life Journey of slick mob lawyer, James.

James spends his life doing good for very bad people. One day, he goes too far and he must face the music in more ways than one.

Also by D.P. Conway

Plus
Starry Night, A Magical Tale
Free at the end of this book

Judgment

The Angel Sagas

&

The Journey of James

by D. P. Conway

After Life Series
Book 3

What is the After Life Series

This is the start of an epic story of Lords, Angels, Dark Angels, and Humans. There are two types of stories in the series: The Angel Sagas and the After Life Journeys.

THE ANGEL SAGAS tell the story of Creation from the beginning of time to the coming end of time. Long before the earth, or Adam and Eve were created, the Lords created the male and female Angels and the Heavens where they were supposed to live in harmony.

But when the Dark Lord rises and discontent is sown, the dreams of the Lords begin to fall apart, and everyone must choose a side. The Archangel Sagas spans all 15 books, but in books 1 through 12, the exciting After Life Journeys of our Human characters are also presented.

THE AFTER LIFE JOURNEYS dramatically tell individual tales of 15 modern-day people's lives and journeys to the After Life. There is an autistic young man, a mob lawyer, a girl with Rett's disease, a middle-aged divorcee, a rigid Baptist preacher, a U.S. Senator, a Muslim American soldier, a woman who suffers abuse as a child, and even an avowed atheist who survived the shark-infested waters after the sinking of the U.S.S. Indianapolis.

Each person lives life the best they can, but suddenly, and often unexpectedly, death crashes into their plans. Many never get to say goodbye or attain the hopes and dreams they often desperately desired.

Some are cautionary tales, like the mob lawyer's story. Even the 9/11 hijackers are addressed in book 12, because the series is not only about Heaven but also about Hell, and about a place in between, for those who don't quite fit into Heaven or Hell. The series is about second chances, and life on the other side, a life we all someday want.

All 15 human stories converge in the last three books of the series, as the Angels, the Heavens, and the Earth race toward their destiny, and all are hurled toward the final showdown between good and evil.

Now, I invite you to sit back… and let me tell you a story.

D.P. Conway Advent Season during the Great Pandemic

Books in the After Life Series (Read in Order)

Book 1: Dawn of Days
The Angel Sagas & Journey of Nancy

Book 2: Rebellion
The Angel Sagas & the Journey of Duncan

Book 3: Judgment
The Angel Sagas & the Journey of James

Book 4: Empire
The Angel Sagas & the Journey of Julie

Book 5: The Innocents
The Angel Sagas & the Journey of Laura

Book 6: Revelation
The Angel Sagas & the Journey of Katie

Book 7: Memento Vivere
The Angel Sagas & the Journey of Susan

Book 8: Rise of Legion
The Angel Sagas & the Journey of Brittany

Book 9: Revenge of the Damned
The Angel Sagas & the Journey of Jill

Book 10: Crucible
The Angel Sagas & the Journey of Kyle

Book 11: Deliverance
The Angel Sagas & the Journey of Lena

Book 12 : Title to Be Determined
The Angel Sagas & the Journey of John

Book 13: Title to Be Determined
Series Conclusion Part 1

Book 14: Prophecy
Series Conclusion Part 2

Book 15: Kingdom Come
Series Conclusion Part 3

AFTER LIFE CHARACTERS - HUMANS & THEIR GUARDIAN ANGELS

JULIE

Julie is a middle age woman who, due to the lack of affections from her husband, becomes discontent in her marriage and is tempted to go outside the boundaries to meet her needs.

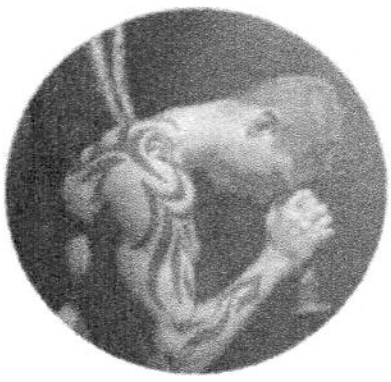

ANGEL JARIO

Angel in the 1st Heavenly Realm.

Julie's Guardian Angel

DUNCAN

Duncan is a young man with severe Autism who one day meets a special visitor who changes his destiny forever.

ANGEL LINDA

Angel in the 5th Heavenly Realm

Duncan's Guardian Angel

LAURA

Laura is the principal of an elementary school, who leads the fight in stopping an unprecedented attack on her, her peers, and her innocent young students.

ANGEL JOSEPH

Angel of the 4th Heavenly Realm.

Laura's Guardian Angel

AMIR

Amir, a young American Muslim who is caught up in the tide of resentment after 9/11, goes the extra mile to save his fellow soldiers

ANGEL SADIE

Host Commander in the 5th Heavenly Realm

Amir's Guardian Angel

JAMES

James is a crooked mob lawyer who goes too far in defending his boss against a rival mob family.

ANGEL MERCIO

Host Commander in the 5th Heavenly Realm

James' Guardian Angel

KATIE

Katie, a young girl whose dreams of love and happiness are threatened by a terrible disease, discovers a destiny she never imagined.

ANGEL ROSIE

Host Commander in the 3rd Heavenly Realm

Katie's Guardian Angel

AFTER LIFE CHARACTERS - HUMANS & THEIR GUARDIAN ANGELS

BRITTANY

Brittany, abandoned by her father, is an emotionally troubled teen who becomes the girlfriend of a gang leader.

ANGEL CAROLYN

Angel in the 2nd Heavenly Realm

Brittany's Guardian Angel

NANCY

Nancy, an old woman in a nursing home, is visited by a special person and reminisces back to the days when America was shaped by the Great Depression.

ANGEL THOMAS

Angel in the 4th Heavenly Realm

Nancy's Guardian Angel

JOHN

John is a WWII veteran who loses so much during the war that is sends him on a journey few could imagine taking.

ANGEL MARY LEE

Angel in the 7th Heavenly Realm

John's Guardian Angel

JILL & GIRLS

Jill and her daughters are faced with an unbelievable nightmare which will ultimately lead to something they never expected.

ANGEL VERIA

Angel in the 6th Heavenly Realm

Jill's Guardian Angel

APRIL

April is a young African American girl with special promise who is asaulted at a party and loses sight of all her dreams.

ANGEL DARIAN

Angel in the 1st Heavenly Realm

April's Guardian Angel

RICK

Rick is an American Baptist preacher who learns that there is more to life than he was taught to believe.

ANGEL INDIRA

Angel in the 7th Heavenly Realm

Rick's Guardian Angel

AFTER LIFE CHARACTERS - HUMANS & THEIR GUARDIAN ANGELS

KYLE

Kyle is an American man who was plagued with an addiction that is threatening to dissolve his marriage.

ANGEL RAFIELA

Angel in the 3rd Heavenly Realm

Kyle's Guardian Angel

LINA

Lina is the daughter of Italian immigrants who faces a private ordeal, as well as circumstances that challenge her will to live.

ANGEL MARCO

Angel in the 6th Heavenly Realm

Lina's Guardian Angel

SENATOR SUSAN

Senator Susan Davis is the daughter of a Jewish Rabbi. She becomes a Senator and now must face a personal show down involving her families long held beliefs.

ANGEL DAVID

Angel in the 3rd Heavenly Realm

Susan's Guardian Angel

AFTER LIFE CHARACTERS - THE LORDS

ADON

Ancient hunter, Lord of the Forest, and Lord of the Heavens and the Earth. Loving, caring, realistic as to what must be done for their plan to work out.

CALLA

Lord of the Wind and Sky, and Lord of the Heavens and the Earth. Loved intensely for her soft feminine beauty, and respected for her fierce warrior instincts.

YESHUA

Lord of the Sea and Lord of the Heavens and the Earth. The steadying force in the relationship with the other Lords. Tall, athletic, muscular, and closely attuned to the needs of the other Lords.

LEGION

The mysterious, dark, 4th Lord, created as an opposite reaction by the collective will of the Lords during the act of the 1st Creation.

AFTER LIFE CHARACTERS - THE ARCHANGELS

1st of the Archangels.

Caught up in an age, old love affair with her first love, Luminé.

SPLENDORA

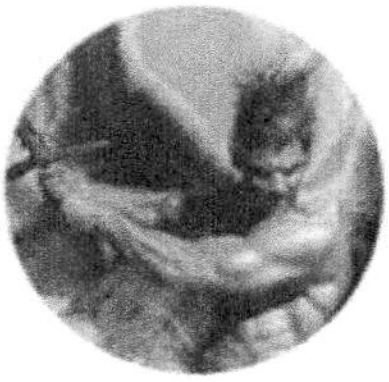

The most popular Angel in the Heavens.

Leader of the 2nd Heavenly Realm, and one of the favorites of the Lords.

LUMINE

3rd of the Archangels.

Tall, muscular, among the greatest warriors in the Heavens.

MICHAEL

Archangel of the 4th Heavenly Realm.

A charismatic, strong, and brave warrior.

RAPHAEL

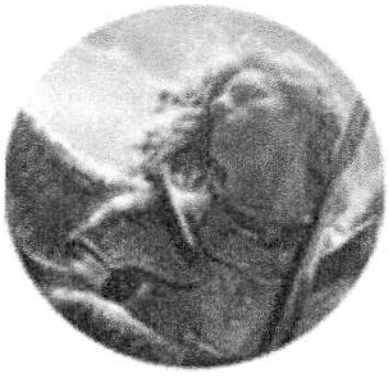

Archangel of the 5th Heavenly Realm.

Wisest of the Archangels.

Leader of 1st Special Mission Angel Team.

GABRIEL

Archangel of the 6th Heavenly Realm.

Secretly in love with the leader of the Dark forces.

RANA

AFTER LIFE CHARACTERS - IRISH ANGEL BIRGADE

Fearless leader of the Irish Brigade who camps atop Slie Mor mountain and are known for their bravery in fighting the forces of Darkness

DANIEL

2nd in command of the Irish Brigade and not always in agreement with his leader.

ANGUS

Fierce warrior for centuries as a member of the Irish Brigade.

ANNIE

AFTER LIFE CHARACTERS - THE DARK ANGELS

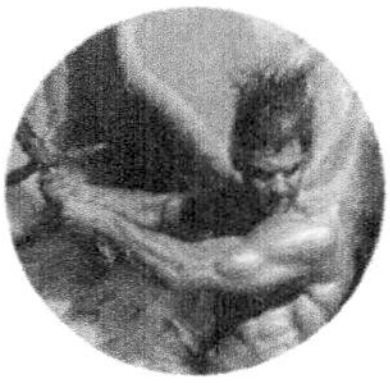

Lumine is the leader of the Dark Angels and finds that what he has so desperately sought is not what he was looking for.

LUMINE

Oxana finds her way to the pinnacle of power only to realize she needs more.

OXANA

Antonio is the most trusted commander in Luminare but discontent leads him to do the unthinkable.

ANTONIO

The Dark Fourth Lord is able to transform his appearance at will.

LEGION TRANSFORMED

Sylvia does what she must to survive in Luminare and becomes a servant to Legion.

SYLVIA

Sansa becomes one of Legion's favorite consorts and is forced to do his dark deeds.

SANSA

Tira finds herself caught up in the epic struggle of evil in Luminare.

TIRA

Thomas finds himself trapped in Luminare and faces a day he never dreamed of.

THOMAS

Jasper finds himself trapped under the dome and must decide if he will stay or escape.

JASPER

Sparkis finds himself in partnership with a most unlikely Dark Angel and must decide if he will cooperate till the end.

SPARKIS

Nina is tasked for a special mission she neither wants nor can fail in if she is to survive.

NINA

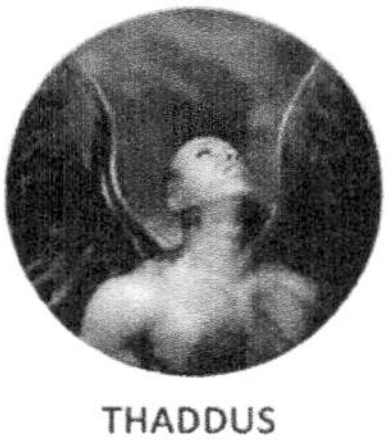

Thaddus finds himself in the unlucky predicament of keeping a secret that could destroy him forever.

THADDUS

AFTER LIFE CHARACTERS - SPECIAL MISSION ANGEL TEAM

SADIE

Sadie is the go-to Angel for trouble in the Heavens and is tasked with leading a team in an all important mission.

ROSIE

Rosie is chosen to be a member of the Special Mission Angel Team.

JOEY

Joey, Sadie's 2nd in comand, is chosen to be a member of the Special Mission Angel Team.

DAVID

David is chosen to be a member of the Special Mission Angel Team.

MICHAEL-SWORDSMAN

Michael, known as the swordsman, is chosen to be a member of the Special Mission Angel Team.

Dedications

For Marisa
We have deeply shared life's journey.
Cara Femmina, Solo Tu
Io Ti Amo Sempre

For Colleen
my faithful daughter
The years of your encouragement
and help on this series
can never be repaid,
because they carried me
through the darkest of times.

Love, Dad

The Prophecy

In the tree, the secret lies
The ancient seed, bearing life
Whose fruits reveal both dark and light
And opens eyes to the age of strife.

When sea doeth yield the Golden Sword,
Forged and burnished from the fire.
The virgin warrior again will rise.
Bringing hope to listless band.

When armies face eternal doom
And the holy one is lost for good
The feared day has now arrived
Darkness reigns, yet even still…

The fiery column signals time
Seven days, no more may pass
But yea, cannot beyond delay
For sunset yields eternal night

If the fire consumes the host
Unto the end, the dark must go
And Sacrifice will save the day,
And Sacrifice will save the day.

Say My Name

Darkening skies and growing storm clouds rolled in from the East, settling above the heads of over 235,000 Angels gathered at the shore of Luminé's 2nd Heavenly Realm. The Angels were waiting for their leader, Luminé, to come and lead them away to their new homeland.

Today was the most exciting day in many of these Angels' lives. None of them ever imagined leaving the Heavens, but all felt justified in their doing so. Most were discontent at the special privileges the Humans had been given not just of creating new life by having babies; it was much more than discontent that ruled this day. Following Luminé, the greatest of the Archangels, to a new world was a thrilling adventure that promised to be filled with wonder and excitement.

It had all happened so fast. Only ten days earlier, the announcement had been made that they were free to leave. No one imagined that a third of the Angels would go, but here they all were, anxiously waiting with great anticipation.

The scene at the beach was escalating in tenor and nearing a fever pitch. The time was near, imminent, and Angels jostled with each other, laughing, talking excitedly, speaking of what they would do when they arrived at Luminé's new kingdom: One thing they all agreed on. They would be finally free of the domination of the Archangels and Host Commanders they were leaving behind. In their new land, they would be ruled by Luminé, the greatest and most daring of all the Archangels. They would welcome his rule.

~ ~ ~ ~

Oxana lifted her head high and walked out of her quarters and into Luminé's 2nd Heavenly Realm's Headquarters Compound. She was dressed in a beautiful skin-tight gold-and-black uniform with a silver-colored belt holding her sword sheath.

Today was the day she had dreamed of for years, and nothing was going to stop her rise to power. She drew in a deep breath, savoring the feeling of exhilaration, then turned to the hundred Angels, stationed on the walls of the compound, holding large maroon-colored banners. They were stationed on the wall so they would be visible to those on the beach. They would soon wave those banners, sending the message to the mass of Angels on the beach that it was time to set the great day in motion. The drummers and trumpeters she had organized were also there on the beach, at the front, waiting for their cue to launch the departure with pomp and fanfare. Oxana planned it all this way, to ensure all would feel the elation she felt, that Luminé's new kingdom awaited them.

It would be a different kingdom, not one saddled by Heaven's silly rules, nor structured in a way that the Humans were of first concern. No, this would be their own kingdom, one in which they could do whatever they pleased.

It was almost time for Luminé to emerge from their living quarters. With a gleam in her eye, she raised her arm high above her head, holding it there for all to see, then waved. All at once, a hundred Angels stationed on the walls stood tall, raising the massive maroon-colored banners high into the air, and began joyfully waving them to and fro, sending the first signal to all on the beach to get ready.

She watched the spectacle then listened to the immense roar from the beach. It sent shivers up her spine, and she knew they would now assemble in tight formations, readying themselves for her and Luminé to join them, waiting for Luminé to conduct his review of their lines. It would be his last act in the Heavens before leaving for their new realm.

Oxana turned and looked at the Headquarters' large arched entryway where Luminé would stride out any moment, ready to embrace his destiny. She glanced up at the faint sun behind the clouds to gauge the time, nervously chewing the inside of her cheek.

He was taking too long.

The moments were beginning to feel like hours, and her heartbeat quickened noticeably in her chest as inevitable apprehension set in.

She glanced around, half-smiling at all who were waiting inside the compound, knowing there was no way she could show even a flicker of her growing concern.

Several minutes passed with no sign of him. She glanced up again at the location of the sun barely visible through the darkening skies. Was this an omen? Was this a sign that it was to all be stopped, that the Angels would lose their will? Was Luminé having second thoughts? It would be the end for her. She would be relegated back into obscurity, back to being nothing more than a lowly Angel. She would face Legion's wrath, too, the punishment for failure.

Her teeth clenched tightly, stopping a look of concern from breaking through her stoic smile. She decided to do the only thing she could do. She whispered a prayer, though strangely it did not feel like a prayer, that Luminé would not turn his back on his new Kingdom.

Then, she waited.

They all waited.

~ ~ ~ ~

Luminé opened the door slowly and stepped out onto the portico of his Headquarters. He stood still, his shoulders squared, his chin held high, his jawline set and determined. He was dressed in his Archangel uniform, with gold breastplate, gold-trimmed white tunic, and dark brown sandals laced up his muscular calves to just below his knee.

He raised his eyes to the sky, noticing the dark storm clouds. He had hoped for sun this day, and it had been here earlier, but it didn't matter. Nothing was going to stop him. He looked across the compound at Oxana. She was standing as tall and straight as he had ever seen, with her eyes fixed on him. Her chin was tilted up, her hand on the handle of her silver sword. Her whole countenance spoke of success. Luminé thought for a brief moment, that today in many ways, belonged to her too, the great organizer, the one who pulled it all together; rallying them all to come together in this epic moment in the history of Angels.

He looked up at the walls, to the hundred Angels waving their banners in unison, all of them looking at him, proudly smiling. It all looked so regal, and why should it not? He was the greatest of Archangels, and ever since the very first day, he knew he was superior to the rest of them. He knew he was destined to rule.

He nodded to Oxana and watched her subtly nod, then elegantly turn, and stride across the courtyard toward him. As she drew near, she raised her hand in the air, beckoning for him to step down and accept his destiny.

Luminé took her hand and walked down the stairs, but he paused as his feet touched the ground. His stomach fluttered as the demons he had wrestled all night within his mind were back. He felt his eyes narrow as he glanced around at the Angels on the walls again, searching his mind for answers. Yes, it was all magnificent, but was he making a mistake? If he were, it would be the biggest mistake of his life. He would be leaving the Lords, leaving the Heavens, leaving it all for good this time. He told his mind to stop, but the last thought would not stay quiet. He was leaving Splendora, too.

Oxana stepped forward and held out her hand, waiting for him to take it. He looked intensely into her eyes, searching for the reassurance he desperately needed. Then he remembered the Humans, and how he would become their servants, and how he was greater than this. He was more than a simple servant. He was the greatest of Archangels, and he deserved everything he was getting.

He bowed his head, working through it one more time, then slowly lifted his eyes to meet hers as a broad smile spread across his face. He grasped Oxana's hand tightly, then stepped forward, leading the way now, with her just behind him. They lifted into the air and flew past all the flag-waving revelers to the waiting crowd of Angels at the beach.

~ ~ ~ ~

Splendora and Arcano raced through the sky across the Heavenly Sea toward the 2nd Realm, thinking there was still time. But as the immense crowd of Luminé's Angels, waiting on the beach, came into view, she and Arcano stopped for a moment, unsure if it was too late. Arcano looked over at her, out of breath, and hastily asked, "Are you sure you want to do this? Maybe you should just forget about him."

"Don't you understand, Arcano? This is not about me. This is about everything. The foundations of the very Heavens are about to be destroyed forever."

Arcano put his head down, nodding, embarrassed he had not himself seen this.

Splendora did not wait for his reply. She took off, flying ahead of him, waving for him to follow. She was not going to let Luminé leave without answering to her, without making sure he had one more chance to hear her plea. Oxana had obviously swayed him, but there was time to persuade him again, back to her. She knew he would listen to her. He had to. Their love had been real, and because of it, he owed her one more hearing.

~ ~ ~ ~

The army of 235,666 Angels stood at full attention and in absolute silence, arranged in perfect rows, 30 columns wide, just as Oxana had ordered the night before.

Sparkis was at the front of one of the columns. He had reserved his spot by coming very early. He wanted to be as close to Luminé as he could. He imagined that since he and Luminé had been friends for so very long, that following him to his kingdom would ensure he would be given a prominent place. But just being here on this epic morning was beginning to feel like a reward in and of itself. Sparkis had never felt so proud. He felt bigger and taller than he ever remembered.

He looked around at the others and could tell they felt the same way. All the Angels, male and female alike, stood straight and tall, their chests puffed out, their eyes wide and determined, their chins lifted slightly to one side, as Oxana had ordered the night before. Sparkis never had seen such a spectacle in all of his life.

Suddenly, Luminé and Oxana flew in from the sky and landed on a small hill overlooking the beach. They both stood tall, with their hands on their hips and legs spread apart, facing down at the throng below.

Absolute silence held sway, as Oxana had given strict instructions on how she wanted this moment to unfold. She and Luminé walked up through the center of them, as row after row parted in perfect time to let them pass, then closed ranks immediately afterward.

There was newness and excitement in every Angel's eyes. It didn't matter that the sun was not there, yielding perceived glory to the day. The shining brightness in the faces of the Angels, male and female alike, created their own glory.

When Luminé and Oxana reached the front of the crowd, they stopped and looked out ahead into their future. A strong wind from the South blew, causing Luminé's and Oxana's hair to flow backward in the breeze. Luminé turned to Oxana, his brow furrowed, and his gaze and jaw set like steel.

Oxana smiled and nodded, then lifted her hand, signaling the start. All at once, over 1,000 drums began beating loudly, and trumpeters began trumpeting. Dancers and banner wavers leaped into the air, circling and twirling wildly, forming up on two sides, creating a long canopy path in the air for all to travel through.

Oxana waited for it to escalate, and for the tensions to mount, then she and Luminé joined hands and lifted up into the air, flying away, the first ones through the canopy of drummers, dancers, and trumpeters. Right behind them, row after row of Angels leaped into the air, one row at a time in perfect unison, following those in front of them, passing through the spectacle, out away from the shoreline of their former home and out over the open sea toward the Southern Realm.

~ ~ ~ ~

Splendora and Arcano finally drew close enough to see the epic moment unfolding. Splendora stopped suddenly. Luminé was holding Oxana's hand, already out over the sea, leading the mass of Angels through the sky. Her chin lowered to her chest.

"Come on, we have to catch him," Arcano shouted, "There is still time!"

Splendora shuddered and shook her head slowly, as a tear fell down her cheek. Her tense shoulders and arms, ready for the fight, let go and hung at her side, as her entire body quivered in despair. She closed her eyes, turning away slightly so Arcano would not see her tears. He and everyone would think it was about her, but it was not, and it was too late. Luminé had done it. He had destroyed the Heavens, he had destroyed the Earth, he had forever tarnished everything that was supposed to come, and this time he had done it for good.

Why had she let him return to Oxana? Why didn't they go and see the Lords together? Whether she had loved him truly or not was at issue. His being true to who he was meant to be, to all that was meant to be, was lost now, and he with it, and it would be forever.

With wide eyes, Arcano cried out in a quickened, shallow breath, "Splendora, it's not too late! We can catch up to him."

"No, Arcano," she replied, turning to face him now, "It is too late. He will never turn back. All has been lost." She turned again to watch Luminé and Oxana for one long moment until they faded into the distant sky.

"Let's go home," she said, her shoulders slumped and her head down.

Arcano turned as well but then turned back one more time to see the throng. Realizing Splendora's words about the foundations of the Heavens being destroyed was indeed true. He said, "Everything good we have ever known is suddenly in the past. All of our history means nothing anymore."

Splendora listened to him, unwilling to look back, and left.

~ ~ ~ ~

Rana was lost in the throng. The crowd was so massive, so full of expectation and excitement, that nobody was really paying attention to where their arms and feet and wings were, and she found herself tangled up in the atmosphere. She recognized a few faces, former commanders, and even some people she had once called friends, and she realized suddenly that she could not, under any circumstances, imagine life among them.

So she had snuck away without anyone noticing, because something felt wrong, a voice within her was warning her. She had fooled herself into thinking that somehow, being the only Archangel to leave with Luminé would give her a special place with him. He had already promised her she would be his 1st of Archangels. She loved Luminé, and more, she loved the excitement that always surrounded him. His kingdom would be one of thrills and fulfillment.

But there was something she was leaving behind, something she never imagined having, something that might mean she was making a mistake. She desperately needed to think. She knew exactly where to go.

She landed in the yard of a large mansion, ran up the steps, and knocked loudly on the door. Moments later, Michael opened the door, with raised eyebrows, clearly showing he was surprised.

He asked, "Rana, what are you doing here?"

She sighed and shook her head, not knowing what to say. She felt so confused, and she knew she couldn't hide it from him. There was no time to adorn masks.

"Is everything all right?" he asked.

"I was just… well… I came to say goodbye."

"Where are you going?"

"I am going with Luminé."

Michael froze. He had not known she had even been considering leaving. He repeated her words back to her. "You are going with Luminé. Today."

She repeated hers, right back, unwilling to say what she wanted to say, "Yes… and I came to say goodbye."

"I see." He cleared his throat and looked at the ground. Rana could have sworn he made a move toward her, to stop her, to keep her in place, but when she looked again, he was still frozen, empty-eyed, seeming to gather his words. She wanted him to cry out, to sweep her into his arms—but instead, he stayed still and silent.

Until he looked up and stepped forward, "I don't want you to go." His eyes were zeroed in on hers, trying to connect.

"Why not?" she said hesitantly, afraid he would not give her the only answer that could save her from leaving. She waited, though it was quickly dawning on her there was no longer any reason to. She lowered her head, turned and walked down the stairs. She had thought there was a reason to stay. Now she knew there was none.

Suddenly, she heard his heavy footsteps running down the stairs, "Wait, Rana," he called out in a desperate voice.

Before she could turn, he took her shoulders and turned her to face him, "I can't let you leave. I won't let you leave."

"Michael… but I… I told Lumi… "

He put his finger gently on her lips, "Rana, forget about Luminé. Stay here… with me."

He lowered his lips to meet hers and kissed her. She felt the passion and strength in this kiss, unlike she had ever felt before. Her whole being rejoiced inside of her, and she let herself fall into his broad arms without another thought of leaving.

Let the Festivities Begin

The endless white sand beaches of the Southern Realm came into view. They had left the dark skies and storm clouds behind. The sun was peering through the remnants of the clouds, illuminating the lush trees and endless shoreline. Luminé was surprised to see large tents dotting a three-mile swath of the beach. He turned to Oxana, "What are those for?"

"You said we needed to celebrate, so I arranged a three-day-long festive celebration."

Luminé subtly nodded, feeling the elation, as a wide smile crept over his face. This vast land, it was his, all his, his kingdom. He said, "Yes, we must celebrate."

He headed down with haste, waving the multitude forward. They landed haphazardly along a mile-long swath of beach, and immediately wine casks were opened, and the party began. The trumpets announced the revelry, and the drummers and dancers took up along the entire beach. Smaller tents were set up around the larger tents to allow Angels to have privacy for the carnal relations, which would surely ensue during three days of revelry. The old order, the old rules on Seasons of Love, were now gone. Now, carnal desires would have their full reign, and one would partake of it all according to one's appetite, not in accordance with any sense of temperance or prudence as the Lords had taught. As night drew near, fires were lit, and the beating of the drums only grew louder.

Luminé, Oxana, and many of his key commanders sat in his tent, facing the large bonfire outside with the front flap open. Everywhere beyond them, Angels were stumbling past, laughing and shouting, most drunk. Male Angels were snatching up willing females and carrying them into the woods or into the surf or further down to the beach's secluded areas. Oxana's friend Sansa walked past, peering in, when an Angel grabbed her, lifting her, carrying her to a nearby tent. She kicked and screamed, but only in playful resistance.

Luminé laughed and raised his glass of wine, directing it toward Oxana, "Here is to you, my Queen! Your belief in me allowed me to survive while I was in exile, and your belief that I deserved my own kingdom helped me to obtain all of this!"

Oxana looked deeply into his eyes, stood, and reached down her hand. All eyes in the room looked to Luminé as he smiled and took her hand, standing to the sudden eyebrow raises of all present. Oxana pranced slowly and seductively out of the tent, with Luminé in tow, as he looked back, like a helpless victim.

Oxana walked Luminé past a few smaller tents. Inside Luminé could hear the sounds of Angels making love. As they passed the last one, he saw Sansa through an open tent flap. She was facing away from him, standing before an Angel lying on a bed watching her. She dropped her tunic to the floor. Luminé marveled at her sleek, naked backside and voluptuous curves and legs. He watched her seductively climb up onto the Angel. Then, Oxana grabbed him by the sleeve, pulled him away, and took him to the next tent, where she lay with him.

~ ~ ~ ~

By the second night, things were getting out of control. The Angels had easily learned what it meant to indulge. Without the boundaries and the rigid rules of the Lords' realms, they found it easy to get carried away. One swig of wine turned to two, which turned to three, and then four, and soon the Angels found themselves reaching out, clasping hands, embracing.

Oxana had already passed out. She was sleeping in the main tent not far from the fire. Luminé was restless and also very drunk, so he went for a walk along the beach. He journeyed beyond the tents, beyond the area of the party, to the distant shore. He needed to be alone. It was a grand celebration and yet he knew this would never have happened in the Heavens. There had never been a party like this, and while it gave him a sense of freedom, it also gave him a feeling of emptiness.

Luminé finally stopped and sat in the sand, finishing his flask of wine, watching the waves gently wash ashore. Then he saw her. It was Sansa, drunk, walking alone down the beach with her feet just in the water. She walked up to him, "Luminé, I see you are all alone."

He looked up at her beautiful body, swaying in the moonlight. Sansa was petite with well-defined curves accentuating every part of her body. Luminé had always found her intriguing. He thought about her body, seeing it naked the night before, and he wanted her.

She walked past him, then turned facing away from him, as if she could read his mind. She dropped her tunic to her feet, giving him another chance to see her naked, all of her, just as she had purposefully done the night before.

He reached up and took her hand, pulling her onto the sand, as she laughed, pretending to want to get away. Suddenly, he heard Oxana's voice calling from a distance. He pushed Sansa away and said, "Get out of here, quickly." She looked down the beach, then grabbed her tunic, and scampered into the woodline. He heard Oxana again, and waited a few moments, then called out, "over here."

A minute later, Oxana walked up, asking, "What are you doing way over here?"

"I just went for a walk, then grew tired."

Oxana yawned and said, "Let us go and sleep, Luminé. Tomorrow we must choose the spot for our Throne Room."

"Yes, our own Throne Room," he said, closing his eyes, laying his head back in the sand again. None of it seemed real to him. It was like a dream come true, and yet, something deep within was worrying him.

~ ~ ~ ~

Sparkis walked alongside over a hundred other Angels on the beach, all carrying sacks, all picking up various scraps of food, bottles, goblets, pieces of clothing, necklaces, and an occasional lost sword or dagger.

They were charged with scouring the beach to clean up after the festivities. His red hair was pointing in every direction, and his eyes were sunken, drained of hydration from three days of heavy drinking.

He saw his friend Thaddus with a cohort of over 50 Angels dismantling one of the large tents in the distance. "Hey, Thaddus," he said, waving.

"Sparkis," Thaddus called out, turning his head while he held up a tent pole that another Angel on a makeshift wooden ladder was slipping the ropes off.

Sparkis walked up, "Hello there, Thaddus. So, did you enjoy the festivities?"

Thaddus breathed in deeply, shaking his head, "More than you know, Sparkis. I met the most amazing female Angel, Rhonda was her name. She is so eloquent, and so, well, let me say, incredibly sensuous. We practically spent the entire three days in the tents."

"Oh, wow. I think I know who you are talking about. Does she have long curly blondish-brown hair that hangs down her back?"

"Yes, she does."

"Was she a commander in Rana's Realm?"

"Yes, that is her."

"Oh, yeah. She is gorgeous. Are you going to start a Season of Love with her?"

Thaddus hesitated to answer. He looked out to sea, then down at the ground, "I'm not sure."

"Well, why not?"

The other Angel chimed in, gruffly, "There are no Seasons of Love here! We can all do what we want, and… who we want."

Sparkis smiled, nodding, but he noticed Thaddus was not really smiling. The look on his face was forced as if he had to go along with the comment yet did not want to. And Sparkis thought he understood why. Thaddus probably liked her, but here in Luminé's Kingdom, there were to be no commitments, no rules, no boundaries. How then could there be love? Sparkis tipped his hand off his forehead, saying, "Well, guys, I have to get to it."

"Yeah, consider yourself lucky," said the Angel on the ladder. "We will be working hard for the next week."

"Doing what, may I ask?"

"No, you can't ask," the Angel said, laughing.

Thaddus gave the Angel a scowl and said, "Luminé wants us to move these tents up onto the bluff over there." He pointed to a high bluff overlooking the sea. "He's setting five of them up temporarily as his Throne Room, administrative offices, and living quarters. As soon as we are done, there are over a thousand of us tasked with building the compound."

"Wow," said Sparkis. "That is going to be awesome."

"What's so awesome about cutting down thousands of trees and working our asses off?" the other Angel growled as he glared at Sparkis.

"Well, we are in a chipper mood this morning," Sparkis said.

The Angel jumped down, "Why don't you get the hell out of here?"

Sparkis dropped his sack, raising his hands in the air, "Okay, okay sorry." Sparkis remembered his promise to himself, to be more assertive here in the new kingdom.

When the Angel turned to climb the ladder, Sparkis jumped onto his back, pulling at his eyes from behind, pummelling the side of his head with his fists, shouting, "Get out of here, huh, how is this for you, huh?"

They fell to the ground, and Thaddus jumped down and pulled Sparkis off, shouting, "Stop it, Sparkis."

Sparkis huffed, breathing heavily, intentionally calming his breath with several exhales. He looked down at the Angel laying on the ground, curled up, holding his bleeding ears.

Sparkis shrugged Thaddus off and picked up his sack, and said, "Have a good day, Thaddus."

The Archangels

Luminé and Oxana spent the next several days directing thousands of Angels to remove trees, to start building the compound walls, and begin laying the foundations for their living quarters, Throne Room, and guest quarters in the rear of the compound. The Throne Room was planned to be a large, open-air structure, 50 feet long by 100 feet wide. Angels from his kingdom would gather in the skies above, with a view of the sea. It was to have smooth polished wood floors, be built 15 feet off the ground, set on top of massive vertical logs supporting the perimeter, with massive long crossbeam logs supporting the center. A great widening staircase would climb from the ground to a large balcony that would overlook the entire compound and be high enough to see over the 10-foot-tall compound walls. Luminé imagined himself in the future, standing proudly next to Oxana, as he had stood on the eve of their departure, giving rousing speeches to his multitude of followers, waving to them, accepting their accolades for the pronouncements and rulings he would give as their new society formed. The chants of *Luminé, Luminé, Luminé* would be heard from that balcony for all time.

Next to the raised Throne Room, also raised up 15 feet from the ground, administrative offices were to be built. These were designed to be spacious with room for many offices where he and Oxana imagined they would closely monitor the activities of everyone in their kingdom. Oxana would have her own office, with a window looking out to the sea. The central feature of the administrative offices, though, would be Luminé's office. It was to be 30 feet long by 25 feet wide, double the size of his old Archangel Office. A large desk and conference table with 12 chairs was ordered to be built. A massive window would be at the rear of the office, looking down over the compound, in the coastline's direction.

Their living quarters were also large, with two bedrooms, one each for Luminé and Oxana, a large living room, dining hall with a large fireplace, kitchen area, and hall at the entrance. Oxana ordered that no opulent feature was to be spared. She wanted it to be the most regal living quarters ever created.

All of this, though, would take some months to complete. However, their plans had been made, and directions had been given to a thousand Angels who would begin by clearing the forest and the land.

A massive temporary Throne Room tent was then erected. It was a white tent, with several large poles lining the center, 25 feet in the air. Inside, it spanned 30 feet wide by thirty feet long. Carpets were laid on every part of the floor so nothing touched the ground below it. Two thrones were set upon a slightly raised wooden stage at the far end, and all the sides of the tent were tied to the ground tightly, while the entranceway was set with an extended maroon canopy from where all would enter and exit.

When all was ready, Luminé and Oxana walked alone down the blue carpet runway under the maroon canopy into their temporary Throne Room. They joined their hands at the entrance and walked across the carpeted floor to sit on their thrones for the first time.

Both of them sat, looking around the massive tent, imagining their subjects standing at attention, ready to do their will.

Oxana asked, "How do you want your subjects to address you?"

Luminé thought for a moment, looking out the tent's front entrance to a distant beach, full of Angels who were indeed, now his subjects, busily organizing. The word 'Lord' crossed his mind, and a smile crept over his face. "I was thinking, Lord Luminé, but then I thought it would not be original enough. Instead, they can call me King Luminé, or Great Luminé. Which do you prefer?" he asked with his chin held high, ready to ascend to his new title.

Oxana bowed reverentially and said, "Great Luminé, you are already their King. They shall call you, Great Luminé, King of Luminare. How shall they address me?"

"I want them to call you who you are, my Queen. Queen Oxana is your name."

Oxana stood up, stepped in front of him, and bowed, "Behold, your Queen, Great Luminé."

Luminé said to her, "The first thing we must do is choose our Archangels."

Oxana said, "I was thinking, why don't we call them Ruling Angels instead of Archangels."

"No, I don't like that," Luminé replied abruptly. "It implies they will have authority. I alone," he paused, realizing he needed to include her, "with your help of course, I will be the sole ruler here. No, I think we can stay with Archangels. We must decide who will be first among our Archangels."

"Good, I agree. I would like Antonio to take that spot. He is our most capable and our most loyal Angel. He helped me immensely during the year of your exile."

"I am sorry, Oxana, but I have already promised this honor to Rana. She will be an important asset to us here because she is the only other Archangel to come with us."

Oxana had been waiting for him to bring her up. She was fully aware of his history with her. She replied, flippantly, "Oh, you did not hear? She didn't come."

"What do you mean?" Luminé said, his eyes narrowed. "But I saw her and her commanders in the crowd."

"Oh yes, her commanders came, but she turned back."

Luminé swallowed hard, doubt suddenly gripping him, trying desperately not to let Oxana notice. He conceded, "Then let it be Antonio."

"Good, we will need six others. I have several in mind."

"No, not six others, only five. I don't want seven Archangels. I want six. I think it is a more perfect number."

Oxana said, "I would like, "Dyanna, and Rodrigo and Lito."

"They are all acceptable to me," said Luminé.

"Sparkis?" Oxana asked.

Luminé shook his head, "No, as much as I like Sparkis. He is not a leader." Luminé laughed, "Amusing, and, useful, yes, but not a leader. Instead, let's consider Sansa?"

Oxana's face recoiled, and she replied adamantly, "Sansa? No!"

"Why not Sansa?" Luminé said, "She is quite capable."

Oxana snapped back, "Capable for what? No! She is not a leader." Oxana was fully aware of Luminé gazing at her in the tent during the festivities. She also had been wondering whose footsteps were in the sand the night she found Luminé.

Luminé angrily replied, "Well, it seems you already have this all figured out."

"I know who we can trust, Luminé. And we must have Angels we can absolutely trust."

Luminé paused, considering her words, and asked,"Who else, then?"

"Thaddus and Lisala should be our final picks."

~ ~ ~ ~

Antonio, Dyanna, Thaddus, Lito, Lisala and Rodrigo stood at attention inside the large tent, waiting for the meeting. Luminé and Oxana walked in from the back of the tent and took their seats on their thrones. Luminé said, "I have called you all here to confer upon you a special honor." He paused for effect, "You have been chosen to be our Archangels."

Luminé waited, watching the smiles come over their faces as they looked at each other, with looks of satisfaction and accomplishment. He then said, "These appointments will be kept by you, as long as you serve us well. Don't make me regret appointing you, or you will be sorry."

An immediate hush fell over the tent. All the momentary looks of satisfaction turned to chagrin. Even Oxana seemed caught off guard by the demeaning statement.

Luminé continued, "Antonio, step forward."

Antonio stepped forward and bowed his head. Luminé said, "Antonio, I have decided that you will be 1st of the Archangels in my Kingdom."

Antonio bowed low, "Thank you, Great Luminé."

Luminé did not reply but motioned for him to step back in line. He then continued, "We will be establishing 6 sections of land where each of you will be able to establish your headquarters. From there, you will be in charge of the Angels we will place under you. But you will send reports to me daily of the occurrences and issues in your land. Is that clear?"

The atmosphere of chagrin deepened, as did the looks on all of their faces. Luminé then said, "Now, let us go down to the beach and tell my subjects."

~ ~ ~ ~

As they flew down to make their announcement, the Southern Realm beach scene was chaotic, as everywhere partying, fighting, and much debauchery was on display. Many of the Angels were scantily clad, with a good number not wearing clothes at all. They were gathered in large groups, staggering and stumbling and raising their voices. Luminé and Oxana, and their new Archangels hovered high in the sky, shocked at the melee going on below them. Fires raged from haphazard fire pits. Thundering, booming voices demanding more wine. Occasionally, a piercing scream could be heard.

Oxana leaned over to Luminé and quietly said, "Luminé, you need to establish order now before things get out of control."

He flew down closer and raised his hand high, shouting out, "Everyone, stop!"

Slowly, Angels began noticing, pointing up, turning, pulling others along, spilling goblets, stumbling over each other, telling others to stop. It all unfolded painfully slow.

Finally, after several long, loud minutes, Luminé had their attention. He pointed to the new Archangels and shouted, "These are your new leaders, your new Archangels. All of you will be assigned to one of their realms." He smiled, looking out, waiting for some reaction. But the reaction was uneventfully silent. The crowd of Angels seemed unfazed by Luminé's great first act. Indeed, it took a long time for the news to spread, as Angels in the middle and back could not even hear, as one could see Angels turning to explain to those behind them what had been said. Slowly but surely, it became clear that the old standards would not abide. He could hear gruff, irritated scoffs and small cries of, "Absolutely not!" and "I don't think so!"

A steady uncertainty fell over the crowd. Angels started to raise their voices, to shout out in disapproval. Luminé looked at Oxana, their eyes conveying the disappointment they felt. He was beginning to boil with anger. He shouted his next announcement, "All former Host Commanders come forward."

The scene unfolded like molasses, though the news made its way back somewhat faster. Luminé suddenly felt inept. He had imagined giving a great speech and being rewarded with the applause of all. When the Lords spoke, things happened instantly, as if everyone at once heard them. He could not believe a simple announcement would take so long. Finally, the former Host Commanders were gathered in front of him.

Luminé shouted louder this time, "Host Commanders, the seven Archangels will now select you, one by one, to join their respective realms. After that, you and they will select, again, one by one, the rest of the Angels to fill out your realms." That's when it started, a low, steady rumble. He couldn't quite believe it at first, but by the time it filled his ears it was clear: His subjects were booing him. Some were hissing.

Luminé turned, motioning for Oxana to follow. They returned to the compound and went into a temporary tent for their living quarters. Luminé drew out his sword and slammed it into the ground, "What just happened there!" he screamed, in as forceful a voice as could be allowed behind such flimsy walls.

"They are all out of control," Oxana replied, her face etched in the same frustration he felt.

Luminé kicked the sword across the room, his face scrunched in anger. He turned, "We must crack down, Oxana. We cannot have this disrespect."

She swallowed hard. All her grandiose plans seemed to have suddenly unraveled.

He snapped, "Did you anticipate this? This... this... outright insubordination!"

"No! of course not!" Her breathing grew shallow, more rapid. She not only felt threatened by what had happened; now Luminé was attacking her. Then, she thought of Legion, and her chest relaxed, drawing several deep breaths, as a feeling of calm began to descend on her. "Luminé, we do not need to panic. As you have already said, we need a crackdown. We need to assert our authority early, and we will."

Palace Guard

The following day, Luminé went into the section of the tent where Oxana was sleeping. He crawled into her bed, "Oxana, are you awake?"

She turned over, opening her eyes, "Luminé, I am sleeping."

"Wake up, I need you," he said, as he placed his hand on her lower abdomen and began caressing her. Oxana thrust her head back, raising her arms in a long cat-like stretch, then pulled up her nightgown and opened her legs, letting him have his way with her.

When they had finished, they laid awake, silent, staring up at the white canopy ceiling of the tent. Luminé interrupted the silence, "Oxana, I have an idea I want to run past you."

"What is it?"

"I am going to form a special unit, a palace guard. Initially, we will have them build our compound and Headquarters, but as soon as they are finished, we will employ them to be the enforcers of our wishes. We will empower them to raise a network of informants throughout the kingdom. They will be our eyes and ears, our... our secret police. What do you think?"

Oxana sat up, her mouth open and her eyes wide, "It is brilliant, Luminé. I love it. How did you think of it?"

"Well, I thought of what the Lords did not have. They trusted us, they trusted their Angels. Look at what that got them."

"It is fantastic. We should start immediately."

~ ~ ~ ~

Later, a summons was sent to the six Archangels.

To the Six Archangels,

You are ordered to select 400 of your best Angels and send them to the headquarters. We will be using them to form a special unit that will build the headquarters and form the Palace Guard. I need to stress that you send your finest Angels for this task. Any candidates sent who seem unworthy will be held against you. They are to report for duty tomorrow morning, dressed in their full uniforms.

Signed by my hand, the hand of the King,

Luminé

When all 2,400 Angels arrived, Luminé had them begin construction of the stockade fence around his headquarters. He ordered that three sides be built, each 700 feet long. The Headquarters' back was set along a heavily wooded area and was not closed in but left open to the wilderness behind.

At one end of the compound, they were also to construct simple living quarters where up to 400 of them at a time could stay while on guard duty.

Four days later, the stockade was completed, and all members of his special unit stood in the vast courtyard waiting for the next announcement. Luminé came out, followed by Oxana.

"Angels, you have all been specially chosen to become my Palace Guards. You will be an elite unit who will all have special privileges here in my Kingdom. Your next task will be to build my palace. I have laid out the designs on these parchments. After the palace is completed, you will all be given choice pieces of land here in my kingdom, where you will be able to build your own homes. I will leave the parchments here on this table. Lastly, work together. That is all."

Luminé put the parchments onto a table in the compound and unfurled the designs he and Oxana had drawn up. He then stepped back and joined Oxana on the steps of their makeshift Throne, watching it all set in motion. He was curious to see how things would commence and show the natural leadership skills that would be taken into account when he chose who would become the elite group's leaders.

"What's going on over there?" Oxana said, interrupting him from his observations. On the far side of the compound, a tall female Angel with long black hair that hung down to her perfectly curved waist, and long, shapely legs that accentuated her curves, was conversing in a highly animated fashion with two male Angels. After a few moments, she stopped and turned to walk away. One of the males lurched forward and slapped her on the ass. She stopped, gritting her teeth, then turned. She walked forward forcefully, grabbed him by the neck, and lifted him into the air. She took her dagger and thrust it into his stomach. The other Angel reached for his sword, but she leveled a high kick to his head, knocking him to the ground. She stood on his neck, talking to him, then let him up as he scampered away, leaving his wounded friend writhing on the ground.

Luminé turned to Oxana, who stood angrily and said, "We cannot tolerate this in our kingdom, Luminé."

"Just a moment, Oxana. I see something far more interesting," he said, as he stood and called out, "You! Come over here."

Everyone grew silent around them, and the female Angel looked over, then walked unremorsefully across the compound. Everyone watched in anticipation, expecting her to be severely punished. When she reached their thrones, she stood tall and asked, "What is it, Great Luminé?"

Luminé examined her for a moment, marveling at her thin black eyebrows and dark, almost black colored eyes set above high gently curved cheekbones. It was more than her beauty he admired. She stood tall, with a look of confidence etched onto her face. She pleased him greatly. He asked, "Why did you do that to those Angels?"

"They disrespected me."

"Is that so?" asked Luminé.

Luminé considered her words for a moment, acting in the seat of his first judgment, then said, "You were right to do what you did... perhaps a bit humiliating and volatile for them... but a good strong response. What is your name?"

"My name is Vamorda, Great Luminé," she said, as a seductive smile graced her lips.

"Whose realm were you with?"

"I was part of Raphael's realm, though he refused to make me one of his commanders. It is why I left."

"And whose realm are you in, here, in my kingdom?"

"Thaddus's. He promised to make me a Host Commander."

Luminé glanced back at Oxana for a moment, feigning to include her in his decision. He could tell even she was intimidated by the presence of this tall female powerhouse. Luminé said, "Well, Vamorda, you no longer work for Thaddus. You work for me. You are the new Commander of the Palace Guard."

Vamorda's seductive smile only deepened, and she bowed. "Thank you, Great Luminé."

The Golden Sword

"Faster Willow," Calla yelled, the wind cleansing her face as she pushed her horse to the limit of its strength. The sun was just rising over the Eastern horizon, and the grass was warm, the heat of a summer day having already settled upon it. The smell of the air was fresh but dry, the kind that frequently beckoned her to go to the sea to swim, but there was no time for relaxation today. She was on her way to the Dark Mountain. Her dream the night before beckoned her to go there. The disappearance of the still missing Angel Mylia long ago had been forgotten by most, but not by Calla. She was determined to find her.

In the distance, the Dark Mountain came into view. "Whoa," she said, pulling back on the reigns. The very first day of Creation flashed into her mind, the day they discovered that the creature Legion had been created. Adon had wisely suggested they create this Dark Mountain and Dark Lake to bind him. But that was before Adon had freed him, all by himself, setting in motion the chaos and trouble. It broke her heart in so many ways. Her love for Adon was all she ever wanted, indeed, all she ever needed, but his rogue actions had cast an irreparable shadow over everything.

She gently kicked Willow's sides and galloped the remaining miles to the edge of the Dark Lake. Upon reaching the shoreline, she dismounted and got into one of the boats. It was an eerily quiet ride across the calm dark waters, giving Calla the same ominous feeling that always gripped her when she neared Legion's presence. She wondered where he was. He had been quiet for a while now, with no one being able to find him. And no wonder, he had scored a major accomplishment in splitting the Heavens. Calla now realized that somehow he had planned it all and succeeded perfectly. But what was his next move? Surely he had one. But one thing she knew for sure: If Adon had acted alone in setting him free, she would find a way to act alone to kill Legion without the consent of the other Lords.

When she reached the other side, two Angels stepped out of the woods. "Lord Calla, we did not expect you."

"Good morning," she said, "Who is in charge?"

"Michael."

"Take me to him."

They began the long walk up the dark mountain path that winded through the dense forest up to the barren plateau. All along the way, Calla could see Angels on guard at various places. The dark mountain, covered with dense trees except at the very top, was well guarded on all fronts. When they reached the plateau, Calla saw Michael in the distance, smiling, speaking to someone in his command. He looked strong and tall, happier, more confident than she had ever remembered seeing him. He turned, saw her, and shouted, "Attention!"

At once, all the Angels stood at attention. Michael came across the plateau, with a gleam in his eye, proud of his guard. He bowed, "Good morning, Lord Calla. What brings you here?"

"There is something I need to see without anyone around. Michael, can you please have everyone go down to the base of the mountain? You may stay here, but no one else can know."

"Absolutely," He stood tall and looked about, "All right everyone. I want all Angels to assemble at the base of the mountain, by the transfer point. I will be down shortly for further instructions."

Once all the Angels left, Calla walked over to the watery abyss and peered in, just as she had done in her dream. The waters were still and dark, almost resembling a looking glass, and the eternal flame was extinguished. She looked over at the place where they had found the tuft of hair and cringed.

Michael asked, "May I ask what you are looking for, Lord Calla?"

"I don't know exactly," she said, as she squatted down closer, trying to see into the water. "There," she said, pointing.

"What is it?"

"I don't know. Something glimmered… like a rock or something. Do you see it?"

Michael squatted next to her, his eyes determined and serious, searching the waters. He said, "No, I can't."

He reached his hand into the water, trying to move it, trying to see deeper. But after a few moments, he pulled his hand back, as if something had burned him. "That's funny. It started to burn me."

Calla looked around to make sure no one else was watching them. She put her hands over the water and closed her eyes. At the bottom of the 30 foot deep abyss, the white object began moving up through the waters, becoming clearer and clearer with each second.

"I see it," exclaimed Michael.

Calla nodded, "Let me do it. She kept her eyes closed, drawing the object upward, until finally a white, stony looking object, smoothly curved, like half a cup, with holes on one side burst through the surface. It rolled and bobbed, settling and floating on top of the water.

Michael watched it bob and asked slowly as if he did not want to know, "What is it?" When Calla did not answer, he looked over and saw the look of horror on her face.

She felt his stare and said, "It is a skull, the remains of… an Angel."

Michael stepped back quickly, dumbfounded, "An Angel? What… how can that be an…?" He stopped as he watched Calla reach into the water with both hands and pull it out, wincing at the pain she felt from the water. She still did not understand the mystery as to why the water caused her pain.

Calla stood up, her hands trembling, and closed her eyes. A vision appeared in her mind. It was Mylia, with her blonde hair waving in the wind, standing next to the plateau. Legion was next to her, holding a golden sword. Suddenly Legion thrust it into Mylia's stomach. She screamed, grasping the sword, cutting her hands, trying to remove it. Legion dug it deeper, twisting it, then pushed her into the water. Calla watched with horror-filled eyes as Mylia slowly began to disintegrate in the water. She writhed wildly, pleading with Legion to help her. Calla shouted aloud, "No!" as Legion took the end of the sword and pushed Mylia's head downward until she sank under the surface and descended to the bottom of the abyss.

Calla fell to one knee, tears running down her face. The sorrow of the tarnished world was one thing, but to now have one of her eternal creatures, one of her beloved Angels to have been snuffed out by Legion, was too much to bear.

Michael knelt next to her, "What is it, Lord Calla? What has happened?"

She looked up at him with a look he had never seen, a look of fear, of hopelessness. "It is the missing Angel Mylia. Legion has killed her."

Michael said nothing but only glanced into the waters, then back at the skull. Calla continued, "He has the Golden Sword. We must find him. We must find and kill Legion at all costs."

"What sword?" Michael asked, realizing what it was as soon as the words left his mouth. "The Sword of the Prophecy," he said aloud.

Calla nodded, "Yes, he has it." Her mind began whirling with possibilities, dire possibilities. In Legion's hands, the sword changed the balance of power in the Heavens. It was clear now. It had the power to kill eternal life. Everyone was at risk, including her and the other Lords. They had to find a way to stop him. But how?

She looked up, "Michael, no one can know what you saw and learned today."

He stood at attention and said, "Yes, my Lord, you have my word."

Adon

Adon reached his two-story forest-edge mansion overlooking the sea. He had built the mansion with his own hands, using logs from the forest and the carpentry help of his friend, Yeshua, a long time ago.

The mansion was two stories tall, made of mostly pine wood. Its ceilings were 15 feet tall, all stained with a honey color Adon had made from herbs in the forest. Large lanterns were hung along the pillars of the vast interior rooms. At night they gave off not only light but warmth. There was also an abundance of windows, so natural sunlight bathed all the rooms during the day. Fine cloth couches, chairs, and pine end tables were neatly arranged in the living areas, and oak tables and chairs, stained with the color of cherry, adorned the dining areas.

He walked across his yard and hoisted the body of the large limp buck onto a stand, and went inside. He went to his room and looked in the mirror, reconsidering what he already was determined to do. His brown hair and beard were disheveled from the hunt, but it was his eyes that he noticed. They were sullen, sunken, having endured too much worry over the past several years, and especially lately with the decision that he was contemplating. It was Calla's reaction that worried him, and yet, he knew it would ultimately make no difference.

She was upset with him and doing what he was about to do, for better or worse, would not change that.

He took up a sharp knife and began cutting off his beard. A half-hour later, he pulled the sharp blade over his cheeks one more time and smiled into the mirror at his new clean-shaven face. "Hmmm… I believe I still have it." He laughed, thinking back to before all this, at a time when he did not have his beard, and Calla thought he looked so dashing.

There was a knock at the door.

He went to the bedroom window and looked down. Yeshua's horse Sundance was eating grass near his porch. Adon smiled and made his way downstairs and out the door.

"Welcome, Yeshua! How are you?"

"I am good… What did you do to your face?" Yeshua said, smiling.

"What's wrong with my face?" Adon said, holding back a smile.

"Where's your beard?"

"Oh, that," he said, rubbing his chaffed chin, "I got tired of it."

Yeshua started laughing, slowly at first, but then erupted in hearty laughter. "You mean, after *all* these years, you finally grew tired of it? That's a long time."

"Well," Adon said, holding back his laughter, "How do I look?"

"Like a… like a new man!"

Yeshua walked up to him and grabbed him by the shoulders, shaking him, "But I can still take you in a battle, with or without the beard, old-timer."

"You think so, huh!"

They both laughed. Yeshua said, "I aim to go fishing. Would you like to join me? "

Adon frowned, "I'm afraid I can't today. But… " his smile reappeared, "but I will join you tomorrow?"

"Tomorrow's fine," said Yeshua, "What are you doing today?"

Adon looked over at his horse, "I promised Hunter I'd take him for a ride."

"You promised Hunter?" Yeshua said, with an astonished look on his face.

Adon knew it was not a good enough reason, but he stuck with it. ."Yes," he said, "and… as you can see… he's waiting by the stable. But I will come by your place early tomorrow morning to go fishing."

Neither Yeshua nor Calla would ever approve of his methods. He trusted them, though, and if they failed, he would pay the price. He would not let his friends down.

Yeshua shook his head, smiling, "Sounds good, old boy. I will see you in the morning."

Adon waited until Yeshua was on his way home, then whistled for his horse Hunter. When the magnificent horse arrived, he jumped on. He pulled an old ripped tunic from his satchel and threw it on. "Are you ready, Hunter? We have a long journey."

Hunter neighed loudly, and Adon kicked the horse's sides. They raced toward across the pasture down toward the overlook to the Heavenly Sea. "Yaaah!" yelled Adon, pushing Hunter forward, "Now, Hunter, now!" They leaped off the cliff overlooking the sea and cascaded into the air, then turned south.

The Rally

Luminé stepped out of his newly built palace's Headquarters, took Oxana by the hand, and flew toward the beach. Anxiously waiting for them were all the Angels of the Southern Realm assembled in the sand and the skies of the beach. In front were his Seven Archangels. All around the perimeter were the new Palace Guards, adorned in their black uniforms, ready to discipline any outbreaks militantly.

As the mass of Angels had been instructed, when Luminé arrived, they began to chant, "Luminé, Luminé, Luminé, Luminé!" Luminé waved to them all, as the crowd burst into thunderous applause.

Luminé stepped onto the small stage, smiling. He was happy they respected him. This was what he envisioned from the beginning of his grand idea, constantly receiving accolades and admiration from his followers. He shouted, "Angels, today I come to you with several announcements, the first of which regards our new kingdom. From this day forward, this place will be called Luminare because I was the one to secure it for you from the Lords."

A loud cheer went up. After a few moments, Luminé raised his hand, quieting the crowd.

"As you can see, a new Palace Guard has been established," he pointed to the guards surrounding them, "and the Angel Vamorda will head them. These guards are an elite unit who will protect our Headquarters from all its enemies and at my command, discipline, anyone who does not follow orders." Luminé pointed to Vamorda, raising his hand, calling for all to applaud.

Most applauded, drowning out the dissenters who could be heard faintly shouting, "Who made you king?"

Luminé raised his hand to quiet the applause. He had to deliver one more pronouncement. Otherwise, he risked them finding out first. They were not allowed back. It was the Lords' decree, but he had failed to inform them. He shouted, "Finally, is the most important announcement. No one who came here will be allowed to go to the Heavens. We will build our world here, as we have no need of the Heavens any longer. We must show ourselves as superior to those we left."

A voice, deep within the crowd, shouted, "Who are you to tell us what to do!" Luminé turned to try and see who it was,

This last announcement was received with only modest applause, mixed with faint murmurings. Luminé was satisfied, though. He had laid down his law. He would deal with the dissenters later.

Vamorda, who was standing behind Luminé, leaned over to one of the Palace Guards and whispered, "Over there, behind the bushes on the hill. Someone is spying on us. Do you see them?"

"Yes,"

"Circle around with a few others and subdue him."

Luminé finished his speech and walked out to the crowd, shaking hands and enjoying the feeling of being on top as a swarm of admirers seeking his favor ran up to him.

In the back of the crowd, yelling and commotion was coming from the surrounding hillside. Four Angels pulled tightly on a net and lifted someone into the air for all to see.

Vamorda flew to his side and whispered in Luminé's ear, "Great Luminé, we have captured a spy!"

Immediately clamoring and shouting erupted from the crowd, all watching the captured Angel writhing in the net. Luminé looked on, worried, suddenly feeling the eyes of thousands descend on him, eyes wanting to see what he would do. He raised his hand high and shouted, "Take him to the Throne Room."

All of a sudden, thousands upon thousands of Angels raced through the sky to the Throne Room, hoping to get a glimpse of what would transpire. Four of the Palace Guards, led by Vamorda, carried the net into the courtyard, flying just above the crowd, as thousands poked at the net and jeered at the hooded Angel inside. They dropped the net in front of the waiting Luminé and Oxana in front of the Throne Room.

Luminé stepped forward and signaled for the others to undo the net. Vamorda grabbed the seated Angel by the shoulders and lifted him to a standing position. Vamorda took her dagger and held it to his throat, "Tell us your name."

Oxana saw Vamorda taking the limelight from Luminé, so she nudged him forward. Luminé nodded and intervened, "Put down your dagger, Vamorda. I will take it from here." He walked up to the Angel, eyeing him with a severe look, putting on his first show for the masses. He said, "Why are you here, spying on us? Who sent you?"

"No one sent me. I wanted to see how things were going."

"Tell us your name," Luminé demanded.

The Angel sighed and removed his hood so all could better see. His disguise had worked, and Luminé said, "Adon." With his beard gone, no one had recognized him.

Luminé's eyes froze, and Oxana put her hand over her mouth. Vamorda stepped back, as did the guards, as a collective gasp shot through the crowd, rolling along as fast as the turning and murmuring could carry it. Then all grew silent and turned to see Luminé's reaction.

Luminé gathered himself, feeling the need to be a ruler, "Lord Adon. Why have you come here to spy on us?"

"I am sorry," Adon said, "I wanted to see how things were going."

Someone shouted, "He deserves to be punished," And all at once, the crowd began clamoring, growing uneasy, shouting and jeering at Adon. The sudden shift in the mood and the disdain for their former Lord surprised Luminé. Indeed his Angels were not that vengeful?

And vengeful for what? He turned to Oxana, hoping she might know what to do, but he could see the worry on her face.

"Vamorda!" he said. "Tie up the prisoner's hands and take him into my Throne Room. Then, disperse the crowd."

Vamorda looked at Adon, worried he might resist her. She held no animosity towards the Lords and did not want to be put in a situation where she had to confront him.

Adon saw her trepidation, and compliantly held his hands out as Vamorda grabbed a piece of rope and tied his hands. She then led him inside to the Throne Room, followed by Luminé and Oxana. She came back out and signaled for her guards to move into action and send the crowds home. Before long, the crowd was gone, and the gates were closed.

Inside the Throne Room, Luminé closed the doors, leaving Adon alone with him and Oxana. He cut the rope and said, "I am sorry, Lord Adon."

"It is okay, Luminé. I should not have come." Adon wanted to tell him the truth that he came for their sake. He was worried that Legion would already be at work, trying to find a way to use them. He needed to see for himself what the situation was. Perhaps, he should tell them. They were alone.

Oxana sternly interrupted his thoughts, "You should not have come. You see how angry it made everyone."

Luminé's lips tightened as he snapped, "Stop, Oxana. I will… "

"No Luminé, you stop! This makes you look weak. It is wrong."

Luminé gritted his teeth, "Oxana, I will… "

Adon interrupted him and said in a disarming tone, "Luminé, please. Oxana is right. I have no place here, and I will not come again. If… I can retrieve my horse. I will be on my way."

Oxana scoffed, "Your horse! Where is it?"

"At the other end of the southern realm by the mountain range."

Oxana slowly rolled her eyes and looked to Luminé. "I will take you there," Luminé said.

"No," said Oxana, sternly standing. "It will not look good for you to do so. Your authority will be questioned. Lord Adon, Antonio will take you there now, but out the back way."

Adon nodded, "Very well."

Legion

Legion snapped awake. *Calla is looking for the sword.* He looked to the sky. There were still two hours before daybreak. He needed to try one more time before it was too late. They would find it before too long, and his chance to wield its power would have passed.

When he arrived at the Land of the Lords, it was still dark. He flew low now toward his former home, the Dark Mountain, but this time he went toward the bank of the Dark Lake along the backside of the mountain, near the place where he had hidden the Golden Sword. He landed near some trees and slowly approached the bank's edge to get a closer look across it. There was no movement. Swimming across would be best, as it would give him the best chance of not being seen, but it would be exhausting and weaken him as he was not at full power. He started into the water, then stopped. Across the lake, he saw movement. There was an Angel on guard. He thought, *I could probably subdue him quickly. Still, if he makes any sound, it will alert others, others undoubtedly nearby. They will wonder then why I came across here.* He grimaced, knowing it was too dangerous. He needed help, help from the inside. He reluctantly turned and left.

~ ~ ~ ~

The following day, Oxana walked through Luminare's compound, thinking about Adon's surprise visit yesterday. It was hard to believe she had been standing in front of him on equal terms, both of them, rulers of a Kingdom. The thought of that made her shudder, for she knew how utterly powerless she and Luminé were before him. But it was more than that which disturbed her. He had been kind in every aspect of the meeting, even while under the net, even while having the knife held to his throat, even while apologizing. There was a quiet strength about him which, as a lowly Angel in the Heavens, she had never been privy to. Perhaps they had made a mistake by leaving, perhaps... She felt a jolt in her mind and stopped, as a dark quivering sensation raced down her spine into her loins. It was Legion, summoning her, beckoning her.

She looked up at the sun. It was still early enough. Luminé was off with Antonio inspecting the section of land Antonio would claim and call his realm. She went inside and quickly freshened up, then flew to Legion's lair hidden on the Earth.

It was easy to find this time, as she recognized the high mountain, next to the smaller peak and rocky stream that marked the entrance. Her entire body warmed as she walked down the hidden pathway of the dense pine forest. The last time she was here, she rejected his advances, but she would not today. Today, the dark pleasure she had experienced only with Legion was beckoning her, drawing her, and she needed to recruit its power.

"Oxana," came the voice from behind her.

Oxana turned, "Lord Legion, you startled me," she said seductively.

"You felt my summons. I am pleased." Legion was dressed in a long tan robe with sandals on his feet. His long blonde hair was pushed behind his shoulders, accenting his tan skin. It was darker than the last time she saw him, and it made him look even more desirable.

Legion smiled and stepped closer, "I have something very important for you to do."

"Anything, my Lord." She bowed.

"We must retrieve the Golden Sword from the Dark Mountain."

"But I do not know what this is."

"It is the sword from the prophecy. I have found it, but someone must go and get it."

"Why can't you get it?" she asked.

"It is on the Dark Mountain, being guarded by Michael and Rana's Angels. It must be someone else. Perhaps, Rana."

Oxana was outraged to hear Rana's name, as well as his need to involve her. He meant, get Luminé involved too. She thought for a moment, wondering what Legion was about to say next. She was a Queen now, no longer an errand Angel, running about doing Legion's tasks, nor Luminé's for that matter. "Why do we need the sword?"

Legion's face grew cross, "Do you question me, Oxana?"

"Yes, I do," she said confidently, knowing she was in a place of power as he was asking her for help.

He smiled, "The Golden Sword will give power to whoever possesses it. It also has to power to kill any Angel or any Lord."

Oxana listened calmy, but inwardly she was shuddering. *The power to kill,* she gulped. "Is that all? It does not seem that important."

Legion gritted his teeth, "Are you listening, Oxana?"

"You forget Legion. I am a Queen already. What do I want of a sword?"

"The Lords will try to unseat you, Oxana. That is why. Do you think they are happy Luminé broke away? They will try to undermine him… and you. I have seen this in my dreams. Calla will take revenge on all who left."

Oxana tried not to show her growing apprehension. Adon himself had already been caught in Luminare. Legion was right.

"If I agree to help you. How do I get it?"

He said, "Luminé was in love, or should I say, in lust with Rana, was he not?"

Oxana's blood boiled all at once as she snapped, "What has this to do with me?"

"Rana, Michael, and the Angels under them are guarding the Dark Mountain. The sword is hidden there. Luminé must convince Rana to bring it to him as she has access and the trust of Michael."

"That is outrageous! I will not… "

Legion cut her off by putting a knife to her throat, "Do not question me. You will be destroyed, Oxana. You and Luminé will be destroyed unless you possess the sword."

Oxana swallowed. Legion was not doing this for them. He wanted the sword for himself. He was using her and Luminé and would most likely kill them both when the opportunity presented itself. Yet, Legion would not be so open about the sword unless it truly possessed the powers he professed it did.

Legion stepped forward, slowly pressing her, "You must do this."

She nodded, "I will do it."

Lito

The Archangel Lito, one of the six appointed by Luminé, marched across Luminare's headquarter compound accompanied by his second in command, Yuki, and five of their Host Commanders.

Lito was a dark looking, secretive Angel. He had belonged to Gabriel's realm before deciding at the last moment to leave. He was exceedingly muscular and strong, good looking as well. Immensely popular with the Angels in Heaven, he had once been thought of as a possible replacement for Luminé. That was, of course, until the news of the Humans being able to bear children. It struck Lito with the same jealousy as it had for most of those who left. Once Oxana found out that he was among her recruits, she immediately set her sights on grooming him to be one of their leaders.

Yuki was another surprise recruit. She was a slender female, strong and athletic, with lightly tanned skin and shiny black hair. Her eyes were her most stunning feature, narrow and brown, adorned with thin, even darker eyebrows. She had trained with Calla for over a year in all aspects of the Martial Arts, and she had been one of Calla's favorite students. It was said that she was secretly in love with Lito, which was why she had followed Luminé out of the Heavens. This was only a rumor, though.

As Lito and his entourage reached the entrance, several of the Palace Guards, dressed in crisp black uniforms, stopped them, asking, "What business do you have here?"

"I demand to see Luminé immediately."

"Demand?" The guard said. He was a tall, muscular guard. Obviously, one of the top recruits Luminé had required. He turned to the other and laughed, then turned back to Lito. "You cannot see him without an appointment."

Lito grabbed him by the shirt collar and lifted him off his feet. The other guards drew their swords, but Yuki and Lito's commanders quickly disarmed them. Lito said, "Go tell Luminé I need to see him now!"

The guard went in and came out a few anxious minutes later. "He will see you now."

Lito confidently smiled at his followers, and they went up the wide stairway to the elevated, newly completed, Throne Room, standing 15 feet in the air. It was not nearly as large as the Throne Room in the Heavens. It was still majestic in its own right, open at the top with magnificent side views looking over the compound wall to the sea and all the surrounding lands. Twenty Palace Guards, their faces set and determined, came in and stood at attention along the surrounding walls. Lito, Yuki, and their commanders, suddenly greatly outnumbered, stood in front of the empty thrones waiting for Luminé.

The side door opened, and Luminé and Oxana walked in and across the floor without looking up. Their faces showed no emotion, except perhaps a tint of aggravation at being suddenly summoned. They took their seats on the thrones and said nothing for several moments. Finally, he asked, "What do you want, Lito?"

"We need more land than has been apportioned to us."

Luminé did not reply but only glared at him, with the corners of his mouth clamped stiffly together. He asked, "What is wrong with the land you have?"

"Not enough of it overlooks the sea. Antonio's realm has almost twice as much coastal land."

Luminé stood abruptly and snapped, "Antonio is my lead Archangel. He has special apportionments for a reason."

"He is no better than I, Luminé. Now give the land we want, or we will take it by force."

Luminé glared. He looked at Yuki, and the other commanders, then back at Lito, "Take it by force?" His voice now began to raise, "Do you know who you are talking to, Lito?"

"Yes, I do, Luminé. You are nothing more than an Angel like me. You may have been an Archangel in Heaven, but you are not here."

Luminé slammed his fist, shouting, "I am in charge here, Lito!"

Lito stood firm, unmoved, glaring back at Luminé defiantly, and asked, "Are you going to grant the land, or not?"

Luminé's chest puffed out as he bared his teeth, ready to answer, but just then, Oxana put her hand on his arm, pausing him. She said, "We will take the matter under advisement and let you know tomorrow. Come back tomorrow here, at the same time, and we will have your answer."

At The Haldansa

It was evening, and the low warming rays of the sun cast their golden light across the stone floor of the Haldansa, the great meeting hall the Lords had built for banquets and dancing.

Calla stood in the center of the raised marble stage, getting ready for her announcement. Next to her, seated in chairs, were Adon and Yeshua. To the side of them, also seated, where the six remaining Archangels. Though there were over 400,000 Angels gathered, the place looked empty. It had been built to hold 700,000 Angels comfortably. It had been built to be a place of celebration and fun, but that was when the Angels were all one, and there was no trouble or division in the Heavens.

Calla stepped to the front of the stage and waited a moment for all to quiet down. She said, "Angels of Heaven: We have two important announcements. First, we wanted to inform you all that the Angels that followed Luminé to the Southern Realm are not allowed back into the Heavens. By the same token, none of you are allowed to go to the Southern Realm. The Archangels will begin establishing a guard system to ensure that this is followed."

Murmurs went through the crowd. Most of the Angels had friends, and some of them lovers, who they were suddenly being told they could no longer see.

Calla raised her hand again, "There is one more announcement. We have chosen a new Archangel to replace Luminé. It came down to two Angels, who actually know each other very well. They are both deserving, and our only regret is that we could only choose one. It came down to a decision between two of our truly finest Angels, Sadie and Marcellus." Calla scanned the crowd. She spotted Marcellus, but strangely, Sadie was not with him. She turned to look briefly at Adon and Yeshua, and the other Archangels standing on the stage her and whispered, "Where is Sadie?"

They all shrugged and scanned the gathering. Calla nodded and turned back to the crowd, "Well, I was hoping to acknowledge them both before the announcement. But, we have decided that the new

Archangel of the 2nd Heavenly Realm is Marcellus. Marcellus, please come forward."

A loud cheer went up, and everyone began to congratulate Marcellus as he made his way through the immense crowd.

Splendora leaned over to Gabriel and said, "I think it should have been Sadie. I hope she is not upset at being passed over a second time."

Gabriel grimly nodded, "She may be at that. Where is she?"

"I don't know. Maybe she is with Eve?"

Marcellus came onto the stage and received a special sword from Calla. He was congratulated by all and ushered over to stand next to the other Archangels as everyone applauded.

~ ~ ~ ~

A festive evening of music, dancing, they were reconnecting. Trays of fresh fruits, bread, and freshly cooked meats were plentiful. Several flavors of wine and teas and coffees were available at all corners of the great open-air mountain top hall.

As the night wore on, Sadie landed on the western edge of the Haldansa and immediately began making her way through the crowd, looking for Calla. She found her speaking to a group of Angels. Calla turned, "Sadie, where have you been?"

"I was busy, my Lord."

"I need to speak with you," Calla said, smiling.

Sadie nodded, then walked up to her and whispered in her ear.

Calla listened intently, and then her eyes lit up with a hopeful smile on her face. She said, "The great day has come." She then leaned forward and said quietly, "Sadie, go get Splendora and meet me at the home of Adam and Eve. I will tell the other Lords. Tell no one."

"At once, my Lord," Sadie replied, as she turned and went looking for Splendora. When she found her, she was near the stage, speaking to Rana and Michael. Sadie dreaded having to go anywhere near Rana. Rana had cheated in the Angel Games and stolen Sadie's rightful place to be the Seventh Archangel. After the stress of what happened to Adam and Eve, and the stress of Luminé shattering the Heavens by taking a third of the Angels, she was in no mood to be nice. She honestly did not trust herself out of fear; she might lose her temper and let Rana have what she deserved.

Rana looked at her stunning self, with her white Archangel uniform, short skirt, long tan legs, and long wavy blonde hair. She never impressed Sadie, though, because Sadie knew inside she was not as beautiful and not as strong as she looked. Sadie stopped a few feet away from them and called out, "Splendora?"

Rana turned, "Oh, Sadie. It's you. I'm sorry you didn't get chosen."

Sadie kept her lips compressed, trying desperately not to say what she wanted to. "What do you mean, chosen?"

"Well, to replace Luminé. They chose Marcellus instead of you."

Sadie smirked and brushed her hand through the air, "Oh, I am happy for him, Rana, *and* happier still that he didn't have to cheat!" Sadie's smirk turned to a glare.

Rana's eyes narrowed, "It's not my fault you weren't paying attention, Sadie, or should I call you, just, Angel Sadie."

"Well, if you would… "

Splendora stepped in, "All right, that's enough. What is it you need, Sadie?"

"Calla needs you. You are to come with me at once."

"Where are we going?"

Sadie looked to Rana and replied with a half-smile, "It's a secret."

Sadie turned, and Splendora followed. As they walked away, she heard Rana say loudly to Michael, "I don't like her."

~ ~ ~ ~

Sadie and Splendora raced toward the Earth. They landed inside the compound where Adam and Eve lived. It was dusk now, and the night was growing dark. The sounds of the animals of the night were coming alive outside the compound walls. These sounds were never welcome to Adam and Eve because they were wild and dangerous. As they crossed the compound, they heard loud moans coming from the hut.

Splendora placed her hand on Sadie's arm, stopping her, and asked, "What's going on?"

"I don't think anything is wrong. I think she is having her baby. Calla said it would not be easy. Let's hurry." They hustled over the remaining steps and climbed up the ladder into the front room of the large hut. They could see Eve in the backroom, lying on the bed, with her waist covered by a blanket. Her face showed great anguish, and tears were running down her reddened cheeks. Adam was sitting next to her, holding her hand and holding her neck up. At the edge of the bed was Calla, sitting, with a concerned look on her face. The sleeves of her tunic were rolled up past her elbows. She was gently rubbing Eve's stomach, talking to her softly, encouraging her.

Calla turned, her eyes wide, and her brow wrinkled with worry. She hastily said, "Sadie, go get water from the stream. Splendora, gather some fresh cloth. Hurry."

Sadie and Splendora raced out, both worried by the look on Calla's face. When they returned, Eve was moaning even louder. Calla was urging her, "That's it, Eve, push... yes, that's it... you can do this... " Suddenly, Eve began to lurch forward slightly, bearing down, pushing even harder.

Calla's eyes lit up, "Here it comes," she said, as her hands reached down and gently took hold of a small head and body that emerged from between Eve's legs. Calla pulled the blood-covered infant out, first its shoulders and arms, then its midsection, and finally its legs. She held the tiny Human upside down, marveling for a moment, then slapped it on the backside, and the child began to wail. Calla turned to all, "It is a male child."

Splendora gasped and turned to Sadie just in time to see Sadie's eyes roll to the back of her head as she fainted and fell to the floor, knocking over a bowl of fruit on a nearby table.

"Sadie!" exclaimed Splendora. She jumped down next to her, picking her head off the floor, asking, "Sadie! Are you okay?"

Calla turned to look at the commotion, her face full with a broad smile, and said, "She'll be fine. Give me the water and cloth. Adam, give me your knife."

Calla took Adam's knife and cut the long tube that ran from Eve's womb to the middle of the baby. Then she carefully tied the cord and tucked it into the baby's stomach. Splendora and Adam looked on in amazement. The baby was washed quickly and bundled and placed in Eve's arms.

Eve began to cry as her pain suddenly turned to immense joy. Adam, too, had tears running down his face as he pressed his wet cheek against Eve's. Calla and Splendora wiped the tears from their eyes, and both looked down at Sadie, who was still out and chuckled to each other. Suddenly Eve's eyes widened, and she looked at Calla and started moaning again.

Calla shouted, "Adam, take the baby. Something is wrong."

Sadie woke, looking around, and was helped up by Splendora. She went over to Adam and looked closely at the baby. "Oh, my goodness. Look at... at..." she looked up at Adam. Is it a male child or a female?"

"A male child," replied Adam proudly.

Sadie then heard Eve moaning. She asked in an alarmed tone, "Lord Calla, what is happening?"

"I think another baby is coming."

"Another!" Sadie again began to faint. This time Splendora was ready and caught her.

"Sadie, stay with us. We need you."

Sadie revived herself and sat next to Eve while Adam stood behind them, holding the baby. Sadie grabbed Eve's hand, tears running down both their faces, as Eve moaned louder and louder. Sadie said, "Eve, you are going to be okay. Did you see that beautiful little man child?"

Eve turned to Sadie and started to smile widely but was pulled back into her labor.

"Here it comes!" Calla exclaimed for the second time.

Moments later, Calla held the second child aloft, slapped it on the backside, and amidst the new round of wailing, proclaimed, "We have a beautiful female child."

Splendora handed Calla Adam's knife as she cut the cord and immersed the child in the water. She handed the female infant to Splendora. Splendora laid the little girl on the clean cloth, marveling at her beauty, and carefully wrapped her up. She brought her to Eve and placed her gently in Eve's arms.

Eve broke down crying, unable to contain her joy. The male child was then handed to her, and she held them both, crying, laughing, talking to the cooing infants.

Eve looked to Calla, "How will we take care of them?"

Calla smiled, "Well, the first thing we have to do is feed them."

"But how? They are so little."

Calla went over and helped Eve to loosen the top of her tunic. "Eve, we have made provision for you to provide your babies with all the food they need. Your breasts will produce milk for them. This will only be until they grow old enough to begin eating normal food, such as fruits, vegetables, grains, and meats. Here, place the child's mouth by your breast."

Everyone watched in amazement as the little infant began to gently suck on Eve's breast. Eve watched in wonderment, then looked up into the eyes of all, astounded at everything that had occurred.

Calla then said, "Sadie, you were under consideration to replace Luminé as the newest Archangel. However, we did not choose you for a reason. I would like to ask you to keep with what you are doing here. Eve will need help for a while, and I can think of no better Angel to help them. Will you?"

Sadie's wiped the tears of joy from her own cheeks. "I will, Lord Calla."

"Good. Then we will go. Sadie, stay here tonight and assist them with caring for the little ones."

"But how do I care for them?" Sadie asked.

"Oh, you will see. They have lots of needs." Calla laughed, "Don't worry, Sadie. It is all very natural."

She then turned to Adam and Eve and asked, "What will you call your children?"

Eve looked up, "We have already decided on a male name and a female name, Lord Calla."

"Oh, what are they?"

Adam said, "The male child will be called Cain. The female child will be called Luluwana."

"That's beautiful." Calla went to the babies and placed her hand on their heads, whispering words of blessing. Then, she and Splendora left to go and tell Adon and Yeshua.

Round Up

The Archangel Lito woke. Something was moving across the room. He sat up quietly, reached down for his sword, and felt a hand wrap around his forehead while a sharp blade pressed into his neck. A female voice whispered, "Stay perfectly still, or I will slice your throat open."

Lito stayed still as the blade lifted up, forcing him to stand. For a moment, he felt fear, but then it turned to anger. Luminé was behind this, and Luminé would pay dearly.

"Bind him," came the command. Suddenly two other Angels grabbed his arms, wrenching them behind his back, tying them tightly with a rope. His mouth was gagged with a large cloth and a hood thrust over his head. From behind, a dagger was placed between his shoulder blades, and the command was given, "Take him."

Lito was dragged outside of his hut and thrust inside some sort of cart with caged sides. Inside the cart with his hands bound, he vowed he would seek revenge. But then, a tinge of fear shot through him. If Luminé had dared to take him as a prisoner in the middle of the night, what fate did he have planned? The ride in the cart was long, down bumpy roads. It seemed to him they must be taking him to the Headquarters.

He felt the cart stop and the cart door open. Several hands grabbed hold of him, dragging him with a thud out and onto the ground, then dragging him across the compound ground's dirt. All around him, he could see torches burning. He was taken to a spot, still outdoors, and forced onto his knees. He moaned, trying to talk through the gag in his mouth. He heard others moaning close by. Then he waited in the darkness, frightened and disoriented by the hood.

Suddenly, the hood was yanked off. Before him stood Luminé and Oxana outside their Headquarters, their faces stiff with angry resolve, illuminated by the nearby torches' flickering light. Standing next to them were at least 10 Palace Guards, all dressed in their black uniforms, all holding their swords in their hands, all their faces bearing down on Lito. Lito looked to his left and saw six other Angels, all wearing black hoods, all with their arms behind their backs tied up with rope, all trembling, writhing to get free. Lito shuddered, realizing that Luminé was using the one thing Angels feared more than anything, darkness; and it was working.

One by one, the hoods were yanked off by someone behind them. Lito strained to see who was removing the hoods. It was Vamorda, standing tall, a foreboding figure in the night. He could see her eyes were fixed, and so was the smile on her face.

When she removed the last hood, Lito's face appeared, tears streaming down his face, his chest rising and falling rapidly, trying to breathe through his gagged mouth. Between him and her were the five commanders who were with him yesterday. Vamorda walked back in front of the line over to Lito and pulled the gag out of his mouth. He gasped, trying to calm his fear, and said, "What... what is the meaning of this?"

Luminé walked up and stood in front of him, glaring. He then said, in a low tone, "You and your companions are here to be judged."

"Judged! You cannot judge me!" Lito said through gritted teeth. Vamorda stepped forward and whacked the back of his head with the handle of her sword, yelling, shouting, "Silence, before the Great Luminé."

The other Angels looked over, still unable to speak, but their eyes showed worry. One, a commander named Michelle, was the worst. Her eyes were closed tightly, with tears running out of them. Her body shivered uncontrollably as if she knew some dire punishment was about to befall them.

Luminé turned to the side, looking back toward the dark area of his compound, "Bring the first cage."

Three palace guards walked over, carrying a wooden four-foot by four-foot square cage, draped in black cloth. It was set down, and a door was opened, revealing a pitch-black interior. Suddenly, Lito understood, and his entire being trembled. It had always been known that complete darkness was to be feared. Even being under the black hood had severely frightened them all. To be put inside a dark box would surely drive any Angel to the point of insanity.

Lito looked into the cage and swallowed hard, his heart sinking within him. He looked up, his eyes no longer trying to be strong, pleaded, as he said, "No, Luminé. Please, we… we… "

"Silence, before the Great Luminé!" said Vamorda, as she smacked the back of his head again with the handle of her sword, this time drawing blood.

Luminé's face did not indicate feeling or remorse, as he uttered the words, "You are sentenced to one year in a Dark Cage for defying my rule."

Lito's widening eyes drifted into the blackness of the cage, then back to Luminé, "No…no… please… Luminé, please!"

Three of the Palace Guards lifted him, shoved him inside, cut the rope from his hands, and closed the door, the pitch-black darkness rendering him powerless to resist. All eyes, even those of the guards, cringed as they heard the desperate cries from within the cage to open the door.

Luminé turned to the next Angel, Michelle. "You are also sentenced to one year in a Dark Cage for defying my rule." Her eyes opened wide, then closed in despair, as they yanked the gag out of her mouth. They dragged her over, shoving her in. Her feeble voice could be heard saying, "Oh my God. No. no!" as the door slammed shut, and what followed could only be described as a long, continuous, bone-chilling scream.

Luminé went down the line, sentencing each of the commanders to the same fate, as the Palace Guards thrust them into cages. Finally, he came to Yuki, Lito's 2nd in command. The gag was removed from her mouth. Luminé asked, "Yuki since you are second in command, you will receive the same sentence as Lito."

She gasped but was already trying to visibly slow her breathing as if preparing to endure the darkness.

"However," said Luminé. "Oxana thinks you have potential. She thinks you are not as foolish as Lito. Are you as foolish as he was?"

"No… no Great… Luminé. I am not," she replied, desperately wanting to know if she could genuinely avoid the horrible fate of the others.

"Stand up," said Luminé.

Vamorda stepped behind her and pulled her up.

Luminé walked up to her, examining her face, assessing her fear, contemplating his plan. He asked, "Will you ever defy me again, Yuki?"

"No," she replied, her knees shaking almost uncontrollably.

"Will you tell others what happens to those who oppose me?"

"No, I won't."

Luminé gritted his teeth and leaned closer, "Yes, you will tell them. You will tell them all what happened here. Do you understand?"

"Yes, I will tell them." She swallowed, hoping he would not change his mind.

"Good. You are now the newest Archangel in my realm and will take over Lito's possessions. Now, go with my Palace Guards and see where they will hang the cages."

Luminé turned to Vamorda. "Hang them in the back, place a guard around them at all times, and put the sign up. 'Here are the Angels who dared to oppose Luminé.'"

Oxana

The next day, Oxana watched from the Headquarters ' window as Angels from all over came and looked at the six Dark Cages hanging in the woods behind. A heavy guard had been established, with over 30 Angels assigned to the duty. The cages were to be guarded night and day. Six of them swung gently in the breeze. A large sign had been made out of wood. It read, "Behold those who dare to defy Luminé."

All the gaping onlookers were forced to remain at a distance by the Palace Guard, allowed only close enough to read the large sign and hear the periodic muffled cries from within the cages.

Oxana could tell by how the onlookers spoke to each other, there was a mixture of anger and fear. She was pleased. This excellent idea she and Luminé had concocted, to make an example out of such a popular Angel as Lito would indeed send a message that no one was safe. Allowing Yuki to return to her command also ensured that the story of Lito's absolute terror and the others would not remain a secret of that night.

~ ~ ~ ~

Over the next several days, Luminé was busy inspecting the Angels' progress in building the Headquarters' offices and living quarters. Oxana kept watching on the steady stream of Angels who had come to see for themselves Lito and his commanders inside the Dark Cages.

The mood and tone had begun to change. The mixture of anger and fear she had seen over the first few days was now changing to anger and rage. More and more, Angels were approaching the place with anger and malice on their faces. She began to worry. She looked beyond the gathered crowd at the collection of open cages sitting on the ground underneath those hanging in the trees above. Luminé had ordered them built and put there, as a reminder to all, that they could also end up in one. Now, for a moment, she imagined her and Luminé being dragged from their Headquarters, across the compound and locked inside one themselves.

She shuddered, and went outside and decided to go down to a quiet place on the shoreline. She needed to think.

When she arrived at the shore, it was midday. The waves were low today, gently washing onto the sandy beach. Some Angels were not too far away, swimming, so Oxana walked in the opposite direction. She breathed in the sea air, trying to remember herself. For so long now, she had been acting, it seemed, cast into some role as the Queen, the confidant of the Great Luminé. Oh, if the others only knew how fragile she really was, and Luminé too, for that matter.

Here, alone on this beach, she was just herself, and part of her missed those simpler days when she had no pretenses to hide.

The growing mood of the masses worried her. It had been a few weeks since Legion had spoken to her about the sword. Even after he had, she knew she would not act right away. She needed to let Legion realize he was not her Lord, and certainly not one who could command her every move.

But it was more than that. Up until now, she had dismissed Legion's far fetched idea, or command rather, that Luminé was to use Rana to retrieve the Golden Sword. Now, seeing those Angels' faces, and peering into the blackness of the open Dark Cages, she was beginning to realize just how powerless she and Luminé were. If what Legion said was true, the Golden Sword's power could change everything. It could provide the edge her and Luminé might very well need.

The following morning she watched from the corner of the upstairs Throne Room window, careful not to be seen from below, pondering her plan.

"Oxana? What are you looking at?"

Her eyes widened, and she calmed her heart, then turned, offering a fake half-smile, and said, "Luminé, you startled me."

"I am sorry. What are you looking at?"

She leaned back, careful to stay out of the views of those below, and said, "I am watching the reactions of the Angels. They are angry, Luminé. I am not sure this was a good idea."

"Don't worry," he said in a dismissive tone. "We had to send a message, and we did."

"But, Luminé, you don't understand. We do not have power like the Lords have. We will need this power if we are going to survive."

"Survive?"

"Look at them, Luminé. I can feel a rebellion in the air."

Luminé's face grew cross, and he walked over to the window, looking outside. He observed several Angels looking, pointing, scoffing with angry looks on their faces. He too, stepped back.

Oxana could see the momentary fear on his face. He asked her, "What are we supposed to do? We have to keep order."

Oxana was quiet for a moment, pondering how she would explain it all without implicating herself. She decided it was the best time. She stepped further away from the window, then walked across the great hall and sat on her Throne. Luminé followed and stood in front of her. She crossed her legs and leaned forward, looking out the side of the open-air throne out to sea, pretending to be in deep thought.

"What is it, Oxana?" he asked.

"I have hesitated to tell you this, but I believe there is something we can do."

"What?" he said, in a tone full of doubt.

"Do you remember the Golden Sword from the Prophecy?"

Luminé's brow furrowed, "Yes, I know the sword from the Prophecy? I haven't heard that in a long time."

Now his tone turned to one of interrogation, "Why do you mention it?"

"I know where it is."

Luminé scoffed, "You know where it is? That is absurd. How could you possibly know?"

Oxana hesitated, but she was committed already. So she just said it, "Legion told me."

Luminé froze, and a blank, questioning look filled his face as he stared at the floor. Oxana could see the wheels in his mind turning with a million thoughts. She knew where they were all headed, back to the wooden crate in which the creature Serpe had been brought into the Garden of Eden. Oxana had sworn she had nothing to do with it, yet now she had openly admitted she *had* talked to Legion.

"What do you mean, Legion told you?" Luminé asked in a probing, angry tone.

"Luminé, listen to me. I have never spoken to him in my life before now. A few weeks ago, he cornered me while I was flying by the Earth. I had no choice but to listen to him. Once he told me about the sword, I dismissed it and vowed in my heart to stay away from the Earth, for fear I would see him again. But now, seeing those Angels' faces, and knowing how powerless we truly are against all of them, I decided I must tell you what he told me, and... I have come to a conclusion. You and I need to possess that sword.

"So, you consult with Legion now?"

"Luminé, forget about Legion. He seems weak to me, but that does not matter. It is the sword of the Prophecy! It makes sense. We need to get the Golden Sword in order to stay in power. He said it would make us as powerful as the Lords. He told me he has it hidden, but he knows how we can get it."

"Where is it?" Luminé asked.

"It is on the Dark Mountain. Michael and Rana's Angels are guarding it. Legion said you would convince Rana to get it for you."

The mention of Rana's name stirred Luminé. Her beautiful body flashed into his mind for a moment, but he put it aside.

Oxana seductively stepped closer, taking his broad shoulders into her hands, "Luminé, forget about Legion. He must think he is using me to get to you. Let him! I love you. I am loyal to only you. He obviously wants the sword for himself, but we will hide it. In fact… " Her eyes widened and she looked out the window, thinking it through. She looked back at him, "Once we have it, we will make a duplicate, so we can give him the fake one and keep the real sword without anyone knowing!"

Luminé studied her face carefully. He seemed to trust her. "What will this sword do for us?"

"It must have immense value. It is the sword of the Prophecy. Legion said it has the power to take Eternal Life away, to power to kill an enemy forever. We can use it as a bargaining chip. He also said whoever possesses it would have special powers, Lordly powers."

Luminé began nodding. "Alright, tell me where it is exactly."

Rana

Michael opened his eyes and reached over, feeling the empty spot in the bed next to him. He lifted his head and smiled. "Good morning, beautiful."

Rana was standing naked in front of the mirror, fixing her hair. She turned, "Good morning, Michael."

He closed his eyes, taking in a deep breath, feeling the deep peace wash over him. He was falling in love with Rana, something he never imagined doing. He knew all the rumors were probably true about how she had cheated Sadie at the Angel Games and stole her Archangel title. How she was intimately involved with Luminé and to what degree was complicit in his fall, no one really knew. But none of that mattered because she was exciting, kind, seductive, and despite her questionable lapses in character, amazing in almost every way.

Rana turned around, crossed her feet, and leaned against the dresser, showing off her body. "And what do you have going on this morning?"

"I am just going to stay right here and watch you for a while."

Rana laughed, "Oh, is that so."

He thrust the sheet aside, "Yes, that is so."

"Well, perhaps you would like a closer look then."

Michael sat up and held his hand out, beckoning her.

Rana waited a moment, thinking, then walked over and took it, climbed back into bed.

~ ~ ~ ~

An hour later, Rana landed in the yard of her seaside home. She paused to take in the beauty of the sun still in its ascent over the Heavenly Sea. She was glad she had not left for the Southern Realm with Luminé and was pleasantly surprised by her new love affair with Michael. He was strong, caring, good looking, and solid in his convictions and desire to do what was right. That was the thing she liked the most. His physical prowess was unmatched, but it was the innate goodness that possessed its own strength. This was something she had never understood and now loving him was opening her eyes to all of it.

She walked to her door slowly, mesmerized. Suddenly she gasped. There was a ribbon on the door. Luminé used to leave one to let her know he was there. She walked down the hall and stopped. Luminé was sitting on a chair, smiling.

"Luminé! What are you doing here?"

He stood up slowly, "Hello, Rana. I am sorry to surprise you.

She exhaled slowly, trying to process the myriad of emotions and questions running all at once through her mind. What was he doing here? Was he there to try to seduce her? Was he there to admonish her for not going with him? And, he was not even allowed to be in the Heavens? She said, "Luminé, you are not allowed to be here."

"I know that, but… I snuck in anyway. I am more powerful than you may think," he said, as he walked across the room toward her.

She turned away slightly and went to a chair across from him and sat down. "Luminé, sit down, please. Let's talk."

"Where were you?" he asked.

"I was… out."

"Do you have a new lover?"

"Well, of course, I do."

Luminé smiled. He was not in control now, and he sensed it. He inwardly cringed.

Rana gulped, unsure of what to say or do as silence ensued. Luminé was the first she had ever loved, and he was the one she would always love. Her daringness kept her visiting him while he was in exile, which allowed him to keep his sanity. At least, that was what he had constantly told her. And by the hunger he always greeted her with, she believed him fully. She had let him down, though, in the end, by turning away, turning her back on his promise, to make her his 1st of Archangels.

Luminé interrupted her thoughts with the question she dreaded, "Why didn't you come?"

"I don't know why… I changed my mind." She felt the opposition and trepidation in her voice but saying the words made her stronger. "Why are you here, Luminé?"

Luminé knew there was more to her excuse, but he wasn't ready to have that conversation with her. He needed her. He could not risk angering her. "I need your help. There is a sword that is said to possess power. We have trouble down in the Southern Realm. There are rumors the Lords are going to confront us to overcome us, and we are too weak right now to handle this."

"What! I have not heard any of this." Rana stood in disbelief at his comment. He had never lied to her before. Was he lying now? No, he would not, he loved her, and deep down, she would always love him.

"Just last week, Adon was caught at one of our rallies. He was spying on us."

"Caught? Adon? That makes no sense."

Luminé stood up and began to pace. "I have to have the sword as a bargaining chip. It possesses power. I need this power to keep things under control to bargain with the Lords."

"Why do you need me to help?"

"Because it is hidden on the Dark Mountain. I cannot get to it."

"But how did it get there?"

"I don't know how it got there, but I have found it, and it does not matter. I must have it, or I will have no power. Will you get it for me?"

Rana stopped. Something was wrong. She felt it. But what? In the old days, she would do anything for Luminé. Was it her love for Michael? Was it his influence on "I don't know if..."

"Rana, please. We have been friends and lovers from the beginning. We have always been destined to be for each other. I am asking you one last favor. As remediation for you... for you not coming with me... " He looked down, hoping he had swayed her.

Rana had disappointed him once. She would do this, and then be done with him. She said, "Alright. I will get it. Tell me where it is. I will bring it here tonight after midnight."

Discontent

Luminé raced back to the Southern Realm, flying various routes to remain unseen. The guard network established by the Archangels was centered over the normal routes between lands. They did not imagine Luminé would fly right over the various realms, in plain sight, wearing only a modest covering on his head as a disguise. As he flew, he looked down over the villages and cities of Heaven's realms. They seemed so much more vibrant and alive than his own land. Life was teeming and active. His kingdom seemed to be stalled, full of chaos. Perhaps, they just needed time to get organized. It was beginning to anger him, and in his mind, he began blaming his inept Archangels.

But then, he dismissed his thoughts and focused on what was at hand. Tonight he would have the Golden Sword and all the power it possessed. He was not sure what he would do with it, but he was well aware of the Prophecy. Possessing it had to come with power, and in the very least, bargaining power. It would allow him to keep Legion at bay by denying him the thing he wanted most. It would also give him an ace in negotiations with the Lords, negotiations he was sure would ensue for a myriad of reasons.

As he made his way to the final stretch of the open sea, he headed far west to allude any possible guard activity. He then headed across the sea to Luminare. As he neared, he could see a crowd of Angels in the courtyard of his palace, angrily rioting. He landed in their midst and shouted, "What is the meaning of this!"

"You promised us a better life, Luminé!" one Angel said. "Now, we barely have enough land!"

Luminé's face grew enraged, and he shouted, "All of you go back to your homes. I will meet with the Archangels tomorrow to find out what needs to be done."

"I will tell you what needs to be done!" one Angel said, as he drew his sword. Luminé stepped up, skillfully drawing his sword, hopping forward, and knocked the sword out of his hands in three quick maneuvers. He put the point of his sword at the stunned Angel's neck, clenched his mouth, and said, "Would you like to join those Angels over there in the Dark Cages?"

"No… no," came the quivering reply.

Luminé pressed the sword in, cutting his neck, then kicked him away. "Go now, all of you. There will be an announcement tomorrow night."

The crowd dwindled away.

Luminé stormed up the stairs and into the Throne Room. Oxana was waiting, sitting calmly on her throne.

"What happened?" he demanded.

" The Angels are not content for many reasons."

"What are they upset about?"

"They gave me their list." She unfurled a parchment and began to read. "For one thing, they all have to build their own homes. In Heaven, everything was provided for them. They also are complaining that there is not as much land available as there was in Heaven."

"There is plenty of land!" he said scoffing.

"I know there is, but they are comparing it to Heaven, Luminé."

Luminé gritted his teeth and walked to the window. He had not expected all these headaches. With his voice filled with frustrated rage, he shouted, "Call a meeting with the Archangels now."

Oxana nodded, "Of course, but before we do, there is one more problem you need to be aware of."

Luminé turned, "What?"

Oxana glanced down at the bottom of the parchment, then looked back up, saying, "There are not enough females."

"What are you talking about?"

"When we left, a great deal more male Angels came than females."

"Well... what do I care? They have to figure it out."

"It's a problem. I have heard of many of the females being taken advantage of. There is an undercurrent of vile lawlessness growing." She paused, watching his reaction, not wishing to alarm him, yet needing for him to take it seriously. She finally added, "It scares me."

Luminé turned back to the window, scanning the horizon of his kingdom. "We will deal with them all. Do not worry. I have secured a way to get the Golden Sword tonight."

Oxana's eyes widened, "She agreed?"

"Yes, she did. It was too easy to convince her. I am to go there tonight after midnight."

"Be careful. They are establishing guards all along the border. I have heard it is getting very difficult to get through."

"Heard from who?"

Oxana smiled, "I have my spies, Luminé. Former friends, loyal to me. Go to the Earth first. From there, go to the Heavens from the North. The guard is weak there in the evening."

Luminé gazed into her eyes. She was beautiful, cunning, capable, and once again anticipating his every need. He pulled her closer, holding her waist. "Oxana, you are truly a Queen."

"You're not so bad yourself." She smiled seductively.

Luminé took her by the hand, "Come, my love."

The Sword

Later that evening, Rana left her home and rode her horse across the 6th Heavenly Realm's dark fields. She wanted to go as far as possible on land to be least noticed. She had no problem with any of the border guards. After all, she was an Archangel and dating an Archangel, and everyone knew it, giving her special permission and access. But still, tonight, it was best to remain under the radar as much as possible. When she reached the coast, she vaulted into the sky to the LAND OF THE LORDS, swinging along the coast to avoid Holy Mountain. She aimed straight toward Dark Mountain where her and Michael's forces were on guard.

She reached the opposite bank and got into a boat and went across. As soon as she landed, two guards with torches came out. "Archangel Rana? What are you doing here?"

"I have to inspect our night defenses. Who is in charge?"

"Timothy. He is up on the plateau."

"Good, give me a torch. I will go up and see him."

Once Rana reached the top, she summoned Timothy. "Timothy, show me where our guards are stationed."

Timothy walked with her around the perimeter of the large plateau, pointing downward to the various parts of the mountain leading up to the dark watery abyss in the center of the plateau. When they were on the North side, Rana said, "Who is down there, along this Northerly Western portion?"

"Two guards are stationed below."

"Good, say nothing. I am going for a walk to see how attentive they are." She started down a path along the side of the mountain, weaving her way to the place Luminé told her he had hidden the sword. A foreboding feeling swept up her spine. Was she doing something wrong here? Would she be better to find the sword and bring it to the Lords, winning the favor of them, as well as Michael? No, she didn't need any of this. Everything was going fine for her, and she owed Luminé. She would do him this favor and be done with him.

When she was nearly halfway down the mountainside, an authoritative female voice rang out, "Halt, who goes there?"

"It is I, Archangel Rana."

"Stay where you are," said the Angel.

Rana waited, listening to the Angel call the other guard, "Hey! Get over here."

Within a few moments, both guards were there. Rana said, "It took entirely too long for you two to discover me. Go at once and tell Timothy that I want at least two more guards put on every side of the mountain. Draw up a plan at once and implement it first thing tomorrow morning."

"But who will guard while we are gone?"

"I will stay here," she replied. "Go! Now!"

"Yes, Archangel Rana." They turned and began climbing to the top.

As soon as they were on their way, Rana turned her attention to find the marker. She had little time. Luminé said it was near a group of very large boulders just off a curved path. Next to them was a large fallen tree. The sword was underneath a group of stones arranged ten feet up the base of the fallen tree. She hustled down the path with her torch, anxiously looking left and right for the obscure markers.

~ ~ ~ ~

Michael woke up suddenly. A cougar had suddenly appeared in his dream and snarled at him. He calmed his racing heart, wondering if the dream had any meaning. His dreams had been fitful lately. Ever since Luminé and his followers had left, he felt uneasy. Many in his own ranks surprised him by going with Luminé, but even more of Rana's realm had done so and abandoned their homes. A good number of them were from the ranks of those assigned to guard the Dark Mountain. He was angry with them all. Fools, who had followed Luminé to their own demise, was the only way he could characterize them.

He looked out at the moon, then rolled over and tried to get back to sleep, but he could not. He decided to check on the guards. He flew to the Dark Mountain, got in a boat, and crossed. When he reached the other side, two guards came out. "Great Michael, what are you doing here?"

"Can I not inspect my guards any time I want?"

"Of course," he bowed. "It's just that Rana is also here doing the same thing."

"Rana? Now?"

"Yes, she went up to see Timothy a little while ago."

Michael took one of their torches, saying, "I need to borrow this."

~ ~ ~ ~

Rana hustled along the path, guiding the torch left and right, desperately looking for the large group of strategically placed boulders. Time was running out as the guards would be back any minute. She needed to get the sword and get out of there. Once she picked it up, she would be in a practically unexplainable predicament if she were caught.

"There they are." She ran over and held the light close, then looked for the fallen tree as she hopped off the path over the boulders and held the torch to the base of the tree. She walked 10 feet along the trunk, holding the light low as it illuminated the ground. The collection of stones sat neatly piled. She dropped to her knees. One by one, she lifted the stones aside, brushing dirt away as she went along. Then she saw it. A glimmer of metal was shining up at her. Her eyes widened as she ran her hands along the golden blade and picked up the sword, marveling at its beauty by the dimming light of the torch.

"Rana!" came a loud familiar shout from not too far away.

She looked up in a panic. It was Michael. She stood up and took her own sword out of its sheath, and placed the Golden Sword in its place. She dropped to her knees again and pressed her own sword into the dirt, then covered it, then hopped back onto the path. "Rana? What are you doing?"

Michael was standing in front of her. Had he seen her come out of the path. "Michael?" she said as she casually placed her tunic over the handle of the sword.

"Why are you here?"

"I… I was testing our defenses. I sent the guards to inform our leaders to come up with a better plan. They completely missed my arrival too slow to respond, not acceptable."

Michael knew something was amiss. Her words were hurried, and her voice was subtly frantic. He had interrupted something.

"Rana, what is really going on?"

She froze. He had said it as if he knew something. "Nothing is going on." she said adamantly. "Except that the guards are not doing their jobs!"

Michael sensed she was lying. But why? He said in an authoritative tone. "We will speak to them together then."

Rana nodded and walked past him, heading up the path. Michael glanced over at the place he had seen her come out of the woods, then followed her up the path.

"Rana!" he called out. She stopped and turned, careful to conceal the sword.

"I have been thinking about us."

"What about us?"

"Yes. I want to take a break. I need some time to think things over."

Rana felt her heart drop within her. She turned and stormed off.

Luminé Waits

Luminé waited at the shore not far from the entrance to Rana's seaside home. He had been there for several hours and was growing anxious. Suddenly he saw her. She was hunched over, walking at a slow, deliberate pace. She looked bothered, aggravated. He had never before seen her like this, and he knew he had asked her to do the impossible. Perhaps she had failed. He would have to convince her to try again.

He watched her go into her home. He waited a few more moments to assure no one was watching, then went to the door. She opened with a tired look on her face. The light she always had when their eyes met was long gone, gone in a way that made Luminé realize it would never return.

He asked, "Do you have it?"

"Yes, I have it." Her words felt far away. She pulled the Golden Sword out of her sheath and brandished it in the air. "Here. Here is your damn sword."

Luminé reached for it, but she stepped back. "No, Luminé. You don't just get what you want and get to leave."

"Don't be silly, Rana."

She pointed the sword at him and pointed it into his stomach. She thought of losing Michael, and she wanted to ram it right through Luminé's gut. Her eyes narrowed, and she readied herself, "Will you continue to bother me, asking me to do what I don't want to?"

"Look Rana, you owed me… "

She thrust the sword at him, piercing his skin, then swiped, cutting his arm. Luminé shouted in pain, and she screamed, "I owe you nothing!" She threw the sword at him, shouting, "Get out!"

~ ~ ~ ~

As he flew towards Luminare, he had expected to feel triumphant, like a conquerer. Still, he felt low, having had to beg, and hide, and travel in secret. Even now, upon his arrival back to his kingdom, there was no one to share in the glorious thing he had accomplished. He had the Golden Sword, the sword of the Prophecy. Accolades and applause should be his, but he had nothing but trouble and discontentedness. He was worried about Oxana's true allegiance too. Her casual conversation with Legion had to be more than she was eluding to. He was unsure if he could truly trust her. Yes, she had professed her undying allegiance, but why did Legion keep crossing her path?

He walked into the compound with his eyes down and his shoulders tense, ignoring the greetings of his guards, and went in to see Oxana.

Oxana was sitting in their temporary living quarters, going over some of the building drawings when she saw him. She stood up, expectedly, and asked, "Do you have it?"

"Yes, I have it."

"Let me see it!" she said.

He pulled it out and brandished it in front of her.

Oxana's eyes marveled at it, "It is magnificent, Luminé. Where will we keep it?"

"I have not decided yet." He secretly knew he would hide it someplace she would not know. "Perhaps my quarters would be safest." He lied, watching her soak it in, knowing something was amiss. He would keep this power to himself. He may use her to help him discover what powers it truly held, or who perhaps they should wield those powers to, but she would never possess it.

He held it aloft, brandishing it, feeling a sense of power he had never felt before. Later that evening, after Oxana had excused herself, he went to his room and opened a large wooden chest. He pulled out a parchment where he had written down the Prophecy long ago and went back to his living room, and sat down to slowly read it.

The Prophecy

In the tree the secret lies
The ancient seed, bearing life
Whose fruits reveal both dark and light
And opens eyes to the age of strife.

When sea doeth yield the Golden Sword,
Forged and burnished from the fire,
The virgin warrior again will rise.
Bringing hope to listless band.

When armies face eternal doom
And the holy one is lost for good
The feared day has now arrived
Darkness reigns, yet even still…

The fiery column signals time
Seven days, no more may pass
But yea, cannot beyond delay
For sunset yields eternal night

If the fire consumes the host,
Unto the end, the dark must go
And Sacrifice will save the day,
And Sacrifice will save the day.

Luminé looked up, confused, and said aloud, "Why would the sea yield the Golden Sword? I have it here in my hands. This makes no sense." He pondered it for a while. No one had ever been able to make sense of it.

Regardless, he had it. The long talked of and sought after the sword was his now, yet it was not safe. He needed it hidden. He needed it close by. He looked around and went to the Throne Room, where he spent most of his time and which was most heavily guarded. There were a few places, but he knew having it out of his sight would wreak havoc on his nerves. *Oxana would undoubtedly be looking in his quarters.* He gritted his teeth, unable to think clearly. He silently moved around the throne and examined the freshly built wooden floor. He moved his Throne aside and lifted back the rug. Then, he took his dagger and quietly pried the floorboard on the stage up, careful not to make noise.

He looked within the space and smiled. It would be perfect. He slid it into the floor, pressed the floorboard down. It was directly in the middle of the two thrones. No one would ever know. It was safe and within his sight. Now, he would have to decide how to use it and how to leverage it and… test it.

Trouble

The Archangel Antonio and the five other Archangels, including the newest, Yuki, filed into the Throne Room for the early morning meeting they had been summoned to. Vamorda stood to the side of the two thrones, standing tall and straight with a calm, collected look on her face. She was watching them carefully, her face revealing no emotion. She glanced periodically at the over 20 Palace Guards stationed around the room. Antonio had heard about her iron-fisted management of the guard. He was glad Luminé had them, but part of him was angry. He was the first of the Archangels, and yet, here was this female Angel that no one had ever heard of, suddenly privy to practically every Throne Room meeting.

He waited with the five others, standing in front of the empty thrones. After a long while, Antonio said to Vamorda, "Where is he?"

Vamorda glared, "He said to wait here for him. Do you wish to defy the Great Luminé?"

"This is outrageous," Antonio said. He was growing tired of Luminé pretending to be a king. He was just an Angel, like the rest of them. Antonio turned to leave, having wasted more than enough time when the doors opened. Luminé and Oxana walked in with a regal stride and took their seats. Luminé noticed Antonio had been walking away. He asked aloud, "Are you going somewhere, Antonio?"

Antonio froze, then turned back to his post at attention. Before Lito had been sent into the Dark Cage, hanging not too very far away, he would have left… but now… he would not directly confront

Luminé. He would have to find another way to operate under what appeared to be a growing dictatorship.

Luminé stood in front of his throne and said, "As you all know, Lito decided to defy me. He and his commanders who were with him are now paying the price." Luminé walked over to the large open wall and pointed to the back of the compound where six black cages ominously hung from trees. He turned to look at them, carefully watching their faces, searching for a reaction. He walked closer to them, as they all stood perfectly still at attention and asked, "Yuki, have you settled your land disputes with Antonio?"

She swallowed, "Yes, Great Luminé." She had not resolved anything but had dropped the matter entirely and informed those under her command they would be wise to do the same.

"So," Luminé said, putting his hands behind his back, stepping down and pacing in front of them all, "What is this I hear about the Angels under your commands being discontent?"

No one replied as an even eerier silence fell amongst them. Luminé turned and paced back in front of them again. He stopped in front of Antonio and glanced down the line, asking in a loud ascending, angry tone, "Have I chosen the right Archangels to share in my wealth and glory? Are they strong enough to administer my rule?"

None of them replied. All felt fear knowing Lito and his commanders were enduring unimaginable torture inside the cramped Dark Cages. Luminé turned to Oxana, "Do you think we have chosen wisely, Queen Oxana?"

Oxana raised her eyebrows some and said, "Lito certainly did not make the cut. I am afraid we will just have to wait and see if anyone else fails." Her voice was icy, cold, and unfeeling. Its weight struck Antonio. Oxana had changed a great deal in the last month. She was becoming like Luminé.

Luminé laughed, glancing out toward the cages, "Yes, that is true. Lito did not make the cut," Luminé said, sighing loudly and unapologetically. He turned to Antonio and asked, "What are the Angels saying, Antonio?"

Antonio looked at him with a clenched jaw. He knew Luminé and Oxana better than anyone. He could not tell if their display here today was a show or was the new nature of the reality they all lived in.

Luminé seemed to possess new and bolder confidence that surprised him. He had always been confident and cocky, but today he was more. Still, he knew the only way to please Luminé was to show strength. At least it used to be that way.

Antonio needed to be brutally honest right now, to show his allegiance. He stepped forward, snapped to attention, and said, "They are saying it is very hard to be here. They are saying they don't have as much land as they used to." He paused for effect and added, "They are saying they have to build their own houses and have to search for their own food, which discontents them."

Luminé scoffed angrily, "So they have to do a little work. What is the big deal?"

Antonio replied, "Great Luminé, the fact is that these things were provided for them, for all of us in Heaven. A growing number of the Angels are saying they were better off in Heaven."

The words shook Luminé though he tried not to show it. "I see." He nodded slowly, returning to the throne, eyeing Oxana as he did. Luminé sat down, thinking.

Oxana sensed the moment of weakness needed to be turned around at once, so she stood up and snapped, "I don't think any of you realize what is at stake here. Are the lords trying to punish us? Adon himself was here spying. Luminé is forming us into a strong, cohesive unit, an Army of Angels stronger than the Angels of Heaven."

Luminé glanced at her, marveling at her gifts and sense of timing. He said, "The work we will do here, together, will make us strong, stronger than those we left behind who have been handed everything. We will provide for ourselves and, nothing will be given to us. Though we will toil, our toil will produce the fruits of our labors, and we will feel the satisfaction that only comes from taking care of one's own needs." His voice now grew heated, "You will convince those under you why we must do what we are doing. Those who give trouble, you must deal with. If they continue, deliver their names to Vamorda, and we will deal with them."

He finished and kept silent, glaring up and down the line, the final reminder of his edicts. Then, he took Oxana by the hand and left.

Mylia

At the Throne Room in Heaven, the seven Archangels stood silently before the three Lords. The mood was neutral. It seemed everything in the Heavens was in neutral since so many had left. There were no clear goals anymore, at least none spoken or given by the Lords. But the Archangels were patient. They knew the Lords themselves needed time to rechart the course.

Calla stood up from her throne with a sorrowful look on her face. She said, "I have some sad news to tell you all. Legion killed the Angel Mylia."

A gasp went up from all, except Michael.

Splendora asked, "Killed? But I thought we could not die?"

Yeshua replied, "The Golden Sword of the Prophecy has been found, Splendora. We believe Legion has it. We also believe it has the power to take life, eternal life from any of us. I am afraid Mylia is gone forever."

All the Archangels were searching their minds to come to grips with such a grim reality. If Mylia could be killed, then any of them could be killed.

Rana's eyes were fixed on the floor in front of her. She had just given the sword to Luminé. She had given him something much more diabolical than she had known. *The power to take eternal life?* She had been tricked.

Michael watched her carefully. She was lost in thought, worried thoughts. He could see her thoughts went beyond what they had been told to them. She was involved with this somehow, but he could not understand how.

When the meeting ended, Michael made his way to the Dark Black Mountain. He crossed over in one of the boats and went to the place on the path where he had found Rana. He walked off the path in the direction she had come from. He saw nothing unusual as he scanned the area, wondering what she could have been doing. He sat down on a boulder and looked. Then he saw it, a place where leaves seemed to be unnaturally placed. He went over and brushed them away. In the ground was the impression of a sword. He looked up into nothingness. *There was a sword here. But… she only had her…* he stopped, unable to fathom the awful possibility. Had she been working with Legion this whole time? Had she betrayed them all, their safety, their love? He took a step back, unwilling and unwanting to consider any of it.

Sadie

Sadie left her home early that morning. It had been well over two years now since the disaster in the Garden of Eden. Since that time, the Angels under her command had been pulling more than double duty guarding three places.

The easiest of their jobs was guarding the now completely overgrown Garden of Eden. In addition, they had their regular duties guarding the Headquarters of Gabriel's Realm, and finally, and perhaps most importantly, they had a full team on duty guarding the compound where Adam, Eve, and their children lived. Only two months earlier, Eve had given birth to another set of twins. Now the couple had four children; two toddlers and two newborns. Sadie was absolutely thrilled to be part of the inner circle helping Eve. The wonder of new human life astounded all the Angels, but with new life came lots of work. Now that the toddlers were suddenly into everything, and keeping them safe was hard. Sadie and the few select Angels she had helping around the home were way over their heads. And it was hard work for her to manage it all; at times she felt very overextended, but it was all worth it.

Sadie had left early this morning. She decided the night before to to stop to see Splendora. She'd not heard from her lately, and it concerned her. It was not like Splendora, although, with both of them being as busy as they were, but perhaps everything was fine.

Sadie landed in the compound of the Splendora's Realm and immediately noticed that no guards approached her. She shook her head and headed up to the office, saying to herself, "No one takes guard duty seriously anymore. I will have to speak with Splendora about this."

She went up the steps and down the hall. She was surprised to see no secretary at the desk outside the office. She knocked on the ajar office door and called out, "Hello? Splendora?"

"Come in," came a voice, but it was a male voice.

Sadie opened to door and saw Arcano, Splendora's second in command, seated at her desk. His smile was put on, and his shoulders were drooped. He was looking over a report laid out on the desk in front of him.

Sadie asked, "Where's Splendora?"

"She hasn't been in lately. I'm just trying to catch up on our paperwork."

"Why hasn't she been in?"

Arcano sighed. "She's not been feeling well for a long time, Sadie. But you're going to have to talk to her."

"Where is she?"

"At home. Brooding."

"Brooding? About what!"

Arcano looked up at her. "Don't you know?"

Sadie nodded. She understood now. She turned to leave, and Arcano stopped her. "Hey," he said, "How are those little humans of Adam and Eve doing?"

Sadie started to chuckle, nodding, "They're a handful is what they are. But they are... well... amazing... and beautiful. Come and see them soon."

Arcano smiled for the first time and said, "Okay, I will."

Sadie flew to the other side of the 1st Heavenly Realm to Splendora's seaside home. She knocked, but when there was no answer, she went in. "Splendora?" she called.

She went to the stairs and called up, "Splendora?"

"Who is it?"

"Sadie."

There was silence for several moments, a silence Sadie was all too familiar with from her own life. It was the silence of someone struggling with depressed feelings.

"Hey, Splendora. Can you come down?"

There was quiet for a moment, then Splendora said in a slow voice."I'll be right down."

Splendora came down, still in her nightclothes with her hair completely disheveled. Splendora reached the bottom step and looked at Sadie with dim eyes, her lips held tightly together

"Splendora, what's going on. You look terrible."

"Thanks… I feel terrible." Her hair was all over the place, and her eyes seemed sunken. She had been crying recently.

They sat down.

Sadie asked, "Why are you sad?"

"I'm just really down."

Sadie knew what it was. "It's Luminé, isn't it?"

Splendora looked out the window. Her whole face seemed to droop a bit, "Yes… It's Luminé… it's been a year… over a year, and I just can't get over him leaving. It wasn't just me, Sadie. He ruined it all. He and I could… "

"I'm sorry," Sadie said.

A tear fell from Splendora's eye, and she quickly wiped it way, only for another, then another to take its place. "He was not supposed to go. We were together. He was supposed to choose me." She looked at Sadie, "We were together the night before. We told each other that we loved each other. He was supposed to go to the Lords. We were going to put everything back together. The entire mess was going to be righted."

She stopped, her head falling into her hands.

Sadie rubbed her shoulder, "Splendora," she said softly, "I know it hurts."

Splendora looked up, "I can't get over it!," she started to cry harder.

Sadie nodded, "I get it." She paused for a long time, silence hanging thickly in the air. "Come with me to see the children."

"I… I…"

Sadie stopped her. "C'mon."

Splendora got up slowly, "Alright."

Legion

Sadie and Splendora spent the rest of the day helping Eve, holding the newborns, and playing with the toddlers. It was a marvelous day of unanticipated fun. It helped Splendora forget her troubles, even if only for a day. As evening approached, there was a glorious sunset. The two decided to fly west (instead of home), toward the sun along the earth's surface, taking in the wondrous, expansive lands, rivers, and lakes. Below them were endless fields filled with lush vegetation. Patches of naturally occurring wheat and corn were scattered throughout. Winding rivers teeming with wildlife, including countless bears and other animals along the banks of them, drinking or resting.

As they flew, Splendora smiled, looking over at Sadie, "Thanks, Sadie. I really needed a day like this."

Sadie smiled, "You're welcome. That's what friends are for. Right?"

"Yes, that's right."

Suddenly Sadie stopped.

"What is it?" asked Splendora.

"Down there. I saw… a man clad in black. He went into the forest."

Splendora's eyes widened. She knew who Sadie was talking about. They looked at each other and flew down to the path that led into a dense pine forest without hesitation. They quietly landed and moved in a few steps, peering in. The evening was descending quickly, and the shadows had grown longer, making visibility poor. Splendora whispered, "We should go for help."

Suddenly there was a movement in the distance, and they both crouched down. Sadie looked at Splendora, mouthing the words, "It's him."

Splendora slowly nodded, raising her finger to her mouth, calling for absolute silence. They could see Legion in a small clearing about a hundred feet away. A disfigured animal hung upside down from a tree motionless and stiff, it's guts spewed on the ground. Smoke was billowing from a fire where a piece of meat looked to be almost cooked. Legion's long blonde hair hung down the back of a dark brown tunic that was as long as his body. He was wearing brown sandals and sitting on a log, looking as though he was about to eat.

Splendora motioned for them to back up, and they slowly crept back a safe distance from him. They had not been seen… Splendora whispered, "We need to get help. We have to tell Calla. He is too strong for us."

"But what if he leaves?"

"You go," Sadie said. "I will keep watch."

Splendora hesitated.

Sadie's eyes widened, and she whispered, "Go, I'll be fine."

"Alright, but be ready to get out of here if he sees you."

"I will."

Splendora took off toward the Heavens, as Sadie crept back into position, a safe distance away, to keep watch. She clutched for her dagger, making sure it was ready to draw. With her other hand, she felt for her sword handle, again, being sure it was at the ready. A chill ran up her spine, but she closed her eyes, telling herself that the most important thing she could ever do around Legion was to show courage. Her breathing slowed, and she waited.

~ ~ ~ ~

As she entered the Heavens, Splendora was stopped by the first line of guards, under Raphael's command. She did not wait for any formalities. "Where is Raphael?"

The guard looked puzzled as to why Splendora was here alone, and unexpected. He replied to her, "He is a few miles away."

Splendora did not wait for any further answer. She stated, "Go at once. Tell him to bring one hundred Angels immediately and meet me back here."

"Yes, Splendora. At once."

Splendora raced to the Throne Room and went directly in without waiting. Yeshua was there alone. "My Lord," Splendora said, "We have found Legion."

"Where?"

"On earth. Sadie is there keeping watch."

Concern crept over Yeshua's face. "Wait here."

He swiftly made his way back to the quarters and returned with Calla. Both of them carried their sword sheaths. Splendora bowed and said, "My Lords, Raphael is meeting us with the Angels."

"Should we send for Adon?" asked Yeshua, knowing Adon was at his mansion and it would take some time to get to him.

"No, there is no time," Calla said.

~ ~ ~ ~

Sadie felt fear trying to hold her as the sun began to dip behind the horizon. She kept one eye on Legion, her attention only diverting toward the sky in the direction Splendora had left. Time was running out. If it grew too dark, he could easily escape into the vast dark pine trees. She closed her eyes for a moment, trying to allay her fears, telling herself all would turn out. Everyone was afraid of Legion, rightly so. But he could be defeated. She believed this, and she would prove it to the rest of them.

She opened her eyes and gasped; he was gone. Her eyes widened as she scanned the distant clearing. The faint billow of smoke was the only thing moving. She tried to swallow, but her throat had clenched shut. Her heart was racing. It was too dark, all of a sudden, and she could no longer see where he was.

Had her seen her and circled around to find her. Playing defense was the only sure way to lose to Legion. So she drew her sword quietly and crept down the path toward the clearing, careful to stay on the pine needles, careful to remain hidden as she crept. A deep pit filled her stomach. There was a movement beyond the clearing. She froze, trying to make out what was going on. Legion was moving, quickly away from her. She sped up her pace, staying as silent as she could, staying crouched, hidden. Now that she saw him, she would not lose him again.

She was now a long way from the entrance. Suddenly she could not find him. He was gone. She stopped, crouching lower, scanning the ever-darkening woods, looking for movement. She stood slightly looking into the fading dusk.

Suddenly, the hair on her neck rose as she felt a warm breath gently brush it, as slow, frightening words whispered into her ear, "Angel Sadie. We meet again."

She swallowed and tried to turn, but a sharp blade jolted forcefully into the back of her ribs, stopping her from turning. Pain piercing her like she had never felt before. She tried to yell, but something hard slammed into the side of her head, and all went black.

~ ~ ~ ~

Calla led them down to the path Splendora had lead them to, motioning for Raphael and his Angels to encircle the forest. She turned to Splendora, whispering, "Where is Sadie?"

"She was here," Splendora said, worried. Looking at the still smoking fire and rotting carcas on the tree. "He must have left, and she followed."

Yeshua turned with his jaw set like flint, and his eyes narrowed and brow furrowed. He drew his long sword and said, "Splendora, come with me."

The encirclement commenced, and at the signal, they began walking inward toward the center of the vast forest. Calla would come from one side, Yeshua and Splendora from the other, with Raphael and all of his Angels filling in all the gaps.

"There!" yelled Calla as she ran forward.

Legion heard them and knew he was in trouble. He rose up into the air, but it too hard to see through the pines. He glanced upward. Many Angels were above, guarding the sky. He had been foolish to return, not realizing Sadie had not been alone. He was only glad he had taken care to hide her body. It would prove his bargaining chip.

"There he is!" one shouted, and Legion bolted downward and flew toward the rear entrance of the forest. Two Angels swooped down on his trail. He turned and slashed both of them with his sword, cutting one's hand completely off. He flew again, upward, then over and down, until he saw the light. His eyes widened as he was moments away from escaping.

Splendora was waiting. She leaped from a tree onto his back, wrapping her arms tightly around his neck and head, pulling his head back to the point of breaking. Legion let out a horrifying roar and thrust his elbow into her gut, knocking her off. In the next moment, Yeshua and several Angels pulled him to the ground and wrapped him in chains.

Calla approached him, her eyes filled with the hatred and disdain she felt for him, and demanded, "Where is Sadie?"

Legion chuckled, "Sadie? Why it wasn't my turn to watch her."

Calla flipped her sword around and clubbed him with the handle.

Legion glared through clenched teeth as blood ran down his forehead.

Yeshua went to Raphael. "Bring 10 of your Angels and come with me. We are taking Legion to the holding cell below the Throne Room. The rest fan out and find Sadie."

Calla turned to Raphael, "Get torches for everyone. I want every inch of this forest searched. We will be here all night if we have to."

Luminé

Luminé sat on the side of the highest hill in Luminare, facing the Heavens, a secluded spot he had discovered his first few days there.

He opened his eyes to see the morning sun reaching across his kingdom, up the mountainside, all of it feeling empty. He thought of all the mistakes he had made. "Why, why was I so stupid!" He slammed his fist into the rock.

Suddenly, he heard a voice. "Luminé?" He turned to see Oxana behind him.

"How did you find me?" He said, startled, bothered his thoughts had been interrupted.

Oxana scoffed, "Luminé, this place is no secret to me. I leave you alone when you come here to respect your space, but there is news that cannot wait."

That this place was no secret after all bothered him, but he let it pass. "What news?" he asked.

"Some of our spies say that the Lords have captured Legion. He is below their Throne Room in chains."

"So what do I care? Legion means nothing to me."

"What if he reveals to the Lords that we have the sword?"

"He does not know that we have it. Does he?" he asked, inquisitively.

"No, he does not. But he knows of the plan."

Luminé gritted his teeth. "Let them find out if they must. They will not possess it either. The sword belongs to me. Now be gone and never come visit me at this place again."

The Lords

"We can't find her!" Calla exclaimed as she walked into the Throne Room, angry and tired, where Adon and Yeshua were waiting for her. It was before dawn the next morning, and they had been looking for Sadie all night. "Raphael and his Angels will resume their search at first light. But I don't think she is in the forest."

"I will go question him," said Adon, standing quickly, feeling guilty he had not been there.

"No," Calla said, "We will all go together. I want to see his reaction. But first, I have an idea." She turned to the guards, "Bring me dark blankets."

"What are you planning?" asked Yeshua.

She looked at Adon, "Our informants have told me that Luminé is employing dark black cages as punishment for his Angels. It seems the darkness paralyzes them. I wonder if it would do the same for Legion."

"How can it?" asked Adon, scoffing at the idea. "He is a Lord."

"You can't surely believe he is a Lord!" Calla snapped. Her words echoed back to her. Legion was strong, yes, but not a Lord, not in her mind. He was not like them.

"We will put him into a Dark Cage," interjected Yeshua, reasoning with Adon, "It can do no harm."

All three made their way down the stairs to the large hidden holding cell beneath the Throne Room. Legion was suspended from the ceiling by his wrists, both arms chained, and both ankles chained to the floor. Calla walked up to the bars, "Tell us where Sadie is and... the Golden Sword."

"Or what?" Legion said, smirking, slowly looking up. "I will be out of here soon. I am growing stronger by the moment, being here, in your presence. Did you not know that?"

Calla cringed. None of them knew how or why Legion possessed the powers he did, nor how he grew stronger. Was he lying, or had he just revealed something important?

"Very well," Calla said, keeping her cool. She would not allow him to see the fear in her. She motioned to the guards, who began draping the cage in complete darkness. Legion laughed, "What is this? An Angel game? You cannot harm me."

"Cover him!" Calla said.

Legion laughed again, "Don't you remember sweet Mylia, her fate? He sighed… Sadie is almost out of time."

Calla grabbed her, dagger, "Open the cage door!"

Adon stopped her, "Calla."

All Calla could think of was her beloved Sadie. Another Angel would not be harmed on her watch. "Cover him, now!" she said, "We will be back tomorrow morning."

The Lords went back up to the Throne Room. Calla was angry… "We must post at least 20 guards all around this Throne Room, and one of us must be here at all times. I propose Adon, and I go help to look for Sadie. Yeshua, you remain here."

~ ~ ~ ~

Inside the darkened cage, Legion screamed with all his might but would not allow a sound to emit from his voice. He screamed silently, cringing in agony. He had not known what such darkness would do to him, but somehow, Calla had known. Or had she? Perhaps she was only guessing. He could not let them know the effect it was having. He felt like his mind was going to explode, leaving him forever in an empty void stripped of all thought.

Hour after agonizing hour went on, and at the moment he was about to go completely insane, he saw something. The terrifying blackness turned to white, beautiful bright white, and he could still think, and he could see. In his mind's eye, he saw Yeshua pacing the Throne Room floor, alone. He saw Calla and Adon riding away on their horses toward the Earth. He saw the guards stationed all along the hall and the steps and at the Throne Room entrance. He relaxed his fear and began to feel a power he had never felt before. His eyes grew red and hot and felt as though they were turning, piercing the darkness, piercing his vision.

He saw the guards nearest the cage begin to cringe, holding their heads, crying out. He saw the others coming near to them. They, too, succumbed to the pain, falling to their knees, unable to make a sound, writhing in agony as he had been. He pictured the guards at the Throne Room entrance, too, falling down, writhing on the ground in pain until they passed out. He was doing this.

He heard the footsteps and could see through the darkness. It was Yeshua. The dark covering was thrust back. "What did you do?" he yelled.

Legion smirked, "I told you I am growing stronger. Let me out of these chains, and I will tell you where Sadie is." He paused for effect, "You know she will die soon if you do not."

Yeshua thought of his words, 'I am growing stronger here in your presence.' He thought of the guards, all of them out cold. He must be telling the truth, and if so, it was better he get out now.

"But what about the sword?" said Yeshua. "You must also give it to me."

"We will duel for it. Me against you. The winner takes all."

"Alright," he said, as he went to the now passed out guard and took the key. He opened the cage door and unlocked the chains, allowing Legion to fall to the floor. Yeshua stepped back into the cage doorway, blocking the way. "Where is she?"

Legion replied, "Due west of the forest is a cliff. On the side of the cliff is a cave. She is tied up inside, and she is badly wounded. The tide will be coming soon, oh, and in the darkness, I might add."

Legion looked at the guards lying in the hall, "Now, if you will hand me a sword and dagger, we can get to our duel."

Yeshua backed away, picking up a sword and dagger, and tossed them to Legion. Legion glared, searching Yeshua's eyes, looking for a sign of weakness. There was none. "Here, in this cramped hall? Let us go to the Throne Room floor."

"No," Yeshua said. "Right here, right now." He thrust forward with his sword, bringing it down hard as Legion skillfully blocked with his sword. There was only one way for Legion to get out, and that was through Yeshua. Legion charged chopping, thrusting, and clanging. Yeshua was surprised at his power. Legion swiped with the dagger, then mounted another assault, but Yeshua was ready. He thrust his sword into Legion's midsection and charged with his legs, knocking him over one of the fallen Angels onto the ground.

Yeshua knelt on top of him and pulled out the sword, "Now tell me where it is."

Legion nodded. He let go of his sword, closing his eyes, wincing in pain, and said softly, "It is... "

Yeshua drew closer to hear, and suddenly Legion lurched up, wide-eyed, and thrust the dagger into the side of Yeshua's neck, pushing him off. Legion jumped up as Yeshua clutched at the dagger ripping his neck. Legion roared as he lept away. "Until next time I kill you." Yeshua lifted up and threw the dagger down the hall, as it buried itself in the back of Legion's shoulders. He shrieked in pain, falling, desperately trying to grab the dagger, then ran out with it still protruding from him. Yeshua lay there gasping. He could not die, he knew this, but the pain was unfathomable. He needed the healing spring.

He was too weak to follow Legion. The guards began to wake. Yeshua yelled, "Sound the alarm. Legion is badly wounded and on the run. And Sadie, she is in a cave west of the forest. Quick, go get her before the tide drowns her."

Legion

Badly wounded, Legion raced through the skies out of the Land of the Lords, suddenly hunted by thousands of Angels. He needed to get somewhere safe. He needed to rest. His duel with Yeshua was the most difficult thing he had done. Yeshua was the strongest of the Lords. Legion knew this now. He had thought one day he would face Adon, as the last living Lord, and defeat him in an epic final struggle. Now he realized it would be Yeshua.

The wound from the dagger that had deeply embedded itself in his back, right next to his spine, hurt more than the sword wound, but it was the sword wound that worried him the most. It was bleeding profusely, and while he nor any of the Lords or Angels had any fear of dying based on a wound, the loss of blood would weaken him for a long time. He needed to bandage it, to clean it, but none of these could happen while he was on the run.

As he circled Earth, hoping to find a place to rest far on the other side of it from where he was, he saw them. Hundreds of Angels in the sky flying in a pattern designed to make it impossible for anyone to go in undetected. Suddenly, he came to. He had passed out momentarily. The drain of blood was weakening him dangerously fast. He held himself together and flew towards the North, back toward the Seven Heavenly Realms, but there were thousands more there. His only choice was to go south. He turned and flew as fast as he could, careful to avoid the dwindling pockets of patrols. When he neared the Southern Realm, he had a new enemy to face, Luminé's guards on duty guarding the entrance to the Southern Realm. This would be much easier, though, as they were not nearly as concerned as the Heavens were about intruders, as well as the fact they were not hunting for him.

He easily skirted their defenses and flew to the Southernmost tip of the Southern Realm, where the mountain ranges were located. Here he found a large cave overlooking the sea. It would be ideal, he imagined, as it was deep within the mountains and faced away from the more populated areas of land occupied by Luminé's Dark Angels. They would be miles away, too far to be able to see him, nor any fire he might light at night. He went into the cave and collapsed from exhaustion. He needed to recover, and he needed to find out how to get the Golden Sword away from Luminé and Oxana.

Sparkis

The Angel Sparkis woke early and traveled four miles from his home in Yuki's realm to Luminé's Headquarters. He knocked on the door. There was no answer. He knocked again when a guard came around the corner. "Hey, what are you doing knocking this early?"

"I need to see Oxana," Sparkis replied.

"Who are you?"

"I am the person to whom you are speaking, none other than, Sparkis."

"What?"

"Sparkis, I said."

"Well, Queen Oxana is asleep. Come back."

Just then, the door opened. It was Oxana. She looked down at the short, stocky red-haired Angel standing smiling in front of her and asked, "Sparkis? What are you doing here?" She turned to the anxious guard and said, "It's okay. We are old friends."

Sparkis smiled at the guard and waited until he marched away. He turned to Oxana, "Hey, why haven't you spoken to me? I've been waiting to hear from you and Luminé?"

"Oh, hmmm, waiting? For what?"

"Well, to have a post here at the Headquarters. I figured Luminé would have something ready for me."

"Yes, he must have forgotten. He has filled all the posts, Sparkis, but I will speak to him."

Sparkis' face grew sad as he repeated her words. "Filled all the posts? Doesn't he have any left? I don't want to be stationed out there with Lito's, I'm sorry, with Yuki's rowdy Angels. We do nothing all day. It's horrible."

Oxana raised her head to the sky, "I'm so sick of hearing about Angels doing nothing but partying."

Sparkis quickly asked her, "How is Lito anyway?"

"What do you mean?" Oxana asked in a heated tone.

"I mean, how is he doing?"

Oxana glared, "Sparkis, Lito is in a Dark Cage. His friends are too. Angels practically go insane inside Dark Cages." She shouted, *"How do you think he's doing?"*

"Oh," Sparkis said, "I didn't know."

There was an uneasy silence, and Sparkis felt bad he had provoked her. He knew she had the power to sway Luminé. She always had.

Oxana broke the silence, "Sparkis, I'm sorry, but… "

"Can't you maybe find something for me to do?"

She remembered his loyalty and all they had been through. "Alright, I will ask Luminé."

"Oh, thanks. Should I come back tomorrow?"

"No. Wait here. I will ask him now."

"Oh, boy. Are you sure?"

"Of course, I'm sure," Oxana snapped. "Now wait here."

She went in, and Sparkis heard them talking, then arguing, then Luminé yelling, then Oxana talking, then Luminé talking. Moments later, Oxana returned. "Sparkis, it's not much, but it is actually very good for you, not the job, but the fringe benefits."

"What is it?"

"I need a full-time gardener. I want a garden on the side of the Headquarters and living quarters. I know that it is not glamorous, but you will actually be around the Headquarters more than anyone. And… the fringe benefits are great. Come up here."

Sparkis' face showed the confusion he felt at being offered such a lowly post. But he walked up. Oxana turned him around and pointed toward the sea, "Do you see that hillside in the distance."

"No, where?"

"See that tree way over there. Beyond it, see that bit of land on that small hill?"

"Yes, I do."

"It's yours. Go ahead and build your home on it. It's a prime location, and on the shoreline."

"Okay. I like that. But it looks small."

"Well, you won't be able to build a large home, but you can put a cottage or something up there, and you will have one of the best views in the Heavens."

"Thank you, Oxana."

"You better start calling me Queen Oxana from now on."

"Yes, Queen Oxana."

"Good, Sparkis. You start tomorrow."

Powers

Legion opened his eyes after two days. He was lying in a pool of dark red sticky blood. He winced as he stood and pulled off his black tunic. He brushed his long blonde hair back, cursing, realizing the blood on his hands was probably now all through his hair. He carried his tunic and went to the entrance of the cave, searching the lands below. Not too distant, perhaps a mile away, was a mountain stream. He walked down the mountainside, naked, and went into the cool stream. He carefully washed his wounds, his body, his hair, and his tunic. Then he walked back toward his cave, still naked, letting his tunic dry in the warm spring-like weather. When he reached the cave entrance, he sat down on a fallen tree—*the powers. I forgot about them.* He closed his eyes, remembering the powers he had that disoriented the guards at the Throne Room to the point of their passing out. He remembered seeing Yeshua coming down the hall even before he had. He tried now to see Yeshua or any of them, but there was nothing.

Arghhh! he shouted into the air. He calmed his nerves and closed his eyes again. Staring into the blackness, he saw a large cow with horns. He zeroed in on it, concentrating his will. The cow turned and began ascending a mountain path. Legion smiled and kept watching it going up the path. Soon he heard it in the near distance. He opened his eyes and watched the beast walk right up to him and kneel down in front of him. Legion laughed and petted its head, then gently grabbed both of its horns and violently twisted them. The cow screeched loudly, its death cry echoing through the canyons of the mountains of the Southern Realm, but only for a second, as it instantly fell to the side with its neck broken.

Yeshua

Calla and Adon received word about Yeshua and Legion as well as Sadie's whereabouts at the same time. They split up, each taking a large contingent of Angels with them. Adon led the way to find Sadie, and Calla raced back to the Throne Room.

When Calla arrived, the scene was largely untouched. Only a few of the Angels had woken up. Most were still passed out from whatever trance Legion had cast over them. She ran into the Throne Room and saw several Angels ministering to other unconscious Angels. She ran down the stairs to the holding cell and found the same scene. Lastly, she stepped over the bodies and headed down the hall to the cell where Legion had been held. Yeshua was lying on the floor, his eyes closed, with a pool of blood surrounding both sides of him. A large bloody wound darkened his neck, with the blood mixed onto his hair, skin, and tunic. She motioned for the Angels to leave and knelt next to him, "Yeshua, are you all right?"

He slowly opened his eyes and tried to talk, but it was difficult. The dagger had pierced his throat. He stopped and nodded, reassuring her with his eyes that he would be ok. Calla could see the intense pain he was enduring, but she could not wait to ask him. She needed to know what they were dealing with.

She asked, "What happened here, Yeshua?"

"I had to… Sadie… he told… "

She stopped him. He was too weak to talk. She said, "Adon has gone to retrieve Sadie. We will take care of everything."

She called out to the waiting Angels, "Take him to the Healing Springs and attend to his needs there."

How did this happen? She thought as she went back down the hall to one of the Angels who had just woken up.

"What happened to all of you?"

The Angel looked at her like a man waking up from a night of drinking. His voice was unsure, faltering, but he told her. "My mind started ringing, Lord Calla, to the point of agony. It was as if a dark cloud had descended into my mind, and then I woke up, just now."

Calla shuddered, though she tried hard not to show it. Legion's words, 'I grow stronger in your presence,' raced through her mind.

~ ~ ~ ~

Adon saw the cliffside cave and flew to the entrance. It was no larger than a cave where a mountain goat might live. He signaled for the other Angels following him to stay back. He moved toward the narrow perch of rock at the entrance and peered into the pitch blackness. It was a deep cave. He could tell that by the feeling of wind blowing out of it. It must have gone through to some other side.

"Sadie?" he called. "Sadie?" he called again, louder. He heard a long, low moan. He bent over and went in, careful not to hit his back on the rocky ceiling. "Sadie?" he called again. The moan was louder now. He kept moving, adjusting his eyes to the darkness. Then he heard her again. He was near. Finally, she moaned one more time, and he knew he was within a few feet of her.

"Sadie," he exclaimed as he reached her. She was bound in chains at her hands and feet, laying on a shelf in the side of the cave. Her clothing was drenched in blood. Sadie opened her dried, crusted eyes and tried to speak through her parched lips, but she could not.

"Adon took hold of the chains and snapped them with his bare hands. He unraveled them and gently lifted her, carrying her through the dark cave toward the light of the entrance. When he got outside, he flew into the air as the hundred Angels waiting looked on anxiously at Sadie's lifeless looking, bloodied body. He took her down to the river bank below the cliff and gently laid her in the stream, giving life and vigor to her weary body. Sadie opened her eyes and took in some of the water, wetting her lips, allowing her throat to feel the first water it had in over a day. After several long minutes of trying to revive, she looked at Adon and, in a labored voice, asked, "Did they catch him?"

Adon hesitated, "Yes, we caught him, Sadie." He did not have the heart to tell her that Legion had since escaped, feeling it would be better if she found out later.

Sadie closed her eyes as a smile came over her face. Suddenly she remembered Eve and the children, whom she had been helping. She opened her eyes, "The children? Who... who is... " She stopped, unable to complete her sentence. Adon brushed her hair back, "They are fine, Sadie. Gabriel is with them."

"Gabriel?" she said, trying to keep her eyes open. Then, she closed her eyes and started to chuckle ever so slightly, careful not to hurt her wounded side.

"What is so funny, Sadie?" asked Adon.

She looked up, "He won't be able... to handle them." She started chuckling again, then stopped as it hurt her ribs.

Adon said, "Close your eyes, Sadie. Rest."

Yuki

Yuki waited to make sure no one was around, then went to the door of Antonio's home in Luminare. She knocked, keeping her eyes on the surrounding area. Yuki was slender, strong, and athletic, with lightly tanned skin and shiny black hair. Having trained under Calla in the Martial Arts, she feared little, and little went unnoticed by her. Still, tonight she needed to be cautious.

Antonio opened the door, "Yuki, what are you doing here?"

"I need to speak with you," she said nervously.

"What about?" he asked as he looked at her carefully, trying to gauge her intent. They both knew full well what happened to those who went against Luminé, and from the trepidation in her face, he suspected this would be that kind of meeting.

"Can I come in?" she asked, scanning the area again.

Antonio opened the door reluctantly and motioned for her to come in. He had known Yuki for some time, but only from a distance, as he mainly had dealt with her former commander, Lito. Her beautiful eyes sparkled in the light of the living room lamp, not with softness, but with a keen strength. He could see within them that she possessed courage, a trait Antonio admired in any female.

"What is this about?" he asked.

Yuki's face was serious, "There is grumbling everywhere, Antonio." She was wringing her hands and scanning the room with her dark eyes.

"I know. I have heard grumblings of my own. But I would not say it is with everyone, perhaps only a few." Antonio knew he was expected to tow the line. He stood tall as he listened, acting his expected part, just in case this was a trap, trying to entice him to go against Luminé.

"It is more than a few, Antonio. It is prevalent!" she replied nervously, "and not just with the lower-level Angels. Most Host Commanders feel the same." She turned, "I came to you in confidence. Trouble is brewing, and we will have to deal with it, one way or another."

"Exactly what kind of trouble?"

Yuki glanced out the window, scanning the horizon. She turned back to him, "A few Angels under my command were arrested for trying to visit the 7th Heavenly Realm. They were told by those who captured them that they are never allowed to go back."

"That's' not true!" Antonio snapped, "Luminé only made us commit to one year."

"Well, I am telling you what was said." She paused, unsure if she should continue, and decided she needed to. Antonio was not getting it. "Antonio, there is talk of mutiny!"

"Mutiny!" he exclaimed as his face grew cross. "Who is talking of mutiny?"

"I can't say," Yuki now knew she had said too much. She had sensed she could trust Antonio. He was so much like Lito had been, strong, independent, unafraid.

Antonio grabbed hold of her arms and lifted her slightly off the ground, shaking her, "If someone is considering mutiny, you need to tell me. Now is not the time for disloyalty."

"Let go," she demanded, as she clenched her teeth and shook free of him. "Do not try to threaten me, Antonio."

"Oh really, why not?"

She leaped backward into the air while lifting her long leg, kicking him lightly on the chin, and landing back on her feet. "I could have kicked you much harder, Antonio."

Antonio's head snapped back, and he felt his chin. She was not afraid of him, and she wanted to trust him. He said, "We should not argue, Yuki. We will help each other. What to do? I am not sure, but we will keep each other informed."

"A pact?" she said as she stepped closer.

"Yes, we will make a pact."

Yuki scanned the horizon from the window again, then left.

Splendora

Splendora opened her eyes. It was mid-morning. Spending time with Sadie a week earlier had lifted her spirits, but it didn't last long. The depressed state which had fallen upon her was still there. It was hard for her to look back at all the mistakes she had made. Mistakes which for an ordinary Angel might not be a big deal, but for her, they had proved costly to the entire Heavens. Not reporting Luminé long ago led to Adam and Eve eating from the forbidden tree. Then, not going with him to speak with the Lords again allowed Luminé to be swayed into leaving. No one, except herself, knew of her failings. They all thought Luminé was to blame, and he was, and yet, in many ways, she was too.

Out of the corner of her eyes, she saw something move. It was a messenger bird standing quietly with a message tied to its foot. She lifted the little bird onto her finger and untied the message.

Splendora

I have been thinking about you. I want to see you and talk with you. Perhaps we can meet on Earth someday soon.

Luminé.

Splendora sighed, not believing her eyes. *How dare he write to her directly.* Seeing him was absolutely against everything she stood for. She needed to be done with him. She needed to move on, to start building the new Heavens, without Luminé or any of his followers. Yet, this letter, his words, they lifted her as they always had lifted her. She needed to see him right now, if for nothing else, but to get herself out of this damnable state she was stuck in.

She wanted to write back, but how? Sparkis. Yes, he will give my letter to Luminé.

She grabbed a quill and some parchment and began to write.

Dear Luminé

Luminé, there is so much to ask, to say. No one can know of our meeting. I will meet you on the Earth, on the Western Continent, at the place of the Great Falls. Do you remember it? We looked at it together one day long ago. I am sure you remember exactly where.

Meet me there in two days at mid-morning.

Splendora

She hesitated, then she wrote another letter.

Sparkis, old friend.

Please give this letter to Luminé for me, in secret, of course.
I am in your debt.

Splendora

She then called a messenger bird and sent both letters off to Sparkis.

~ ~ ~ ~

Two days later, Luminé woke early and headed out. He was nervous. With all his heart, he wanted to see Splendora, and yet, he was ashamed that he had not followed through when they had promised themselves to each other.

He flew to the Earth, to the place he and Splendora had visited together years earlier. He landed near the immense waterfalls on the Western Continent of the Earth and sat on a smooth grassy area of the bank, waiting and admiring the thundering waters and the cool spray they cast into the air.

After a while, he saw her approaching, slowly circling in, wearing her radiant white tunic and white boots, and flashing her warm smile. Luminé stood and watched her circle and float down like a falling feather, landing in front of him. Luminé's heart leaped for joy as he beheld her warm, loving eyes, beckoning him with her glance. He felt happier than he had in a very long time.

He gently approached her and took her in his arms, saying, "I have missed you more than words can ever say." He kissed her, and her tense body softened as she returned the kiss she had longed for with equal passion. They stood next to the thundering waters, kissing, not saying a word. Splendora pulled away, and she turned, walking back a few steps.

She had known this moment would lift her, and it did. She felt the joy that had so long been gone.

Luminé's hand rested on her shoulder, as he said, "Come, let us lay together."

His abruptness caused her pause. "No," she said, brushing his hand off her. "I need to think."

Her body had warmed in anticipation of this meeting, all day, moistness and flutterings were within her, but now she felt her body cool as if a cold wind had blown upon her, telling her what her mind was struggling to grasp. She stepped toward the edge of the rock. Here she was again, taking care of her own needs, while the needs of Heaven languished.

She turned, "Why did you leave? You said we were going to fix all this."

She watched his eyes dart along the ground, searching for what to say, but he had no answer.

"That's what I thought."

"Wait," he said. "Splendora, it is only when I am with you that I am truly myself, who I am meant to be. I… I made a mistake."

She shook her head, "It's too late, Luminé." And she left.

The Cave

Legion stood naked in the flowing mountain stream in the mountains of Luminare, with the water up to his mid-thighs, washing his body. His wounds were healing well. He had been wise to come here where the mountain air and fresh water could work their magic. He stepped out of the stream and dried his long blonde hair, then the rest of his body. He dressed into a clean long brown tunic and fastened his brown leather belt around his waist, finally slipping on his brown sandals.

He went back to his cave to check on the deer meat he was cooking over a small fire. He was excited. The powers he had discovered in the black darkness were growing. Clearly, he had used them to cause the guards to pass out. He had been able to enter their minds torturing them with a terrible screaming sound. Could he harness this dark power on command? He also had the power to see into an immediate future. Then it hit him all at once, and he stood up smiling.

He walked to the front of the cave entrance and looked down over all of Luminare. He roared, "This world and all who are in it will belong to me. I am its Lord!" His voice echoed through the mountains and down onto the distant plains and hills below.

Sparkis

Sparkis invited his friends Cleetus, Sansa, and Sylvia to join him at his new house on the hillside overlooking the sea. "And how exactly did you get such a choice piece of land?" asked Sansa dubiously.

"Well," Sparkis said as he opened their second bottle of wine. "As you all know, I have been close friends with Luminé since the beginning. Splendora too."

"You have at that," Cleetus said, as he took a sip of his wine. Cleetus was one of the Angels in Luminare who fashioned metal. He made swords and daggers in exchange for whatever he could bargain for. He was stocky but taller than Sparkis. He wore his hair close to the scalp and kept slightly unshaven to maintain his ruddy image. He was not one of the most liked Angels, as some felt he drove too hard of a bargain. Still, he was one of the only metal workers who had followed Luminé, so he held his ground in negotiations.

It was quiet for a moment, as it often was in conversations around Luminare when the Heavens were mentioned. Everyone had a place within them that wondered if they had made a mistake by leaving. Cleetus broke the silence, "I haven't heard Splendora's name in ages."

"Oh, we keep in touch," Sparkis said, smiling.

"Really?" Sansa remarked, sensing Sparkis was bragging and lying. "I think you're telling a tall tale, Sparkis."

Sparkis glanced momentarily into the new hut he had just built, pondering if he should prove himself, but he realized he should not. He would betray Splendora's confidence. He replied to her, "You'll just have to take my word for it, Sansa."

Sansa noticed his glance towards his hut and wondered if he was hiding something. She laughed, "Sparkis, will you ever stop making us laugh?"

Cleetus chimed in, "So you are Oxana's new gardener?"

"No! I'm not the gardener. I am the head of the Headquarters' grounds team."

"Oh, that sounds better. Uhhh... who exactly is on your team?" Cleetus said in a questioning tone.

"They are still deciding who will work for me." Sparkis stood up, and raised his short arm, pointing into the distance. "But for now, I got this choice piece of property with a view of the sea on one side," he gracefully turned and pointed in the other direction, "and a full view of the Headquarters on the other." He lifted his glass, prompting them all to do the same, "To my new role, here in Luminare!"

They all drank, and soon another bottle was opened.

Sansa had to know what Sparkis was talking about. He had clearly glanced into his hut while he was contemplating proving himself. When he had fallen asleep by the fire, and the others had left, she crept into his hut and looked around. The inside was neat and tidy. There was one chair next to a small table. His bed was perfectly made with his clothing hung neatly on the wall next to it. Next to his bed was a small table with a parchment sticking out from under a small box sitting on top of it. She lifted the box and picked up the parchment.

Sparkis, old friend.

Please give this letter to Luminé for me, in secret, of course.
I am in your debt.

Splendora

Her eyes widened. She looked under the letter and saw another sealed letter. She carefully picked it up and examined it. She could not open it without getting caught. Suddenly she heard a faint chirp that startled her. She quickly put the letters back and went outside. Sparkis was still asleep. She laid down by the fire, thinking. This would be valuable information to Oxana and could perhaps put her back in Oxana's good graces.

Armies

That night Luminé sat at one end of the large dining table with Oxana seated at the other. It was carved from oak and had just been finished for them. Luminé felt the smoothed wooden top, stained with light brown colors, and declared, "A table fit for a King and Queen," his voice echoing into the silence.

Oxana did not reply, and Luminé found it strange. She was off somewhere, but where, and why? "What is going through that pretty little mind of yours, Oxana?" Luminé said, sipping his wine, watching her closely.

She stumbled out of her thoughts and gently glared at him, "Nothing of any importance."

"I need to ask you about something." He again lifted his wine glass and took a long sip.

"What is it?" She said hesitantly.

"The Angels under us do not seem to be happy. I am concerned."

"Unhappy? I think they are more than unhappy." She looked more intently at him. "There a rumblings of discontent everywhere."

"Yes, I have heard that too," Luminé replied.

Oxana added, "Have you forgotten that the one-year anniversary is coming? They will find out then that they absolutely cannot return. What then?"

Luminé froze, as a sinking feeling fell into the pit of his stomach. He angrily snapped, "Yes, I know it is coming up."

"Within two months, on the last day of the full moon, we need to have a plan."

Luminé slammed his fist into the table, shouting, "What is missing? What is it that they want that they do not have here?"

Oxana stood up, suddenly full of anger, wondering why he did not know the answer for himself. She shouted, "I can't believe you don't see it. They are missing a sense of pride and excitement." She exhaled loudly, calming herself, lowering her voice. "Luminé, ever since the announcement of your new kingdom, a sense of pride left not only the Heavens, but it also fell away from all who followed us here. It's all been forgotten, gone by the wayside. All excitement is gone. From what I hear, the Heavens are in the exact same predicament."

Luminé pondered her words. She was right. He was surprised he had not seen something so obvious. How had he fallen so out of touch with his own world?

Oxana's eyes widened. "Wait, I have an idea." A smile spread over her face, "We have a chance to take advantage of them, Luminé."

"What do you mean?" he said with his brow furrowed.

"We can be better than them, better than the Angels of Heaven who look down on us. We need to instill pride and excitement in our followers. We need to ready ourselves to be more skillful, cunning, and powerful than those in Heaven, just as the Lords trained us for the Angel Games."

He caught her vision and stood up abruptly, shaking from his stupor. He walked to the window, his eyes narrowed, staring at the floor, thinking through the plan that was racing through his mind.

He turned and said excitedly, "Yes, yes, Oxana. It is brilliant! Creating armies and training will give us meaning to our days. And I have another idea. We will disguise this build-up as preparation for our own Luminare Games. We will hold our own contests."

He clenched his fists and closed his eyes, feeling a moment of reprieve from his worry. He looked at Oxana up and down, taking her beauty in. She always amazed him with her cleverness and flare. It was why he was always drawn back to her. No other Angel had what she had.

He said, "Summon all Archangels, Oxana. We will meet with them tomorrow night."

The Plot

The following night, Luminé and Oxana walked from their living quarters, across the compound, and up the wide staircase leading to the Throne Room. Hundreds of torches were lit around the compound and within the Throne Room. Inside, the six Archangels waited, along with Vamorda and over 30 Palace Guards, stationed every 10 feet along the inside of the Throne Room.

Luminé began, "We are going to have a great contest of strength and skill. Each of your realms is going to build its own army. The armies will compete against the others in war games. We will have strategic exercises, actual fighting, arena matches, and battles on the surrounding waters. We shall call these the Luminare Games."

Antonio asked, "How will we do battle on the waters?"

"In ships," Luminé said. "Ships you will build. Each of you will build your realms into formidable armies, capable of bringing immense force to a battle."

Luminé stopped, glancing over to Oxana, as they both watched the reaction of their Archangels.

Yuki asked, "When will the contests begin, Great Luminé?"

"In 90 days," Oxana replied.

A strange quiet descended on the entire room. Luminé looked around and asked, "What is wrong, Antonio? Are 90 days too soon?"

"No, Great Luminé, it's just that... well, the one-year anniversary is drawing near. There are many Angels who want to go back to the Heavens."

Luminé slammed his fist on the armrest of his throne and shouted, "You must focus them, Antonio. The winners of the contest will be given extra land and riches, as well as commands on the south side of the realm. There can be no talk of the one-year anniversary right now."

Oxana added, "Tell them they may decide to return after the Luminare Games are concluded. Anyone who brings it up before this will be punished severely."

There was silence as the faces of the Archangels began to betray their true feelings about the plan. But there was reason to fear Oxana's words. Already, there were more than 30 Dark Cages hanging under heavy guard in the woods behind the Headquarters compound. Some there for lesser offenses than others, but all there because Luminé had decided they needed to be punished.

Luminé was not going to let them leave on this moment of perceived doubt and silence. He stood up, "From this day forward, I want daily reports of the progress you are making in training your realms. Do you understand? Daily. Now, you are all dismissed."

The group seemed to exhale at once, and they filed out. Vamorda too dismissed her guards, and they also filed out, leaving Luminé and Oxana alone.

Neither said a word as they tried to process the definite resistance they had just experienced. The pressure of the coming anniversary was growing. Oxana broke the silence, "What are we going to do, Luminé?"

"We will think of something. Don't worry."

"Don't worry? We have to worry! I could see it all over their faces. We are on the verge of losing power," she said worriedly.

"No, Oxana, we are not. No matter what I have to do, I will not lose power."

Cleetus

Cleetus opened his eyes and sighed. He glanced out the window of his spacious hut to see the sun's rays peering through the forest. He got up and sat on the edge of his bed, closing his eyes, thinking, praying, "Lords of Heaven, please help me. I feel so miserable here in my new life, and I feel oppressed by these new rulers, these supposed Archangels, and our… " He couldn't even get himself to say their names. Like many of his friends, he was growing tired of Luminé and Oxana. Most had already decided they would leave on the very first day they were allowed to. By his calculations, he had less than two months left.

His former lover, Linda, came to mind. Oh, how he missed her. He missed seeing her, enthralled by her touch, as he caressed her soft, beautiful body and stared into her deep blue-green eyes. She had been his only lover, and when Luminé's enterprise was announced, he had begged her to come with him so they could build their life in Luminare. Even when she told him her answer was 'no', it did not phase him. They would continue loving each other. It mattered not that they lived in different kingdoms. But that was before the 'new rule' banning travel between the worlds, a rule that caught them all by surprise.

He had gotten several letters off to her, through the bribe-oriented channels some could afford, but she had not responded. He had lost her, he was sure, and the love he held deep within his heart for her languished.

He had tried to replace her of late, but it seemed no one was interested in commitments here in Luminare. Other than a few trysts arranged with willing females, he had no experience of love here in exchange for a night of choice food and wine. Certainly, these were nothing that could heal the hole in his heart and were no encounter of any lasting memory. It was shallow, as was all of life, it seemed, in Luminare.

Cleetus walked over to his closet and pulled out the tunic he wore while doing his metalworking. He fixed a small fire in the small kitchen hearth he had built against the back wall and put on a pot of water and coffee beans to boil. He then took a few pieces of fruit down from the shelf above his kitchen table. As he was eating and waiting for the coffee beans to boil, a knock at the door was followed by a voice he instantly recognized.

"Cleetus? Are you up yet?"

Cleetus smiled. It was his friend Sparkis. "I'll be right out, Sparkis."

Cleetus took down another mug from his shelf and poured two cups of coffee, then went out. Sparkis was sitting on the logs near the firepit, holding his sword in his hands.

"What brings you here so early, Sparkis?"

"I overheard the news. We are going to have our own version of the Angel Games here. Luminé is calling them, the Luminare Games."

"Well, that figures. Is there anything beyond his vanity?"

"I kind of like it. And… I aim to be a winner in these games. It's why I'm here. Can you lighten up this sword?"

"Why would you do that?"

"I've reasoned that I was not fast enough in the Angel Games. It is why I placed 708."

"There were only 707 finalists, Sparkis."

"I know. I just missed it. Had I been a little lighter on foot, as they say, I believe I would have made it."

Cleetus took the sword from him and brandished it, eyeing the forged blade up and down. "It is a heavy sword. It will be difficult, but I can soften the metal and thin it. But it will cost you."

"How much?"

Cleetus glanced inside his hut at his stores, "A basket of fruit and a basket of greens and a deer."

"That's a high price."

Cleetus again began eyeing the sword blade held aloft above his head, "Well, how badly do you want to win? There are other metal workers in Luminare, you know." Cleetus knew he was the best, and Sparkis would meet his price. He waited.

"Alright, I will do it.

Sansa

The Angel Sansa walked into the courtyard of the Headquarters for her appointment with Oxana. She went up the stairs and into the new administrative offices. There were several partitioned walls with Angels sitting at desks piled high with unfurled parchments, quietly going over reports. She walked down a wide hall and was greeted by another Angel sitting at a desk in the hall outside a large office.

"May I help you?" the female Angel asked.

"I have an appointment with Oxana."

"Oh," she said and pointed down another hall, "Her office is down there."

"Whose office is that?" Sansa asked, glancing in at the large office and picture window visible from the open door.

"This is the office of the Great Luminé."

Sansa felt warm inside and remembered the night on the beach when she had allowed him to see her fully.

Sansa went down the other hall where another office was located, not as large or elaborate as Luminé's. The door was closed. She knocked.

"Who is it?" came the voice. It was Oxana.

"It is Sansa."

"Have a seat. I will be out shortly."

Sansa sat outside the hall waiting, wondering what role Oxana would reward her with at the Headquarters. She would be closer to Luminé, and that suited her fine. He had seemingly forgotten about their night on the beach. Still, she knew as soon as he saw her again, it would all come back to him, and she would have yet another chance to ingratiate herself with him.

Oxana called through the closed door, "Sansa, come in."

Sansa walked in. Oxana was seated at her dark brown oak desk, holding a pen in her hand, writing a message on parchment. Behind her was a large window that overlooked the northern wall of the compound.

"What is it you wanted to see me about?" Oxana asked, without looking up.

"Is Luminé here?"

"No, he is away exploring the south side of the realm. Why?" Oxana asked as she penned a few more words on the parchment.

"Because what I have to say involves him. I just wanted to make sure he was not near."

Oxana looked up, her eyes narrowed, and her face fixed, "Spit it out, now, Sansa."

Sansa was alarmed. She had imagined this being a power grab. The meeting was not heading in the direction she wanted. "I have news. It's something I will hold in confidence, but although it is my duty, perhaps a position of power could be granted to me."

"What is the news?" Oxana demanded, ignoring her request.

Sansa sighed heavily, weighing her options, and decided she needed to talk now. "Luminé has been corresponding with Splendora."

Sansa watched Oxana's eyes widen, and she glanced out the window. Sansa could see the change in countenance from a proud ruler to an insecure lover sweep over her, but only for a moment. In an instant, Oxana's eyes turned back to her, narrowed even more, and her narrow jawline now even more rigid. She demanded, "How do you know?"

"I saw a letter in Sparkis's hut. It read, 'Sparkis, old friend. Please give this to Luminé. Tell no one.' It was signed by Splendora."

Oxana stood up and walked to the window. Sparkis was outside near the back of the compound, digging the soil to create a flower bed along the fence outside. Oxana opened the side panel of the window and leaned out, shouting, "Sparkis!"

Sparkis turned, "Yes, Queen Oxana?"

Oxana turned, glaring at Sansa as if she had an idea. "Never mind!" she said. Oxana turned and walked around her desk. She put her face very close to Sansa's and pointed toward the open window. She whispered in an angry tone, "Do you see those cages where Lito, his commanders, and other troublemakers are hanging, the same ones that Sparkis will be occupying when I am done using him?"

Sansa looked out and nodded, a sinking feeling in her stomach.

Oxana tilted her head, glaring, "You will say nothing to Sparkis. You will keep your eyes on him, and let me know about any other letters. You will report only to me. Is that clear?"

"Yes, Queen Oxana," she bowed.

"Then go."

Oxana waited, then shouted out the window to one of her guards, "Summon the Archangel Antonio."

~ ~ ~ ~

Oxana went to the Throne Room to wait for Antonio. She needed him to hurry as she wanted to send him on his way before Luminé returned. Finally, Antonio walked in. He bowed, "Queen Oxana, you summoned me?"

Oxana watched him carefully, making her final decision. She had always trusted him in the past, but this was a matter of utmost secrecy. Could he be trusted?

"Come in, Antonio, and come closer. I have something very important to discuss with you."

Antonio bowed and walked over, standing directly in front of her. Oxana decided, "Antonio, we have been friends for a long time, have we not?"

"Yes," he said.

"I need you to follow Luminé, and I trust you will do so discreetly."

"My Queen, may I ask why?"

"I cannot tell you why, not yet, but it is important, in fact, he might be in danger."

Antonio nodded, "It would be better if I had one of my men do this. I will be too easily noticed."

Oxana paused, thinking. The mere suggestion of involving someone else meant that the little circle was suddenly becoming wider than she felt comfortable with. She could lose control very quickly. She stood slowly, thinking, "Is there someone you absolutely trust?"

"Yes, Ganus. He is one of my commanders. He can be trusted and sworn to secrecy."

"Very well. He cannot be seen or found out for any reason. Have him report to you any findings, then bring them to me."

"Very well," he nodded and left.

Yuki

Yuki crept through the woods toward Antonio's seaside mansion. A light was on in the backroom, and someone was there talking with him. She crouched down and waited. After a long while, the Angel left out the back door and flew up into the sky, heading out over the sea. She waited a little longer, then went to the back door and knocked.

Moments later, Antonio answered. "Yuki?" He quickly looked behind her, then motioned for her to come in.

"What are you doing here so late?"

"Who was that you were talking to?" she asked.

"One of my commanders. He is going on a special mission."

"I wish I was going on a special mission," she said, "I am getting sick of this place."

Antonio grimly nodded.

"Do you have wine?" she asked.

Antonio nodded, as the hint of a smile crept across his face, "Yes, I do. Come in."

Antonio led her through the large kitchen and into the expansive living room. Yuki looked around at the large rooms, sparsely furnished. There were several oil lamps in the main room where it looked like Antonio spent his evenings. She walked over to the large window at the front of the room that looked down at the shoreline and sea. The moonlight was reflecting across the water. "You have an amazing view. Even at night, it is something."

"Yes, is yours not as nice?"

"Oh, not as nice as this."

Antonio lifted his arm, gesturing for her to sit on the couch, and went back to the kitchen, returning with a bottle of wine and two glasses. He sat down next to her and poured them each a glass of wine.

She accepted it and raised her glass, "What shall we drink to?"

"To the Luminare Games," he said, raising his eyes.

Yuki laughed, shaking her head, "We are going to talk about those in a minute. But first, to the Luminare Games."

They clanged their glasses, and each took a sip.

Yuki set her glass down, carefully eyeing Antonio. He was an attractive male, ruddy, and muscular. She wondered why she had never considered pursuing him. Perhaps, because of Lito. But Lito was gone.

Antonio asked, "So, the games."

Yuki replied, "I don't like it, Antonio. I feel like it is a diversion or something. I just get the feeling there is more to the story."

"There may be," Antonio said. "I will try to find out more. What do the rank and file say?"

"It's mixed. Some are excited, as they have nothing else to be excited about. Some don't care. Some are hell-bent on getting back to Heaven. How about yours?"

"Same," he said.

Yuki crossed her legs and noticed Antonio following them. She smiled. Not tonight, she thought, but maybe. She got up and finished her wine. "I have to go now."

"So soon?"

"Yes, I have lots to do. Next time, we will meet at my home. I have some wine I want to share with you. Will you come?"

"I will," he said as he led her out.

She walked down the steps onto the lawn.

"Yuki!" he called.

She turned with a promising smile, "Yes?"

"We will keep our meetings and our friendship secret. It is best for both of us."

"Oh, I know. Goodbye." She slowly lifted into the air and ascended, turning her head to see that he was watching her.

The Dagger

Luminé glanced over at Oxana, sound asleep, and quietly got out of her bed. He went down the hall and over to his own room. The warmth and scent of her body was still upon him. They had spent over an hour rolling, loving, immersing themselves in each other. They had done so more and more frequently lately. He knew why, too. It was not that their love was deepening. It was they were both feeling increasingly insecure. They only had each other, truly, and they were both clinging fiercely to all they had.

He laid in bed, glancing up at the night sky, thinking. There was too much on his mind to sleep. His visits to the realms earlier had not gone as well as he had expected. Antonio and Dyanna were the only commanders who seemed to have it truly together. Their Angels looked sharp. When he had arrived, there were thousands of Angels near the realm Headquarters, training, marching, dueling, all preparing for the games as Luminé had asked. At the shore, Antonio had already dispatched over a thousand Angels to cut down trees and build ships. Dyanna was starting tomorrow. But the others seemed to be a step behind. Yuki, Thaddus, Lisala, and Rodrigo were not inspiring the Angels under them. They were training, but not with the vigor and energy that was supposed to be present after such a great announcement. Yes, Yuki told him they were going to begin shipbuilding this week. Still, it was not enough to comply with what Luminé had expected.

"I need to replace them," he thought, but only for a moment. He knew things were too fragile to deliver such a bold move against the leaders right now. Discontent was in the air, and it meant only one thing. A day of reckoning was coming for him unless he could find a way out. He would have to tell them all. They would never be allowed back into the Heavens. He sat up, leaning forward, and peered out the windows at the 30 or so Dark Cages hanging still from the trees behind the Headquarters. They were still only because the Angels inside had probably already gone mad. Lito, his followers, and the other troublemakers being made examples of were probably cowering inside, trying desperately not to think about the darkness. Yet, how could they not? It was their ever-present monster. Would he end up in one of those cages? Would Oxana end up there too, examples to the inhabitants of Luminare of leaders who lied? She would never be able to handle it. He needed to find a way to absolve her from blame. If it came to it, he needed to take this blame himself. Stop!

He got out of bed and turned away from the window. No, I will not allow them. I am the great Luminé. There is no Angel or Angels who can triumph over me. I need to act now. But how? He paced across the floor of his room, hands nervously clenched in front of him, laying the moves he might make in front of him. Then it came to him. The sword. Yes, the Golden Sword. But to reveal it now might be too soon. To wield its power, though, yes, that could not come soon enough. Did it possess powers that would strengthen him? Did it give the one who wielded it wisdom, strength? He needed to test it. But how?

Luminé went out of his room in the dark of night and quietly crept into the dark empty Throne Room. He went over to the place on the stage and felt around for a slight edge of the floor's hidden opening. He found it and used his dagger to pry open the floorboard gently. He reached in and took hold of the heavy Golden Sword, then sat on the edge of the stage, running his fingers up and down the blade, marveling at it. He wondered if it could truly deliver power to him. At the very least, it would prove to be a bargaining chip with the Lords. All at once, it came to him, and he began to speak to himself quietly in the empty Throne Room. "A child, yes, a child born of the sword. I will make a dagger from its metal, which I can conceal, one I can carry with me. Who was that Angel that Sparkis knew? Cleetus, the metal worker. He is… oh yes, he is in Lisala's realm. I will go and pay him a visit."

The Game

The following night, after Oxana was asleep, Luminé quietly retrieved the Golden Sword from the Throne Room and went through the woods in the back of his Headquarter's compound. The guards under the Dark Cages were all asleep, and Luminé made a mental note to deal with them in the morning.

Once in the woods, he lifted into the air and headed out over the sea. The moon was only a quarter full tonight and hung high in the sky, shedding little light anywhere, and that suited him fine. Tonight's task must be conducted in secret. As he flew, he marveled at the immensity of the dark landmass below him. This was his kingdom. He alone, of all the Angels, had been given his own land. And while he was still unclear of what purpose his kingdom would serve, he would make certain that it served him. He would cement his authority with an angry iron fist if he had to.

He saw the mountain that signified the northern boundary of Lisala's realm and landed on the shore. He would walk from here so as not to be seen. Suddenly, he heard a rustle in the woods behind him. He crouched down, holding his breath, scanning the dark woods, waiting. *It must have been a bird or an animal.* He quietly stood and crept, further along, making his way out of the woods and onto the dark deserted road, periodically glancing over his shoulder.

He passed home after home, all dark. Some of them were nicer, some still huts, as many of the Angels had gotten lazy and were content with huts. Luminé realized too that it might be a sign they were not planning on staying. Finally, he reached the bend in the road he had been looking for. Set back some 40 feet from the road was a large hut with a thatched roof. Next to his was a brick kiln-type outdoor oven, with numerous tools and iron bars laying against a wooden stand.

.He knocked on the wooden door, and Cleetus answered within moments. "Who is it?" came the voice.

"It is Luminé, Cleetus. Open up."

Cleetus stuttered, "Come in," he bowed. "Great Luminé, what are you doing here?"

Luminé put his finger over his mouth, signaling for him to be quiet. "Cleetus, I have a job for you, but it is secret. I will reward you handsomely."

Cleetus hesitated, unsure of why Luminé had chosen him. "What reward, Great Luminé?"

"I will have Lisala promote you to Host Commander and give you a small plot of land by the coast."

Luminé watched his eyes carefully, trying to ascertain how well he could trust him. Cleetus was thinking, measuring something in his mind. Cleetus seemed to resolve it and said, "Of course, what is the job?"

Luminé pulled out the Golden Sword from beneath his cloak, "You must take this sword and melt off some of the blade, thinning it, to yield enough of its material to forge a dagger. You must do this in the mountains, away from everyone, and no one can know."

"When would you like this finished, Great Luminé?"

"Right now. I will go with you."

"Now?" Cleetus said in a voice full of protest.

Luminé stepped closer and said in a low, unyielding tone, "Yes, Cleetus, right now. We leave at once."

Cleetus looked at the sword. He had never seen one like it in his life. He slowly took it from Luminé's hands and examined it reverently. He began nodding, "Yes, I can do this."

"Good, let's go."

Cleetus's hands were shaking as he grabbed some tools.

They flew up and out over the sea toward the mountains. Luminé pointed to the farthest mountain and landed on its side that faced the barren lands, so no one would see the fire they would build.

It was dark when they landed on a plateau halfway up the mountain. Luminé marked a spot in a clearing, and they both set about gathering wood. When they had enough, Cleetus knelt down to start the necessary fire. As it grew, he kept building it higher and higher, hotter and hotter, until finally, it was ready. He set the long narrow metal tray containing the sword into the fire. They both watched carefully, and for a moment, Luminé thought of pulling it out, worried he might damage its nature, but he kept watching. Purple and blue light emanated from the sword, and Cleetus remarked, "That is strange."

"What," snapped Luminé in a nervous voice.

"The colors of the metal as they burn. They are not the normal colors. Where did you get this sword? I have never seen anything like it."

"No questions, Cleetus. Just do what you have been instructed to do." Luminé said crisply. Cleetus was already asking too many questions.

Cleetus smiled, but his mind was racing. Like all Angels, he had heard of the Prophecy. Luminé, having come in secrecy, placed grave importance on the sword. Could it indeed be the sword from the Prophecy? It was so stunning that it had to be. Cleetus finished scraping thin strands of gold from the sword, shaping it exactly as it had been, allowing the strands of gold to melt in the tray. Next, he set to work, molding the dagger, all the while watching Luminé's eyes greedily glued to his work. Whatever he was doing had immense value to Luminé, and so would his silence have immense value.

After over an hour, he had finished the dagger. He took it out with tongs and placed it in a bucket of water. It hissed loudly, quickly dissipating into silence. Cleetus lifted his finger, signaling they needed to wait. After a few tense moments, he lifted out the dagger and handed it to Luminé.

He watched Luminé marvel at it, then said, "Great Luminé, I know this is the sword of the Prophecy. I would like to be able to choose my land along the coast."

Keeping his eyes fixed on the dagger, Luminé scoffed, "We have a deal, Cleetus. I will give you what has been promised, nothing more."

"Or what?" Cleetus said.

Luminé nodded and said, "Ahh, you are very smart to have figured that out, Cleetus. You are right. You deserve more. I will give you a counter offer." Luminé pointed behind Cleetus to the distant sea visible from their high mountain spot. He said, "Turn around and look at the coastland at the base of those mountains."

Cleetus's eyes widened, and he turned to see what grand gift he had garnered through his bargaining.

Luminé put one hand on his shoulder and said in a friendly tone, "Cleetus, when you play a game with the ruler, you either win, or... you die."

In the swiftest of moments, Cleetus felt the sharp burning pain of a blade thrust deeply and forcefully into his backside. It was more than pain, though. It felt like a volcano had just erupted inside of him. His mind began to shake, and his speech began to waver. He tried to scream, but he had no voice. He clutched for his throat, but it disintegrated in his hands. His head felt limp, his eyes forced to look at his own feet and knees as they turned to dust. He tumbled violently onto the ground. Then his eyes shriveled and fell off his face, and all went black.

Luminé watched Cleetus dissolve into dust before his eyes and stood smiling, staring at the worn tunic and sandals sitting in a pile of dust, all that was left of Cleetus.

Something snapped, and he wheeled around. "Who is there?"

Luminé waited anxiously, but then a bird flew out of a tree, and he relaxed. He kicked the tunic and sandals, all that was left of Cleetus, into the brush. He then threw the remaining water onto the fire, picked up the newly forged Golden Sword and Dagger, and flew back to his Headquarters.

Oxana

Oxana felt the warming of her lower abdomen as a dark pall fell over the forefront of her mind. It was Legion calling her, beckoning her. She had become accustomed to this distinct feeling over the last year. When it came, it signaled to her he was thinking about her. If it were strong, strong enough to wake her, he was summoning her mind to see something.

She got out of bed and quietly walked outside. It was the dark of night, and only the palace guards were awake, standing on and under the walls and along the back by the cages, pacing off their patrols.

She closed her eyes, listening again, trying to see if any vision was accompanying it, further proof that he wanted her to come. In her mind, she saw mountains and a cave. Legion was there, but where? She now recognized the mountain. She opened her eyes and turned to look toward the south. "He is here! In Luminare."

She left without being noticed. Flying through the sky she felt the excitement she always felt when he summoned her. It had been that way since the first time she laid with him, an experience her body would instinctively never forget. Legion possessed dark powers, there was no doubt, but for those lucky enough to be his lover, they were sweetly dark powers. This was not her concern tonight, though. She would probably let Legion have his way with her, only to ingratiate herself further with him. She needed him, not for sexual purposes, but for what was at stake.

Luminé was corresponding with Splendora, to what end, she did not know. Could they be plotting his return? Could they be planning on going to the Lords to beg forgiveness? Oxana had been thinking lately if it would be better to be the Queen of a Dark Lord or end up jilted by Luminé, abandoned and humiliated before all of Heaven. She had decided which would be better or worse. All of this was plan B. Plan A was her primary concern tonight.

She was no fool and knew full well that she and Luminé were involved in a game of pretended power. They ruled Luminare because their Archangels allowed them to. Should the Archangels and the majority of Angels under them revolt, she and Lumiine would have no way to stop them. As much as she disdained Vamorda, and more so the way Luminé watched her, Vamorda and her thousands of Palace Guards could not stop the masses. Once Luminé informed them they could not go back, he might end up in a Dark Cage. They might try to put her in one, too, unless she aligned herself with Legion and took his protection at just the right time. Perhaps, Legion would step up and rule this world, as she had frequently considered might be his aim. Regardless, she would stay close to Legion. She would do his bidding until such time she felt it was no longer needed.

Before long, she was flying up into the mountains on the far southern tip of Luminare. No one had chosen to settle there. It was too mountainous, with too many cliffs and no beach. She spotted the mountain from her vision, circled around it, then spotted the cave, lit by a fire. She landed and walked into a large cave illuminated by the light of the blazing fire. It was furnished lavishly for a cave. Inside was a brown cloth-covered chair, a woven couch, a bed set two feet off the floor, and a table and smaller chair, obviously used for eating. A swine was roasting above the fire, and oranges, lemons, grapes, and greens were set upon narrow tables along the cave wall.

Legion was not there, though. Oxana looked to the back to see if there was another way in, but the cave's back wall was the solid rock of the mountain. She looked around, occasionally glancing at the bed where he would have surely had his way with her this night. But where was he?

Suddenly a voice from the cave entrance, "Oxana, you came."

She turned. Legion stood at the front of the cave in a long black robe with a long golden chain hanging around his neck. His blonde hair fell thickly on his shoulders. In the light of the fire, he indeed looked like a Lord.

"Lord Legion, yes. When did you come here?"

"None of that is important for you, Oxana. Where is the Golden Sword?"

"Luminé has it."

"Where is it!" Legion demanded.

His tone frightened her for a moment. He usually frightened her, and yet, she was beginning to think it was an act. She would be giving him commands in a short while, commands to take her. She replied calmly, "Luminé has hidden it."

Legion nodded and began walking toward her, "Oxana, perhaps I will need to find someone else to be my Queen. It seems you cannot handle even a simple task."

Her eyes narrowed, "I got it here, didn't I? You need to be more patient, Lord Legion."

Legion stood straighter. "Watch your tongue, Oxana. Or… "

"Or what? I will find the sword. I need time." She needed more than time. She needed to decide if she would deliver it to him. She might decide Luminé would be best to hold it, for now.

Legion said, in a low, groveling tone, "You must find it and bring it to me. I am destined to rule this world, Oxana. Luminé will not survive. Now, do you want to be by my side?"

Oxana had him where she wanted him. Asking, not demanding. She replied firmly, "I do want to be at your side."

"Then get the sword. I have new powers, Oxana. Growing powers. Powers over the minds of Angels."

"You do?" she asked. The thought suddenly worried her.

"Yes, just like right now, I can see what you want."

Oxana felt a warmth flutter from her thighs to the top of her head. How did he know? She glanced at his growing manhood under his tunic. He stepped forward and took her by the hand. His words relieved her, though, as she realized he had not seen what was on her mind. He had not read her mind. Still, she was ready for him.

Luminé

Luminé woke in the middle of the night with the dissolving face of Cleetus haunting him. He could not believe he had just taken a life. A sense of deep fear overtook him as if the Lords would know what he did and would come to judge him. He shook it off, saying aloud, "I am not under them anymore." Still, the fear at having done something so evil hung over him like a dark mist. He sat on the edge of his bed and let his head fall into his hands.

He thought of what had happened and realized he now possessed two of the most powerful weapons in the Heavens. He alone now had the power to take Eternal Life.

Luminé ran his hands slowly along Splendora's legs and up her thighs, then rolled on top of her. It was magical, and more than he ever wanted. The joy, the immense feeling of life delivering everything threatened to overwhelm him. She whispered, "I have always loved you," and he let go. They rested, then got up, dressed, and went in search of some fruit.

"Look there!" Splendora said. Not far from the Great Falls was a cluster of peach trees. They flew down and picked some, then flew over to sit on the edge of the falls. They ate their peaches quietly, enjoying their rich nectar, but both sad as they knew their time was coming to an end.

Splendora asked, "So how is it really down there?"

Luminé looked up and half-smiled. He tried to frame the right words, words that would tell her it was going great, but he could not get them out. They were all a lie, and he was through lying to her.

"It's not going well at all."

"What do you mean?"

"I was wrong to leave you. I had it all in the Heavens. Why did I want more? Did I find more? No, I didn't. The truth is, I am very unhappy."

Splendora said, "I'm sorry," she said, staring down into the thundering waters plunging into the basin in the canyon below.

"I can't live without you anymore," he said.

"But I can never come back," Luminé said.

"Then, then I will… " Splendora stood and drew her sword. With two lightning flashed, she slashed both wings off and dove headfirst into the thundering waters. Luminé screamed! "Nooooo!!!!!"

In the next instant, Cleetus's face appeared, his eyes wide, with no skin around them, his teeth were bare, with no gums, the white bones moving them as they chattered. "Luminé! Luminé! I win! I win!"

Luminé lurched up, breathing heavy, his mind in a panic. He had been dreaming.

Vamorda

The following day Luminé received a message. It was from the head of his Palace Guard, Vamorda.

Luminé,

We have captured someone who was spying on you. We are secretly holding him one mile due south of the Headquarters in a forest. Please come as soon as you can. You will want to hear what he has to say.

Vamorda

Luminé was fuming with anger, the humiliation he had just endured still gnawing at him. *Spying on me! Who would dare do such a thing?* He started to get up, then glanced down the hall at Oxana's room. Could she be the one? *She is the only one who would dare.*

He put his new Golden Dagger into its sheath and pulled his shirt over to cover it. He had already wrapped the handle to disguise it further. He did not know when he might use it again, but he needed to know more than that. He needed to know if it would increase his powers.

He went out and around the back of his headquarters, mounted his horse, and quietly trotted into the woods, heading due south.

Within a short time, he saw Vamorda and two of the other guards ahead. They were standing in front of an Angel who was tied to a tree. Luminé road up and dismounted. He recognized the Angel. It was Ganus, one of Antonio's Commanders. Luminé walked up and looked at him. His face and body were bloodied from torture. The ropes were so tight, Luminé could see blood oozing from behind them. Luminé motioned to Vamorda to follow him, and he walked off a short distance for privacy.

"How do you know he was following me?"

"We observed him several days ago following you into the mountains but did not have enough time to tail him ourselves. Then, yesterday, when you left Luminare, he was waiting for you and followed you. I made the decision to arrest him, and we did so upon your return yesterday morning."

Luminé swallowed hard and looked over at the Angel. *Followed me into the mountains? Then he saw me. That was the noise I heard. It was him. He saw me kill the maker of the dagger.*

"What else did he say?" Luminé asked.

"He said he was following orders."

Luminé walked over to him, "Who told you to follow me?"

Ganus lifted his head and muttered, "Antonio did."

"Why would Antonio want me followed?"

He shook his head, gasping, "I don't know. He said it was to be kept secret. I had a feeling he, too, was following orders."

"From who?" asked Luminé.

"I don't know!"

Luminé drew his sword and pressed the point into his chin, lifting him, "Tell me who?"

"Oxana, I think. I am not sure, though!"

Luminé stared into his eyes for several minutes. He could see the fear, fear which could only mean he had seen something he was afraid to share. Luminé turned to Vamorda and said, "Gag him, and put him into a Dark Cage."

"No! Please! I… I won't say anything! Please, Luminé?"

Luminé smiled at him, "No, you won't say anything. You will never say anything."

Antonio

Luminé woke, feeling his hold on power growing ever weaker. Oh, yes, his enforcer, Vamorda, had captured Ganus. But how many others like Ganus were there out there? How many had it out for him?

Now was the time to be decisive, or all would fall apart. Despite training, he sensed the discontent everywhere. His hope of renewed enthusiasm with the announcement of the Luminare Games was not playing out as planned. Yes, the training, sharpening their swords, sharpening their maneuvers and command; but the discontent was still present.

He got out of bed and peered into Oxana's room. She was gone.

Suddenly he heard a knock on the door. He walked into the hall and saw the hulking shadow outside. It was Antonio.

Luminé needed to deal with him, but as of now, he was unsure who else was involved. Ganus was inside a Dark Cage, and no one knew, except Vamorda.

Luminé snapped, "What is it, Antonio?"

"I am afraid there is trouble, Luminé ."

"Trouble? Isn't that why you are 1st of my Archangels, to handle trouble? Really, Antonio, I wonder who you are serving anymore!"

He watched Antonio's reaction carefully. It could tell him much. His eyes said he was still loyal. His eyes said he could still be counted on. Was Ganus lying? Luminé looked around to make certain all of the guards were too far away to hear them.

Antonio replied, "I serve you, Luminé. Fifteen of my Angels, including two commanders, tried to escape to the Heavens this morning. I was lucky to find out, as one of them backed out and told me their plan."

"They must be punished," said Luminé.

Antonio frowned, "Luminé, I can't punish that many of them all at once. There will be a mutiny."

Luminé growled, "Listen to me carefully, Antonio. They must be punished to set an example. Get Vamorda to help, and I want them in Dark Cages within the hour."

"Very well." Antonio nodded with a look of anguish on his face.

Luminé looked at the over 30 Dark Cages hanging near the back woods inside his headquarters' wall. He pointed and said, "Over there, in the space next to the last cage, in those trees. Build 15 more Dark Cages. They are all sentenced to three months inside."

Antonio grimly nodded and replied, "Yes, Luminé, right away."

Antonio turned, then stopped, hesitated, and went on. "I can't really blame them for wanting to leave. Luminé, there is not enough land, and there are not enough females."

Luminé snapped, and with clenched teeth, said loudly, "The rules are the rules, Antonio. Enforce them, or you will be sorry."

As Antonio walked away, Luminé studied him. Antonio had not wavered, not even in the slightest. Why would he have sent Ganus to spy on him? Oxana had to have been involved. But why?

Ganus

Early the next morning, Oxana sat on her throne waiting for Luminé to enter, periodically glancing at the seven Archangels waiting at attention. Last night Luminé had ordered the meeting, but he had not arrived yet, and Oxana knew what this meant. He was holding some kind of show, and for some reason, he had determined to keep the reason secret from her. She disliked the secrets between them lately. There had always been secrets. There would always be secrets. But lately, the secrets felt more important, with much higher stakes.

Vamorda was there, along with 30 of her guards, standing at attention, swords at the ready, stationed around the perimeter of the room. There were normally only 20 of them, and Oxana wondered why there were more. The doors were opened, and two of Vamorda's guards hauled in two empty Dark Cages and set them in the middle of the room.

A tinge of fear shot through Oxana's mind. Had Luminé discovered her allegiance to Legion? Was she now going to be struck down as Queen in the midst of everyone?

Finally, Luminé walked in at a hurried pace, with his head down. He walked out of his way to pass in front of his Archangels, glancing up at them as he passed. He circled back slowly and took his place next to Oxana but kept standing. "So, someone has betrayed me or is planning on betraying me." He turned to Vamorda, "Bring in the prisoner."

Oxana as well as the rest of the Archangels, looked to the entrance as Ganus was dragged in, his legs chained and his hands tied behind his back. His mouth was gagged tightly, and he looked exhausted due to enduring the last 24 hours inside the Dark Cage. They set him on his knees before Luminé and Oxana.

Luminé noticed Oxana looking at Antonio, her eyes wide. Luminé said, "Antonio, does this Angel belong to your realm?"

Antonio stepped forward, "I do recognize him, but I don't understand why he is here?"

Luminé announced, "Someone has sent him to spy on me. I want to know who."

Antonio shook his head, "It was not me, Luminé."

Luminé walked over toward the two open Dark Cages. He bent down, peering inside both, then walked back. "Who would dare to have me followed?"

His glance passed by Oxana, though he would not make eye contact with her. He turned to Oxana and said, "What do you say, Queen Oxana. Should we punish this traitor, caught in the act of spying on me, probably working for the Lords? Or should we ungag him and let him try to lie his way out of this charge?"

Oxana froze and yet tried to keep her cool. Everyone was watching her. She looked into the frightened eyes of Ganus and knew if they took the gag off, he would betray not only her, but Antonio. It would not bode well for anyone, including Luminé. Ganus would have to be sacrificed. She walked down the steps and over to Ganus, whose eyes pleaded with her.

She lifted her chin, eyeing him disdainfully, and said loudly, "He must pay the price. Put him inside the cage. Let him think about his treachery."

Luminé turned to the Archangels, "And none of you want to claim him? To join him inside the other cage?"

No one said a word but only stared straight ahead. Luminé motioned to Vamorda, and her guards grabbed Ganus and pushed him into the cage, removing his gag at the last moment and closing the door tight. Everyone in the hall heard the muffled cries of horror as Vamorda and her guards lifted the cage and carried it.

The Lords

His world was closing in fast. Hundreds of thousands of Angels were growing increasingly discontent. It was on all their faces. It was in all their glances. Luminé would have to tell them, soon, of his great ommission, his failure to tell them they could not return once they all signed up to leave the Heavens. They could never go back. He should have told them, but at the time, he feared losing too many. He feared only a small band would come, and he would have looked like a fool. Once hundreds of thousands had signed on, he could not go out and make such an announcement.

Luminé had only a few plays left in the world that was closing in on him. It was the safest play. It was the one where he would forget about his ambitions and crawl back to the Heavens, unburdened by the increasingly paralyzing fear the Dark Cages held for him. He would fight his way, earn his way back to the top. Oxana... he may or may not love her still. She would no longer be needed, not in the way she had. Splendora might take him back too, someday. She still loved him. His heart told him that, and his recent dream only confirmed his belief. He snuck into the Throne Room and lifted the carpet and floorboard. The Golden Sword shined in the darkness. He took the Golden Dagger and placed it next to it. He wanted to take no chance of the Lords sensing or seeing it.

He flew out towards the boundary of the Heavens, called for a messenger bird, and sent the letter. He then waited. Two hours later, the bird returned. They would see him.

At first light, he was to fly to the Land of the Lords from the west. A Throne Room Guard would be waiting and escort him to the meeting. He tossed and turned all night, realizing in one sense he was giving up all he had strived for, but in another sense, knowing that only headaches awaited him. He finally drifted off and woke in the dead of night. He slipped out the back of the Headquarters, through the wooded area, and flew to the appointed place to meet the guard.

~ ~ ~ ~

Splendora woke to noise at her window. "Who is it?" she called.

Only the sound of chirping was heard. It was a messenger bird. She went to the window and took the tiny scroll from its feet, and unfurled it.

To All the Archangels,

You are summoned to a meeting at once at the Throne Room. It is a highly secret meeting. Come immediately and tell no one.

Calla

She sighed and looked out at the full moon. The dawn would break in a little over an hour. She threw off her blanket, swung her feet onto the floor, and stretched like a cat, yawning loudly. She had been in the middle of a dream, and she remembered now, it had been about Luminé. She smiled, trying to think about the details, but they all escaped her. She rose, put on her uniform, and left for the Throne Room at the Land of the Lords.

~ ~ ~ ~

Luminé was escorted to the Throne Room in silence, as the guard seemed to resent bringing him. Before long, Holy Mountain with its vast Palace and Throne Room on top came into view. A thousand memories rushed back, all the way from the day of Creation to the day of his trial when he had been given a second chance. Then, he remembered the day he stood before the Lords demanding his own Kingdom. Being in the Heavens, with the sounds and smells of the vast fresh fields and streams, made him regret all his actions. He would humble himself before the Lords and hopefully convince them to allow it all to be reversed.

The portico of the entrance was empty and wide, larger than any portico in his Headquarters. Over 20 torches burned brightly, affixed to the walls, illuminating the giant wooden entryway doors. Luminé had not seen these doors in a very long time, and strangely, the sight of them gave him a feeling of peace and security.

The two guards walked him to the doors, and Luminé readied himself. Then, they were opened. Inside the Throne Room, over 50 torches were lit along the left and right, with several behind the three Thrones where the Lords sat waiting. Luminé walked in, wondering when he would see Splendora. As he drew closer to the Thrones, he now saw the faces of the Seven Archangels, including his replacement, his old assistant, Marcellus. He was no Archangel. He could barely keep up as Luminé's assistant. Luminé scoffed inside but kept walking.

The Lords were there too, seated, waiting, looking more regal than he ever remembered. Even though it was night, the entire scene looked spectacularly regal. He had forgotten how beautiful the place was. He kept walking forward, periodically glancing from the Archangels to the Lords, not making direct eye contact with any of them. When he got a look at Splendora, he could read the look of disappointment on her face. She looked upset, but he could not let this sway him or disturb him in the least. This was the most important meeting of his life.

He reached them and bowed low. Adon said in a warm tone, "Welcome, Luminé."

"Good morning, my Lords." He turned to the Archangels, "Good morning, Archangels of the Heavens." He quickly rehearsed the order of his points. He could not ask to be restored as an Archangel of the 2nd Heavenly Realm now. It would prove too contentious. He realized he truly had no bargaining power. He would pursue this goal after he returned. His followers would hail him for getting them back into Heaven, and then he could pursue the idea of creating an 8th Heavenly Realm.

Calla asked, "What is it you wish to see us about, Luminé?"

"My Lords, as you know, things have not gone well in either the Heavens or in the Southern Realm. I admit that to have asked for my own kingdom was a mistake."

He paused, but none of the Lords replied, and the room held silent. Luminé continued, "I believe it would be best for everyone if this whole idea was reversed." He paused, but only for a moment, as he could already sense another moment of dead silence about to ensue. "For this reason, I humbly ask that my followers and I be allowed to return to our realms and our original units. I will gladly endure another time of exile as punishment for my transgression. Further, I will promise to make things right in our efforts to serve the Heavens." He finished, and bowed, then waited, his hand nervously grasping his sword handle.

Adon broke the silence, "Luminé, do you wish to come back simply because you are having trouble?"

"No, my Lord Adon. Yes, it is hard to realize that many Angels who followed me are unhappy. But in another sense, my actions have broken much, and I see this as a way to fix it."

Adon nodded reassuringly. Luminé was right. He doubted Yeshua or Calla would agree, though.

Calla spoke next, "But Luminé, you were told that once you left, neither you nor your followers could ever return. You agreed to that, did you not?"

Luminé swallowed. He had known Calla would be an obstacle as she stated the obvious. He replied, "I did agree to that, my Lord Calla. I was foolish to do so." Out of the corner of his eye, he saw several of the Archangels looking at each other. It was obvious they did not know about the provision to 'never be allowed back.'

Now, all ears subtly tuned to Yeshua, wondering what question he might ask.

Yeshua did not disappoint. He asked, "Luminé, you say your followers will return. Will they all return?"

Luminé nodded respectfully, knowing Calla's stance, "Yes, my Lord. I am fairly certain that they will." He gripped his sword handle tightly. Yeshua was with him. He was certain now.

No one asked any more questions. Adon looked at Yeshua, then Calla, then back to Luminé and said, "We will vote."

Calla quickly interrupted, "I request the Archangels vote with us as well."

Luminé waited impatiently, trying not to show his outrage. His eyes locked with Adon's, trying to convey his ardent desire that only the Lords vote. Adon turned to Calla, and Luminé could see he was going to object. Still, Calla looked back at Adon with just as strong of a subtle facial gesture. Adon relented on his willingness to object. But Yeshua said, "Calla, is this not a matter for the Lords alone?"

"Yes," Luminé said, instantly knowing he had spoken out of turn.

Calla glanced to him, then back to Yeshua, saying, "Yes, it is, but it is just as much a matter for the Archangels. Their lives have been turned upside down, and they will have to deal with what comes next."

Yeshua said, "Then let us vote. I vote yes. They may return."

Adon said, "I too, vote yes."

Calla stood and said, "I vote no." She sat down and turned to look at Michael, who was first in the line of the Archangels, and asked, "Michael, how do you vote?"

Luminé locked eyes with him. He already knew his vote, but he could not avoid watching his old rival try to thwart him.

Michael said, "I vote no."

Luminé looked down at the floor, momentarily, as Raphael said, "I vote no."

Gabriel was next. Luminé casually looked up, knowing he was counting on his old friend. Gabriel would not look at him, though, and instead looked to the Lords and said, "I vote no."

Rana quickly said, "Yes."

Splendora, too, hoping to build momentum, did the same, saying resoundingly, "I vote yes."

Luminé clutched his sword handle tightly. The vote was tied.

Cirianna then paused and said, "No."

Marcellus, Luminé's replacement as Archangel, voted last and also said, "No."

Luminé's mind screamed louder than he thought possible. His whole being wanted to kick, rebel, draw his sword and demand his way, but he stood stoic, casually looking down the line of Archangel faces lit by the torches, until he fell to her face, to Splendora's. She looked away.

Luminé turned to the Archangels, glaring at those who voted against him, then spit on the floor, and stormed out.

No one said a word.

Antonio

Antonio's loyalty to Luminé was fast fading. He knew Luminé better than anyone else, and one thing was clear to him. Luminé was scared. Antonio regretted having followed Luminé, and he had already made up his mind to side with the majority, who would leave as soon as the year-long period was over. He also vowed he would set the Angels in the Dark Cages free before going.

One long, difficult year under the rule of Luminé and Oxana was soon coming to an end. Antonio called private meetings with the Archangels as well as over a hundred of Luminé's most influential commanders. The meeting was held at night in a clearing in the woods along the eastern shoreline. Torches were lit, but only a few. This was a secret meeting.

Antonio stood on a rock and said, "Within a month, we will have reached the end of the year we promised. How many of you wish to return to the Heavens?"

All raised their hand.

"And what of those who follow you? What of the other Angels?" There was not one who wished to stay, and among the rank and file under their command, there were none who wanted to remain.

It was agreed that a large contingent of them, led by Antonio, would go together to inform Luminé and Oxana. They entered the gates of the headquarters, walked up to the door, and knocked. A guard answered and said that Luminé and Oxana were not available.

"Wake them," Antonio said. "It is an urgent matter."

Luminé heard the noise outside and looked out the window. He got up and ran to Oxana's room. "Get up. There is trouble." They both quickly dressed and went outside. "What is the meaning of this, Antonio?"

Antonio began, "Great Luminé. We have news from the Angels in your Kingdom."

"What news? Why do you trouble us in the middle of the night?"

"Luminé, there has been a vote. All of the Angels and I mean all, want to return to the Heavens."

Stammering, he responded, "Well… that is out of the question. There is no way we are going back. Do you hear me? No way!"

"But Luminé… " Antonio pleaded, "It's not working out here. We all agree; it's not what we thought it would be like at all. The food is horrible. This 'working all day' thing has grown old. The weather is not nearly as nice, and that is just the beginning. With all due respect… everyone agrees on this."

Luminé shot back, "Well… tell them all to get over it."

Antonio, wishing to remain loyal and respectful, pleaded, "But Luminé, why not? What does it matter? We can serve you in the 2nd Heavenly Realm like many of us used to."

Luminé glanced at Oxana, then motioned for Antonio to follow him inside. The others waited. Once inside, Luminé, Oxana, and Antonio stood in his living quarters. Luminé said, "Antonio, we cannot go back."

"I don't understand, Luminé. Why not?"

Luminé dropped the bomb. "Because it was one of the conditions."

"What do you mean? What conditions?"

"Don't you get it, Antonio?" Luminé yelled, "We are never allowed back!"

Antonio froze, his face etched in stone, as the dread of the words washed over his body. He turned Oxana, who only looked at the floor.

Antonio turned to Luminé. The year-long charade suddenly became clear. They were never allowed back; there was never such a thing as a one-year commitment. It had all been a lie. Antonio drew his sword and grimaced, "Why didn't you tell us, Luminé ?"

Luminé drew his sword, and Antonio charged forward. In two swift blows, Luminé knocked Antonio's sword from his hands. "Antonio, if you try that again, you will end up in one of those cages." Antonio shook his head, "It is you who should fear the cages Luminé, along with Oxana."

Luminé pressed the sword into Antonio's throat. "Listen to me. You will receive great favor from me and great riches. You will lack for nothing, but you must keep silent. I will find a way to deal with this. We need more land, and we need more females. We will find a way to appease everyone. We need some of the riches of the Heavens for ourselves. We will take them. I will find a way to change our lot, but I need time. Go and convince them that we will begin meetings to plan for the day. It does not arrive for a month anyway."

Antonio realized he had no choice. If the Lords had said they could not go back, there was no point in pressing it. He had to put his fate into Luminé's hands. It was his only choice. He nodded.

Luminé lowered the sword. "We will meet with the Archangels in two days, and I will have a plan. No one can know about our discussion. Is that clear?"

"It is," Antonio said.

Calla

Calla was sunbathing on the deck of her Villa overlooking the vast Heavenly Sea. She was laying on a plush towel, with her eyes closed, performing her periodic ritual of sunning her entire body. Perfect white puffy clouds drifted lazily in the sky. Birds were busily chirping and eating sunflower seeds from her garden. The waves washed ever so gently onto the shore.

Despite the peaceful and serene setting, she was troubled. The dreams of long ago returned over the last several nights. The Golden Sword of the prophecy was in the dreams, and Legion was holding it, laughing.

She leaned up on her elbows and whistled. Within moments, her snowy white owl, Sheeva, flew down from the nearby forest, landing on the deck rail. "Sheeva, bring me parchment and pen, I must write a letter to Adon." She was still angry with Adon. He had been at the heart of all of the trouble. She could not believe he was willing to let Luminé and his rebels waltz right back in. And Yeshua too. Why? Why would he let him?

Sheeva returned and dropped the items to her. Calla rolled over onto her stomach and began to pen the letter.

Adon,

I am worried about Legion. My troubling dreams have returned. And I need to remind you that as of yet, we have not found where the Golden Sword is. This is the sword of the prophecy, and we must possess it.

Adon, I am sorry about all of our disagreements. I'm afraid I still have to disagree with you, but I need to trust that you, too, have reasons.

I miss our days of old.

Calla

She rolled up the parchment and gave it back to Sheeva. "Go swiftly, Sheeva, take this to Adon's mansion in the forest."

~ ~ ~ ~

Adon received the letter from Calla and smiled. With his heart, he wanted to make up with her, and now they would. He quickly sat down and wrote his reply.

Dearest Calla,

I have read your letter. I agree, something has to be done, and we do need to find the sword.

I miss our days of old as well. The memory of them carries me through these dark times.

Yours Forever

Adon

Adon rolled up the parchment, tucked it in the owl's claw, and sent Sheeva on her way. As soon as the bird had left, he moved into action. He needed to find out some information about Luminé. He might need to go back down there.

Run Up

Yeshua rode his horse across the vast plain toward Calla's Villa. As he neared, he could see she was walking by the sea. He slowed to a trot and called her name, "Calla!"

She stopped walking and waved for him to join her. He dismounted and walked down the grassy embankment onto the sandy beach. "Good morning, Calla. How are you today?"

She turned, smiling, as the wind blew her brown hair behind her shoulders, and the sun illuminated her face, "I am doing okay, Yeshua." She turned again to the sea, closing her eyes, taking in the fresh sea air.

Yeshua walked up and hugged her, saying, "Let's walk a while."

"Sure," she said, lifting the hem of her dress, stepping into the surf, and shaking the sand off her feet. She took him by the hand, and they walked along the smooth, dry sand.

Yeshua said, "Calla, I don't understand why you voted against Luminé… and, to be honest, I really don't understand why you had all the Archangels come and vote."

She stopped and turned to face him, "Yeshua, Legion wants them to come back. Don't you see what he did to our guards when he escaped? His powers are growing. The Angels who followed Luminé are marked. Were they to come back, the very Heavens would crumble from within."

"How do you know all of this?"

"It is because of a dream, Yeshua. I saw it all in a dream."

"A dream? I hope you are right, Calla."

She nodded and grasped his hand again, continuing their stroll. "Yeshua, I don't know if you realize this, but Legion is slowly influencing them, and not only them, but Luminé, and Oxana as well. Did you not notice Luminé's eye twitching slightly. It was a nervous twitch. He has lost a step, mentally. He was not himself. It is the influence of Legion upon him, and I am sure he does not even realize it. How is Legion getting to him?"

"We had long suspected he was influencing Oxana. Wasn't Mylia her friend? Perhaps there is a connection?"

Calla shuddered with the thought of poor Mylia being killed, reduced to a small chunk of skull. She grasped Yeshua by the arms and stopped him, saying, "I am afraid this will not end well Yeshua. Legion must be planning something."

Yeshua asked, "Have you told Adon about this?"

"How can I tell him anything? He will not believe me."

"Of course, he will."

Calla frowned and looked out to the sea, "I know you're right. I will go and see him."

~ ~ ~ ~

Oxana stormed into the living quarters where Luminé was sitting on a couch, reading some of his daily reports of their training. Despite the middle of the night meeting with Antonio, the realms were all still training vigorously. He looked up at her, standing with her arms crossed, and asked, "What are we going to do?"

"I haven't decided."

"No, Luminé! You cannot block me out anymore! I am your Queen!"

Luminé looked up and asked frankly, "Was it you who was having me followed?"

"Of course not! Why would you say that, Luminé? Have you forgotten, we are in this together!"

Luminé threw his glass across the room, shattering it against the wall, yelling, "The hell with them! The hell with all of them!"

"Luminé, look out there!" She pointed to the Dark Cages in the backwoods. "We are going to be next if we don't think of something!"

Luminé stopped. Her words sent a momentary fear through him. He asked, "Why do you say that?"

"Because Antonio told me he fears mutiny. He said thousands upon thousands are planning on leaving on the day. What will happen when they are sent back?"

Luminé grabbed the sides of his head, feeling overwhelmed, and shouted, "I don't know!"

Oxana shouted right back. "Well, you better think of something!"

Luminé stood and grabbed her briskly by the shoulders, shouting, "You were the one who told me to leave!"

"Yes!" she shouted back, "Because I saw greatness in you!" She clenched her teeth, holding her eyes fixed on his.

Luminé pondered her words, then set her down. Oxana was the only one who had ever truly believed in him. They had gotten out of messes before.

Oxana's eyes widened, "We need a scapegoat. We need someone to blame."

"Who?"

"The Lords… They betrayed us. They are the ones who won't let us back. We will blame them.

"Yes, they did. They lied to us."

Oxana spoke words that felt foreign to her, "Someone must pay. Someone must die."

Luminé looked at her, confused. Did she know he had killed the maker of the dagger? "Who?" he asked.

"We can blame Lito. We can use the Golden Sword. We can show everyone that you are as powerful as a Lord."

Luminé thought of Heaven's Archangels scoffing at him with their eyes, especially Michael. The thought of the vote, how his own had betrayed him. He needed to redeem himself in front of them all. He needed leverage if he was ever going to be restored. That was why. He had nothing to bargain with. He needed a show of strength. Blame Lito, then go and take what they wanted.

"Yes," he said, his eyes searching the ceiling, working out the sequence. "Lito will pay for betraying us. He was supposed to deliver the message, the announcement. He and Yeshua plotted to keep us here forever. He… he was… yes, he was given permission to return, alone, provided he purposefully failed to tell us."

"Yes," Oxana said exuberantly.

Luminé continued, "But we must show strength, Oxana, not only to our Angels but to the Heavens."

"How?"

"We need more land, do we not?"

"Yes, but what are you saying?"

"We need more females, do we not?

"We must attack the Heavens. We must take one of the Realms."

~ ~ ~ ~

It was a moonless night as Legion sat at the entrance to his meditating in the darkness. Darkness had become his trusted friend. Ever since Calla had thrust him into the Dark Cage, he had discovered a source of power he needed. He laughed, imagining himself thanking Calla for introducing him to such a dear and trustworthy friend as the darkness.

He looked down into the barely visible shadows of the distant valley, forests, and plains of Luminare below him, and his mind pictured all of the Angels in all of the Realms. In his mind, he could now see the small dotted landscape of distant campfires. He pictured all of Luminé's Angels sitting around fires, complaining about their wretched lives. Most of them wanted to return and were anxiously waiting for their Archangels and Commanders to remove the roadblocks.

Legion closed his eyes tightly, dwelling on their thoughts, their minds, feeling myriads upon myriads of discontented feelings. He concentrated in the darkness, spreading his dark seed further upon them. It was subtle, and yet Legion could feel It was real. The dark seeds he had sewn on them on the long-ago Day of Creation while being led to the Dark Mountain were slowly coming alive. He could feel the Angels' dumbed-down thoughts, incoherent, disturbed, confused, becoming increasingly irrational. None of them were Heaven's Angels anymore. They were fallen beings, sinking into lewdness and debauchery. None of them knew it yet, but they were becoming his Angels.

~ ~ ~ ~

Luminé stood next to Oxana, on the porch of their headquarters, both of them dressed in their full uniforms. He raised his hands high, silencing the enormous crowd in front of him. He paused for effect, relishing the moment of quiet, then shouted, "As all of you know, we do not have enough land in the Southern Realm. The Angels and Archangels in Heaven openly boast about how we are crowded like animals into a tiny piece of land, while they have enormous tracts of land in the Seven Heavenly Realms. In addition, an imbalance to the natural order exists as you all know; there are not enough female Angels here."

Luminé quieted down and watched the rumblings sweep through the hundreds of thousands of Angels gathered all around the grounds and the skies above his headquarters.

"I have heard that many of you wish to return, but I must tell you now, The Lords have betrayed us! No one can return. Ever."

Shouts, only a few at first, the more, began to spring up. They were murmuring and talking, looks of anger on hundreds of thousands of faces.

Luminé paused, letting their response linger, then shouted, "And one of our own has betrayed us!" He turned to Vamorda, "Bring out the traitor!"

Again he paused, watching the growing anger on many of the faces. He continued, "On the day we left, The Angel Lito was supposed to deliver a message to me. It was from the Lord Yeshua who secretly placed a last-minute condition, stating that, "We could never return to Heaven. Yeshua and Lito crafted this plot. Lito purposefully failed to deliver it. Many of you remember, he was late in joining us. His reward was that he was to be made into an Archangel in the Heavens, taking my place as head of the 2nd Realm. For other reasons, I had him arrested and put into a Dark Cage, preventing him from escaping to receive his reward. But now, he will pay the price."

Luminé nodded, and Vamorda and her guards pulled Lito out. He fell flat on the compound ground, curled up in a ball, with his eyes closed and his whole body quivering. The entire crowd grew silent. No one had ever seen an Angel come out of a Dark Cage. Luminé could see the eyes of all wavering between anger and fear.

Lito was picked up and dragged to two tall wooden stakes that had been placed in the ground for this day. His arms were tied to stakes on either side of him, stretching him out, forcing him onto his knees. He was completely exhausted and barely conscious, as Luminé knew he would be having just emerged from almost a year inside the Dark Cage.

Luminé walked up to him, leaned forward, and whispered, "Confess to your crime, Lito, and I will let you go free. Do you understand? Just confess, and you will be free."

Lito tried to open his eyes, but they closed just as fast.

"Do you understand?" Luminé whispered.

Lito nodded, keeping his eyes closed.

Luminé stepped back. He looked across the breadth of the crowd. All were silent, and it made Luminé nervous. He shouted, "Lito, do you confess to your crime? Tell us all by nodding. Do you confess to this crime of being a traitor?"

Lito swallowed, and lifted his head, then nodded several times, and collapsed in exhaustion.

Luminé drew the Golden Sword from his sword sheath. He held the sword high, pointing it to the sky, shouting to the silent nervous mass of Angels, "I have been growing more and more powerful. As the Lord of Luminare, I now have the power over life and death. We will be taking back what is ours, but first, the traitor must die."

Lito, who had always been friends with Luminé prior to their disagreement a year earlier, swallowed hard, trying to shake off the utter disorientation he felt, trying to understand what Luminé was talking about.

Luminé turned the sword handle in his hands, so it faced downward like a giant long dagger. He glanced at the stunned crowd, then shouted, "Lito, because you betrayed us, you are sentenced to death."

Lito looked up, "But, but I didn't... "

Luminé' violently thrust the Golden Sword downward, driving the razor-sharp blade between the back of Lito's shoulders.

Lito screamed, and his face froze. Blackness descended onto his mind. His knees stammered, trying to get away, but the long impaled blade held him down.

Luminé drew out the blade as the crowd grew silent. Then, Lito's right arm broke in half, and he swung limply to the left. His left arm, too fell apart, and he fell with a loud thud face down into the dust. Slowly, his face and torso began to dissolve. Screams were heard from those closest who could see the details. Blood poured into the dirt as his body fell apart. Then, the pooled blood seemed to sweep itself back together, rolling back toward the shrinking mass of tissue and bone, all dissolving as it did further. Finally, the remains of his legs, arms, skull shriveled further. All that was left was a tunic and a pile of dust.

Oxana covered her mouth in horror, and a horrific cry went up from the entire crowd, followed by silence and murmuring.

~ ~ ~ ~

Legion stood concealed under a hooded tunic inside the compound near the back of the crowd, worried at the reaction. Luminé had not won them over. He had not convinced them, not yet. *Fool!* He thought. You had them, now killing Lito has lost them. This was the critical moment, the moment when Luminé would be turned on, and it was coming too soon. He could not lose Luminé now! Too much had to happen still. He pulled the hood forward, partially covering his forehead and eyes, and covered his hand over his eyes, closing them tightly, entering into the darkness.

He heard Luminé begin to speak, but he needed to push it aside. He needed to sway the Angels. He pictured their faces; he felt the anger in their minds. He felt their shock at being told they could not go back.

~ ~ ~ ~

Luminé stood before the two wooden stakes with the rope dangling in the wind. He stepped over Lito's dust pile, stepping through the stakes, and held the Golden Sword high, letting it shine for all to see. "This is the Golden Sword of the Prophecy. The Lords have made us their prisoners here! The Angels of Heaven think they are better than us. They think we are second-class Angels. We are not their prisoners! We are free-born Angels, who have every right they have. We will not let this stand. We need more land for our kingdom, and we will take what rightfully belongs to us!"

~ ~ ~ ~

Legion felt the swell of indignation from the crowd. They were moving but not fast enough. He began to chant, using his dark powers, sweeping now not through one mind at a time but through whole sections of the crowd. How he thought, and it instantly came to him. The Golden Sword is empowering me. He smiled, eyes shut tight, and began to chant.

As he did, he heard Luminé shout, "We will attack the Heavens, and take the land we need. We will take the 6th and 7th Heavenly Realms for our own!"

"Yes," Legion responded himself. He had not expected this to happen so soon. It was brilliant, and he reminded himself he had chosen wisely so long ago when he chose Luminé. He tried to stay calm, entering deeper into the darkness, feeling the mood of the Angels turning. He began chanting in the darkness of his mind, as if broadcasting to all, "Go to war. Yes, Go to war. Yes. Go to war."

Shouts of approval came from various pockets, only a few at first, then more. Then rumblings and drawing of swords. Legion opened his eyes, basking in the deed he was doing. In every corner of the compound, Angels were shouting, jabbing swords and spears into the air, voices sporadically shouting, one yelled, "Yes, take what is ours!" Another shouted, "We are free!"

Antonio was the first of the Archangels to step forward. He walked out into the clearing where Luminé and Oxana stood and raised his sword high, shouting, "War! War! War!" Soon more joined in, then more, until the thunder of hundreds of thousands of Angels shook the skies with their shouts of 'War!'"

Luminé raised the Golden Sword high and answered them, "Yes! We will go to war!"

Suddenly, the chant shifted, slowly at first. Still, quickly it gained momentum, and soon, it thundered through the entire compound and surrounding skies, 'Luminé. Luminé. Luminé. Luminé."

Luminé turned to Oxana, smiling. He took her by the hand and raised it into the air, taking in the exhilaration he had not felt since the day he had decided to leave Heaven.

~ ~ ~ ~

Legion watched the scene unfold and smiled, *"Yes, go to war, for you will not be victorious, and you will all become mine."*

Preparations

Oxana felt the warming of her lower abdomen strongly as she turned over in her sleep. Darkness flooded her mind, but she wanted to ignore it. She was too tired, too stressed to get out of bed, but she knew she had to. As confused as she felt, she needed more information to make her decision. Earlier in the compound, she had found herself caught up in the euphoria of the chants of war and the cries for Luminé to lead them. It reminded her of the very beginning when she had also feared leaving, but Luminé had bravely led them. Luminé was right, and he had done it. He had found a way for them to get out of not telling the Angels the truth. Now, he was right too, in that a show of strength is exactly what was needed. It would distract the masses.

She threw off her blanket, dressed quietly, and crept down the hall and out the back door of the living quarters, flying into the night sky, to the Mountain cave where Legion was waiting. She needed to read Legion's mind somehow. Luminé was playing a high stakes game, and he very well may fail. What then? Legion would save her, she hoped.

She spotted the mountain and swooped down to the plateau outside the cave entrance. The cave was lit again, with a small fire burning, but Legion was waiting for her this time. He was standing behind the fire, facing her, his broad, muscular chest bare, wearing only a cloth around his waist. His hands were on his hips, and his blonde hair hung down his strong tan back.

She bowed slightly and said, "Greetings, Lord Legion."

She waited as he did not reply but only tilted his head. His eyes glanced momentarily at the bed at the side of the cave wall, then back to her.

Legion smiled, walking around the fire towards her, and said, "It is good Luminé goes to war. He needs to show the Lords who he and his followers truly are and what they are capable of."

Oxana nodded slowly, though she had real fears about what they were about to do.

"Will we succeed?" she asked.

"Oh, yes, I believe you will. This land is not enough to hold Luminé's kingdom."

These were words she needed to hear, but was he telling the truth? She couldn't tell. He interrupted her thoughts.

"Oxana, you have done well, but there is something you must do."

"What is it that I must do?" she asked.

"Luminé cannot bring the Golden Sword with him. You must make sure he does not. And, you must find out where he has it hidden."

"But why not? Won't it help us to win?"

"No, it is not for now. The Golden Sword is the sword of the Prophecy. Yes, it has the power to take eternal life, but it is not for now. It is for me to use when the proper time comes."

Oxana listened, but she was not sure she believed him.

"Come here, Oxana."

She moved forward further into the cave toward him. Legion reached out his hand, running it through her long brown hair, "You are afraid, Oxana. I can see in your mind. You fear being left aside, being abandoned by Luminé."

She pulled back, and yet part of her needed to hear more. He was right. These were exactly her fears. She leaned in again, letting his hands fondle her long hair.

Legion said, "I am a Lord, Oxana. Only I can assure you of never having to fear such things." He paused, carefully watching her reaction, then said sternly, "Go and convince him not to take the sword. Tell him if it falls into the wrong hands, he will lose the only bargaining chip he has. He cannot risk losing it, and it will not help him win the war."

Oxana nodded, "I will convince him, my Lord."

Legion placed his hand gently on the back of her neck, pulling her closer, but Oxana pulled away.

"What is wrong, Oxana?"

"Nothing is wrong. I have to get back."

Legion watched her turn and fly off into the sky above the mountains. He was not used to being rebuffed, and Oxana seemed to be making a habit of it. He would let it be for now.

~ ~ ~ ~

Adon walked out across the dew-laden field to his stable and untied his black horse, Hunter. He led him out into the morning sun and gave him one last drink of water from a bucket, then mounted him and took off across the plains toward the north. He could have flown, but he felt like riding this morning, and Hunter needed exercise. When he reached the sea, he pulled them both into the air and flew across it to the 1st Heavenly Realm. He landed himself and Hunter on the beach, then continued at a slow trot along the smooth sand toward Splendora's seaside home.

He had sent her a message the night before, and as he approached, he could see she was sitting on the porch waiting for him. Adon smiled and waved as he rode up and dismounted. Splendora was one of his favorites, not because she was perfect, but because she had a good heart, one that believed in the power of good to overcome evil. How else could she be so in love with Luminé? Her ability to see the good in him, while few others did, revealed the pureness of her heart, and in Adon's books, that counted for everything.

Splendora stood up, happy to see him, and said, "Good morning, Lord Adon."

"Good morning to you, Splendora. Have you made coffee yet?"

"I have. Come and sit down, and I will pour you a cup."

Splendora went inside, then returned. They sat on her porch, sipping their coffee, looking out at the morning sun peaking over the gently rolling waves, not saying anything. After a while, Splendora asked, "Why did you wish to see me?"

Adon smiled, "Well, I want to understand what is going on with Luminé."

Splendora nodded, momentarily staring into her coffee, trying not to show the sudden resurgence of the heartbreak she had been privately enduring.

Adon watched her and said, "You have always loved him."

She looked into her coffee, nodding.

Adon said nothing. Nothing needed to be said.

She turned, "Lord Adon, no one understands. Yes, I have loved him since the beginning. I wanted him to come back! He wanted to fix all this!" She shook her head, "Why didn't they let him?" She tried to sip her coffee, but she could not hold back the tears of sorrow that would not hold back.

Adon took the coffee from her hand and set it down. He stood and lifted her hand, motioning for her to stand, then hugged her tightly. "I'm sorry, Splendora."

She held him tightly, resting her head on his shoulder, trying not to cry. "They don't understand, my Lord. He is in trouble."

Adon's eyes narrowed, "What trouble?"

"He never told them they could not come back."

Adon pulled away some, "He never told them?"

"No, he said that he didn't know how."

"But... but what does that mean?"

"It means he is afraid when they find out that they are going to put him into a Dark Cage."

Suddenly, Luminé's desperate attempt to meet with them made sense. Adon hugged her tighter, "Splendora, I know this may be hard to believe, but someday, and I don't know when, we are going to fix this mess."

He felt her long shuddering sigh, a release she needed, and he was glad he was there to help her. He let her go and in a concerned voice, asked, "Do you have any eggs here?"

"Yes," she said, wiping her eyes, as a small smile snuck its way onto her face. "Why do you need eggs?"

"Because I am going to make us some breakfast. You sit down. I'll take care of everything." Adon went into the kitchen, trying not to show the worried thoughts racing through his mind. He needed to get back down to Luminare and find out what was going on for himself.

~ ~ ~ ~

The Angel Gabriel knocked at the door of his favorite commander.

"Who is it?" came the reply from Sadie.

"It's your boss!"

Inside he heard lots of shuffling around, then Sadie's voice, "Just a minute!"

Gabriel chuckled to himself. There was just something about Sadie that always made him smile. Finally, the door opened, and Sadie stood before him in her bare feet, with a hastily thrown on, disheveled tunic, and her hair going in multiple directions. She exclaimed, "Gabriel? What are you doing here?"

"I came to see how you're doing? Are you healed up yet?"

"Oh, Gabriel," she replied, in a tone filled with pain and hope at the same time, "I'm getting close."

"Good because I need your help."

"Really, for what?"

"For helping Adam and Eve."

"You've been helping them?"

"Yes, I've filled in a few times. Watching two kids is a nightmare!"

Sadie laughed, "Tell me about it. Welcome to my world, boss."

"Your world. Yes! That has a nice ring to it. When can you start?"

Sadie looked out the window, smiling, "I would love to see them again. I can start tomorrow."

"Are you sure?"

"Yes, I'm actually excited, though I'm sure it will fade once they start running in opposite directions. Have we kept the guard duty up?"

"Yes, I've kept everything going. I've also kept the guard at the Garden of Eden in-step, too."

"No word on Legion?"

"No, I am afraid he is out there somewhere, plotting his next move."

~ ~ ~ ~

Luminé stood in front of his Archangels with the map of the Heavens hanging on the wall. On it, the southernmost 6th and 7th Heavenly Realms were circled. "It is imperative that we secure the entire perimeter of both Realms by nightfall. It is also imperative that all the Angels be captured and either incapacitated through wounds or be put into Dark Cages. To that end, we will spend the rest of the week constructing upwards of 100,000 cages, which we will bring with us. As we attack, we will drop them on the coast. As we capture prisoners, we will begin filling the cages."

He paused, "Any questions so far?"

No one said a word.

"And Antonio, you will form the spearhead that will attack the 6th Heavenly Realm. Rana is the Archangel defending it, and I do not suspect you will have trouble. Yuki, you will lead the spearhead that will accompany me to the 7th Heavenly Realm."

Antonio stepped forward, "What do you think the Heavens will do, Great Luminé?"

"They will divide their forces and attack either the same day, but more than likely the following day. At that point, we will have evened the odds. Heaven will be down to 340,000 Angels, and once they divide that in half, there will be approximately 170,000 attacking 120,000 of us at each Realm. I can deal with those odds, especially since we will be in a defensive posture."

Antonio nodded and stepped back. Despite his knowledge of the truth of Luminé's deception, he was itching to prove himself against Heaven's armies.

Luminé looked at each of them, assessing them, wondering if they could do what would be needed. These were indeed not Heaven's Archangels, they were not the cream of the crop, but they would have to do. He trusted the plan would overcome any shortcomings in their abilities. "Are there any questions?" he asked.

Yuki raised her hand, "What is our goal, Luminé?"

"To capture the 6th and 7th Heavenly Realms!" he snapped.

"But what will we do with it? Will they simply give it to us?"

Luminé knew he had to be careful here because it fit his plan, but ultimately, there was no plan to keep it. "We need the land, Yuki. We will negotiate to keep it."

"With what leverage?"

"Enough!" Luminé said. "I know the Lords better than anyone here. I will have the leverage I need, provided we secure the perimeters of both Realms before nightfall. Is that clear?"

Everyone nodded, except Oxana. She was busy in thought. She knew Luminé had just dodged something, but what? What was he up to? Then it hit her. This, all this, was so he had bargaining power. He was going to give it all back, so he could return, to her, to Splendora.

Luminé continued, "In the morning, at dawn, we will gather at the west end of Luminare on the beach. We will fly low out to sea, then attack from the west, where they will not expect us."

Luminé dismissed them all, then went to his room and closed the door to writing his letter. It would let Splendora know not only to stand down but to understand what his plan was.

My dear Splendora,

My love for you compels me to do what I must do. The humiliation I felt in front of the Archangels and the Lords were too much to bear. I know now that they could not agree to allow me back because they saw me as weak. I am not weak. I am strong, and those who follow me, too, are strong. I am leading them into a show of strength that will convince everyone. I also have something very special, the Golden Sword of the Prophecy. Once I have demonstrated our formidability as an army of Angels, I will go again to the Lords and agree to lay down my sword forever. I will also offer them the Sword of the Prophecy, and they will take me back.

I promise you, Oxana will be no longer with me. I will love only you, and for all time, we will be together as the greatest Archangels in the Heavens.

With all my heart, I pledge this.

Luminé.

He then took the original letter, rolled it up, and tied a ribbon around it. He wanted her to receive it after the battle started, not before, so she had no pressure to report anything. He would send it early in the morning prior to assembling on the shore.

Suddenly Oxana opened the door. "Luminé, I need to… " She stopped, noticing he was concealing something.

"What is it?" he asked.

"It's the Golden Sword. I do not think you should bring it with you tomorrow."

"Why not?"

Oxana knew she had to be convincing, but she did not believe Legion entirely. Still, Legion was right about one thing: The sword would not help them in this battle.

"Because it is too dangerous. What if it falls into the wrong hands? You will lose your leverage, leverage we may need later should things go the wrong way."

Luminé scoffed, "Things are not going to go the wrong way, Oxana. Have you not seen our plan?"

"Luminé, don't let overconfidence blind you. You do not need the sword in this battle. Even your plans say as much."

"I have considered that, Oxana."

"Well, what are you going to do?"

"I haven't decided yet."

"Why haven't you told me where it is?"

"Because I don't want you to be burdened by the knowledge of it."

"But what if something happens to you. Don't you think I should know?"

He sighed, "Not now, Oxana."

"How do you know someone has not already found it?"

A shudder of fear ran through him as his eyes tried to momentarily dart toward the Throne Room, but he stopped. "It is safe, Oxana."

She stormed out and went to her room.

~ ~ ~ ~

Later that night, Oxana lay awake in bed listening. She knew Luminé would go to see the sword, so she waited. She heard him leave his room and listened until he went out the door. She crept down the hall to the door and watched as he crossed the courtyard to the Throne Room. As soon as he entered, she went out and circled around to the back of the Throne Room and flew up to the windows along the back wall. She could see his shadow moving across the floor. He reached his throne and looked back at the door, then moved his throne aside.

He rolled up the carpet and opened a door in the floor. *So, that his where you have it.*

She watched as his shadow lifted the darkened sword. He thrust it around in the air and then sat down thinking. Finally, he placed it back, closed the door, rolled back the carpet, and put his throne back in its place. Oxana raced back into their living quarters and into her room, feigning to be asleep as Luminé quietly crept back into his room. She had one more thing to do before tomorrow.

~ ~ ~ ~

Adon paddled in the darkness through the open sea toward the eastern edge of the Southern Realm. He would enter on the shores near the mountains and stick to the forests to remain unseen. He needed to find out what was going on. It was slow rowing in the choppy sea, and he could have just flown, but he felt he would be less apt to be spotted by Luminé's lookouts who were watching for Angels who would be flying. He stopped for a few moments, taking a sip from his canteen, wiping the sweat from his brow. Gauging by the moon, he had another two hours to go, which would put him there just before daylight.

~ ~ ~ ~

Legion closed his eyes in the darkness of his cave, letting his mind wander over the mass of sleeping Angels in the thousands of huts below. He felt the confusion they felt and knew the day would bring even more. Then he zeroed his thoughts on Oxana. Why hadn't he been able to connect with her? Had she failed in her mission? He needed the sword. He would go himself in the morning to make sure Luminé did not have it. Then he would find it himself if needed.

~ ~ ~ ~

On the morning of the attack, Luminé woke up feeling angry. Was he doing the right thing? Would Splendora understand? Would the Lords understand, bargain, and let him back. He reached into his desk and took out the letter he'd written to Splendora. He signaled for a messenger bird and tied the message to its claws, and sent it out into the early dawn sky, knowing it would be another two hours before she received it. Then he closed his eyes, imagining the victory they would achieve today. He put on his Archangel uniform and went outside to take a walk down to the sea to gather his final thoughts.

~ ~ ~ ~

The Angel Sansa knocked on Oxana's bedroom window. Oxana looked out, then waved her to the back door. Luminé was already down by the beach. She had told him she would be along shortly. Oxana came out, and Sansa handed her the message.

"Did you read it?" Oxana asked.

"No, I did not."

"Good. Go and get ready with the others."

Oxana unfurled the message. It was the letter Luminé had written to Splendora. Her eyes quickly scanned down the letter, then stopped.

Once I have demonstrated our formidability as an army of Angels, I will go again to the Lords and agree to lay down my sword forever. I will also offer them the Sword of the Prophecy, and they will take me back.

I promise you, Oxana will be no longer with me. I will love only you, and for all time, we will be together as the greatest Archangels in the Heavens.

With all my heart, I pledge this.

Luminé

She fell back against the wall, catching herself, saying aloud, "Oxana will no longer… be with me."

Suddenly she realized his entire plan and all his actions. Yes, he wanted to win, but not for her, not for them, for himself. She turned, gained her composure, determined to confront him, and went inside. Then, she stopped. There was only one way to stop this love affair once and for all. She headed for the Throne Room.

~ ~ ~ ~

Adon reached the shore and pulled his canoe up onto the rocky shore. He dragged it into the woods then put on his tunic and a belt to make himself look like one of the Angels. He then headed through the woods along the shoreline toward the center of Luminare. It would take him a few hours. As he walked, he thought of the ancient portal the Lords had placed in each of the Realms. There was no use for them anymore, nor had there ever been, yet somehow they had included them in the design. He did not know why it had come to mind, but he made a note that if his journey went well, he would try to go to it and inspect it.

~ ~ ~ ~

Legion's mind felt a jolt, and he saw a trap door open. The Golden Sword was there, shining brightly, but where? He concentrated, and the floor of Luminé's Throne Room came into view. Oxana was looking inside, then the door closed. "Ahhh, she has indeed found it."

War

The armies of the Archangels of Luminare gathered on the western shores in silence. Each Angel held their sword in hand. Each was dressed in their uniform, each wearing a black bandana tied around their heads to help them distinguish each other from Heaven's Angels. The pomp and fanfare of the last time they were assembled in formation on a beach was when they had left the Heavens. Now, anger replaced joy as the dominant emotion. All were resolved to right this wrong, to win their freedom to move about as they pleased.

Luminé and Oxana flew in front of everyone and paused. Luminé turned to face them, "Today, we reassert our dominion in the Heavens. We must win by nightfall. Is everyone ready?"

With one accord, a loud shout was heard. Luminé turned to face the sky in the west, waiting for first light. As soon as the sun peeked out over the horizon, he raised his sword, held it aloft for a split second, then dropped it, signaling for all to advance. At once, 235,665 Angels took off in two columns, with swords drawn and black bandanas covering their heads. Thousands of them carried Dark Cages for the prisoners they would take, sped out at full speed into the early-morning sky, with Antonio and Yuki each at the head of one column. Their goal was simple: complete victory at each Realm by nightfall.

~ ~ ~ ~

Adon heard a loud noise, as from a crowd, then nothing. He continued walking and found a good number of huts and fires, all smoldering. He found it strange no one was up yet. He stayed in the woods and kept going. The woods were bright and airy, and the sun was peering through in golden slices illuminating the forest floor. Here in the woods, it looked just like the Heavens, but out on the road, the atmosphere felt different, empty, with no sense of hope. Adon knew what it was. It was the influence of Legion on them all.

After another mile or so of passing many huts, all empty, he decided to take a closer look. He walked out of the woods into a clearing of huts and quietly walked up, peering inside. They were all empty. He looked up the road at the next clearing of huts where another fire smoldered. He stayed to the road and walked up, ready to dash back into the woods if needed. *Where is everyone?*

He kept going, gradually going faster down the road, increasingly confident that for some strange reason, he was alone. Finally, he reached the Headquarters, where he peered through the front gates. A few horses were tethered at the side of the Headquarters. Adon carefully approached and went inside. All was empty. He went around to the back and stopped.

He saw no one, but then he heard the cries. He looked up and noticed the Dark Cages hanging, over 50 of them. From inside, he heard anguished cries, and he immediately knew why. He had created the Angels, and he knew full well what darkness and isolation would do to them. Angels were designed to live in the light and to fly freely through the clouds. To be confined in darkness was a sentence of the cruelest proportions. Adon flew up into the air and used his dagger to open each cage.

One by one, exhausted, thin, and frightened Angels fell out and onto the ground, writhing in pain, trembling, trying desperately to catch their breath, all relieved to be free finally.

Adon knelt next to one and asked, "Who did this to you?"

"Luminé," came the reply.

Adon shook his head, angry at hearing Luminé would do such a thing to one of Heaven's Angels. He had vouched for Luminé since the beginning, but had he known he could inflict such cruelty. He wondered if he would again.

He ran to a nearby hut and got some water, and gave it to the Angel.

"Who are you?" asked the Angel.

Adon smiled, "Just someone who cares."

~ ~ ~ ~

Legion watched Luminé and his Angels leave from the woods on the shore. All was working according to his plan. He needed Luminé's followers, but he also needed to get rid of Luminé. What was about to happen now would surely end Luminé's uncanny reign as their leader. They would, of course, lose the war and be sent back here, Luminé with them. Luminé would be thrust into a Dark Cage for the rest of eternity, and Oxana would.... he paused. He was not sure about Oxana, and he would decide about her later. She had the allegiance of many. Would it survive the coming battle? Something about her intrigued him as well as enthralled him. Perhaps because she was the first Angel he had been with intimately.

For now, though, they had gone, and Luminé did not have the Golden Sword with him. Legion laughed and turned, walking down the hillside to the road leading to the headquarters.

~ ~ ~ ~

Adon went inside Luminé's Throne Room, looked around, amazed at how feeble Luminé's efforts to create his own kingdom had been. He felt sad, sad that he had not stopped Luminé from leaving. Calla was right, he knew this now. The misery brought to all because

Legion had been set free, perhaps too soon, was a terrible blow to the Lords plan for everyone to have happiness.

He left the Throne Room and went over to the headquarters looking around with some disappointment at how tarnished things felt outside of the Heavens. Finally, he went into the living quarters, stopping a little way into the entryway, shaking his head, "Luminé, Luminé, why did you give up Heaven for this? Why?" Before the words reached his own ears, Adon felt the answer. It was his fault. All of it was his fault.

~ ~ ~ ~

Legion walked into the empty courtyard of the headquarters, imagining all of it under his command. He would begin by building a worthy palace. He would enslave hundreds of the Angels to serve his every need, night and day, including the most beautiful females.

He went straight to the Throne Room, ready to claim his prize. When he entered, he saw the door at the other side was open. He walked across, looked out, and saw the Angels laying on the ground next to the opened cages. *Who would have let them out?* he thought.

He wheeled around and hastily walked to Luminé's throne, where in his vision he had seen Oxana opening the trap door, looking at it. He moved the throne aside, moved aside the carpet, and pried open the floorboard, revealing the trap door. His eyes lit with anticipation. He opened it, and his eyes suddenly widened in horror. The sword was gone. In its place was a small golden dagger.

He grabbed the dagger and examined it. Suddenly, out of the corner of his eye, he saw something moving outside in the courtyard. He could not believe his eyes. It was Adon. He hid to the side and peered out, watching Adon go around to the side of the Throne Room and untether a horse. Adon hopped on and said something to the Angels still laying on the ground, then pulled the reins and trotted out onto the road outside the compound.

Legion exclaimed, "What is he doing here? Wait! No. Did he have the sword with him? Had Adon taken the sword?" He looked again. Adon had no sword. Luminé must have taken it. But Luminé did not have it. Legion was sure he examined the sword on Luminé's belt. It was not the Golden Sword. His mind raced, thinking of what he had missed. Then it occurred to him. He had not examined Oxana's sword. She must have concealed it. She must have it. But why?

And what was this Golden Dagger? He would figure it out on the way. He had no time to waste. He tucked the dagger into his belt and went outside. He grabbed a horse and headed out to follow Adon. He would keep at a distance and find out why he was there today of all days.

Cirianna

Cirianna, Archangel of the 7th Heavenly Realm, sat alone on the seaside cliff facing the morning sun. It was her favorite spot and the place of her morning prayer time. Each day her custom was to rise before dawn, shower, and head out to some scenic place to pray. The rigors of commanding one of the Heavenly Realms were endless and full of decisions and interactions. This was the one time of the day when she could turn it all off. She cherished this time of solitude.

Behind her back, many called her the forgotten Archangel. She was one of three females but did not enjoy Splendora's notoriety, known for her prowess and rank, or Rana, known for her epic beauty. Cirianna was beautiful in her own right, and she possessed absolute prowess with the sword and with command, but she kept it all low-key. Her brown hair was kept short because it was practical, and she seldom adorned her slim rose-colored lips or light brown eyes with colored herbs, as many of the females did, because it just wasn't necessary. She was happy with who she was and how she was, and it was all enough for her.

As she sat, singing a song of praise to the Lords, she kept hearing two words in her mind: trust and fight. *Trust and fight. I don't understand. What does that mean?* She ended her prayer as she usually did, "Be with me this day, Lord's of Heaven, and bless those under my command. And, as always, help those who are lost, even my old friends, to find you somehow again."

She stood up and gave her body a much-needed stretch. As she turned to leave, she saw something out of the corner of her eye. *Are those birds?* She squinted, focusing her vision, and again asked herself. *Is that a flock of birds?*

She flew toward the distant objects in an effort to make them out. Then she stopped. In the distance, she saw thousands upon thousands of Angels flying as fast as they could. They were headed straight for the frontier of her Realm. *What is... oh no. What are they doing? Are we being attacked?*

She turned and raced through the sky to her headquarters, landing in the still quiet courtyard. She grabbed the trumpet from the guard at the front gate and began blowing the battle sound. At once, all the Angels of the Seventh Realm sprang into action, most directly from their beds. But she was too late. Within mere minutes Luminé and his forces were upon them, and fighting broke out all over the Realm. The battle for the 7th Heavenly Realm had begun.

~ ~ ~ ~

Rana jogged along the wooded path that wound its way like a long snake through the pine forest at the 6th Heavenly Realm's southern edge. She loved to jog here each morning because of the softness of the pine needles that blanketed the path. Her runs had become much more prominent in her life, now that Michael was gone. She regretted helping Luminé and losing Michael. It was all that simple. She had her pick of the very most handsome two Angels in all the Heavens, and she had lost them both. She was unsure when love would ever find her again, and she didn't even want to engage in her past behavior of entering shallow, merely physical relationships. She wanted more. Now, as never before, she understood the Lords' wisdom in establishing not only Seasons of Love, but also Seasons of Reflection. She was in such a season now, and the reflecting was doing her good.

Suddenly an Angel fell onto the path in front of her. A moment later, another Angel wearing a dark bandana landed on top of him, and they commenced fighting. In one swift motion, the dark-clad Angel thrust his sword, pummeling one of her guards through the stomach.

Rana stood still, horrified, as the Angel now turned and saw her. She took off flying through the woods while the Angel pursued her.

Now all around, she could see more and more dark-clad Angels raining down from the sky, attacking her Angels, most of whom were still asleep in their huts.

She neared her Headquarters and started shouting, but suddenly two Angels grabbed her. Their hands were rough and strong, angry, and unyielding. She struggled, shouting, "Let me go!" She kicked one in the groin and broke a hand free, punching the other in the face, but then she felt a heavy blow on the back of her head, and all went black.

~ ~ ~ ~

By late afternoon, both the 6th and 7th Heavenly Realms were in the hands of Luminés' Angels. Both Realms were littered with badly wounded Angels. Those not wounded were inside Dark Cages, including Rana. Luminé's forces had incurred minimal casualties, and all efforts were turned to preparing for the attack that would come either by nightfall or in the morning.

At the Throne Room

Splendora rushed to the Throne Room for the emergency meeting she had been summoned to. She arrived, shaken, having heard the news of the attack on the way. Michael, Gabriel, Raphael, and Marcellus were waiting for her. Splendora exclaimed, "My Lords, what is happening. Is it true? Please tell me that Luminé is not attacking the Heavens?"

Calla angrily replied, "I am afraid he already has."

"Oh, no!" In complete shock, Splendora said, feeling responsible in some strange way because of her secret love affair with him.

"Where is Lord Adon?" Splendora asked.

Yeshua replied, "Adon is nowhere to be found. His horse and animals are there, but he is not.

"Why is he doing this?" Splendora asked as she saw Michael clench his teeth, wanting to reply.

Yeshua answered her, "I am afraid he has become desperate, Splendora. Perhaps we acted hastily in not allowing him to find a way to come back."

Splendora, desperate to somehow make an excuse for Luminé, exclaimed, "Legion is behind this. He clearly has some influence or hold over Luminé. I can't see Luminé doing this on his own. Nevertheless… he is making a huge mistake."

Calla's face grew cross, "It is more than a mistake, Splendora. Luminé has crossed the line, and a line he can never step behind again."

Michael stepped forward, snapped to attention, and said in a booming voice, "My Lords, we are ready to launch a counter-attack."

Calla said, "Yes, we will take back what is ours. Splendora, you and Gabriel will attack the 7th Realm. Michael, you and Raphael will attack the 6th. Marcellus, your army will defend the Land of the Lords and the Throne Room, just in case he is bold enough to come here."

"When will we attack, Lord Calla?" asked Michael.

"Tomorrow just before first light."

No one said a word, as all knew they were suddenly in a fight for the very existence of the Heavens. Splendora interrupted the silence, in a commanding voice, "We should not split up."

Everyone turned to her.

"Why not?" Yeshua asked.

"Luminé would want us to. He has almost 120,000 Angels in each of the Realms. By splitting up, we are practically evening the odds. Together, we should attack at once from all four directions and overwhelm him at one of the Realms. Then, we can turn our attention to the other."

All were quiet as Calla and Yeshua considered her idea.

"It has merit, Splendora."

She asked, "Where is Luminé now?"

"He is in the 7th Realm," Michael said.

"Then there is where we will attack," Splendora said. "It will pin Luminé down, and he will not be able to get reinforcements fast enough."

Calla looked at Michael. "Michael, do you agree?"

"Yes, I do."

"Then, go."

The Ancient Portal

The sun was setting, and nightfall was nearing, so Adon decided to set up camp. He found a good spot and tied up the horse he had borrowed. He built a small fire, pulled some meat from his satchel, unwrapped it, and began to warm it.

As he sat alone in the cold night of Luminare, he could not help but feel sorry for its inhabitants. *I don't know where they all are, but I am sure they will be back.* He felt a sense of compassion for his fallen Angels, having to live in such a dismal home. He thought about Luminé, whom he loved like a son. He knew Legion was pulling him in, but he had to allow it. Free will had to allow it. What surprised him, though, was how fast it happened. *Ahh, yes, Oxana. Oxana must have been seduced. It is the only way she could have fallen so quickly and pulled Luminé down with her.* Still, Adon loved them both. They were his children; all of his Angels were his children.

Calla's letter had given him another reason to come here, not only to check on Luminé but to see if perhaps Legion was here. Clearly, they were not. He would wait till the morning and go quickly to check on the Ancient Portal.

The portals were long-forgotten secret passages from under the sea into all the Realms in the Heavens. The Lords had designed them as an elaborate architectural feature at the beginning of Creation. Still, they were never needed, so they were largely forgotten. They represented a way in, not a way out, and further had to be opened from the inside. Adon wondered if perhaps this portal could become the way he could visit this place more frequently and keep closer tabs on Luminé.

He bedded down, placing his dagger near his side, and tried to fall asleep. But sleep would not come. It was too quiet.

~ ~ ~ ~

Not far away, Legion rested on a bed of grass, keeping a constant eye on Adon's campfire. He, too, was troubled. He knew he should have received word by now how Luminé and Oxana were faring. He tried to summon his presence within Oxana, but it was strangely silent. *Maybe they have failed.* He frowned. *Maybe they have succeeded.*

For the first time he could ever remember, he felt confused. He was sure that Oxana had the Golden Sword. That meant that it was possible, if they lost, the Lords would possess it. Legion had wanted them to lose, but now he realized that he needed Luminé and his army to win because of the sword. The Golden Sword was all that mattered right now.

He looked across at Adon's dwindling fire. He pulled the Golden Dagger out of his waistband and examined it. *Could this have been forged? Could this be made of the same metal as the Golden Sword? It looked like it. Would it, could it, kill Adon, forever?* One less Lord to contend with would certainly even the odds.

He looked again at the fire, almost extinguished. *Adon must be going to sleep. Perhaps I should subdue him now? No, it will be too risky. I must wait for the perfect opportunity.* He laid back down and finally fell asleep.

Legion jolted awake. The sun was up. He jumped up and quietly maneuvered his way toward Adon's camp. Peering at the smoldering fire, he saw that Adon was gone. He looked around and saw hoof marks making a trail. He followed as fast as he could, trying not to make noise, not knowing how far ahead he was.

Legion followed the trail to the top of a hill. From here, he scampered up a tree and peered into the distance. *There he is! Where is he going?*

~ ~ ~ ~

Adon was hurrying to the portal. He had a growing sense he had lingered here too long. A sinking feeling was growing in his stomach that Luminé's desperation may cause him to do something stupid. *But what?* He said to himself, *I have to go back to the Heavens and let the other Lords know about Luminé's predicament. Perhaps, there is still time to fix this.*

He was close to the portal now. He turned the horse to the right, riding into a valley between two large sea-side cliffs that sloped down in a narrow gulley to the water's edge.

~ ~ ~ ~

Legion curiously watched him as Adon dismounted and led his horse into the shallow water. He turned to the left and walked out of sight along the cliffs. *That's strange; there is nothing but cliffs there.* Legion dismounted and ran to the water's edge, peering around the corner. About 100 feet away he saw Adon standing in two feet of water, tugging at something on the side of the cliff as his horse stood behind him in the water. *What is he doing?*

Suddenly, to his amazement, a wide steel door swung open. Adon took the horse's reins and led him in through the wide steel door, and they disappeared into the side of the cliff. Legion waded into the water quietly, inching his way toward the slightly ajar steel door, keeping as close as he could to the cliff wall. He reached the opening and peered in.

About 75 feet in, at the back of the cave, Adon stood looking carefully at some type of large doorway with elaborate writings around it. There was writing engraved above and on the sides, but Legion could not make any of it out. He watched intently as Adon ran his hands along the entire door frame, examining its seal. Legion backed away slowly and reached for the Golden Dagger to contemplate his move.

Day Two

As dawn approached the eastern horizon, Splendora sat atop her white stallion, waiting to give the order. She would head the combined army, an army composed of the armies of herself, Michael, Raphael, and Gabriel. All were assembled in one massive fighting formation, with 240 columns, spread arm's length apart, ready to race to their target.

They were on the Southern shore of the Land of the Lords. From there, they would retake the 7th Heavenly Realm. Each army had 80,000

Angels and combined, there were 240,000 of them, and it would have been more, except Calla was holding Marcellus and his 80,000 Angels in reserve. Splendora hoped this would not harm their chances.

She felt confident, though. She could see the strength, loyalty, and determination in all their faces. They were being called on to defend their homeland, and they would do so at all costs.

Yeshua and Calla were there too, seated upon their horses, watching. They would not be participating directly, but they wanted a close understanding of the plans and their execution.

As soon as the sun crested the eastern horizon, Splendora raised her hand high in the air then waved it forward, signaling the start. She leaped up into the air on her horse, flying high, as all at once 240,000 Angles headed out over the sea as one unit, with Splendora at the head.

~ ~ ~ ~

At the 7th Heavenly Realm, Yuki and the 120,000 Angels under her command waited for an attack they expected for some time. Oxana and Luminé were here too, with them, waiting. They had taken both the 6th and 7th Realms completely by surprise. The fight had been short and violent. There were tens of thousands of incapacitated wounded, mostly from Heaven's side, as none of Heaven's Angels had been prepared for battle. Between the two Realms, over 70,000 of Heaven's Angels were inside Dark Cages along the shorelines, where they would stay until the war was over and the grand bargaining stage began.

Shortly after the sun crested over the horizon, one of the lookouts yelled out, "Here they come."

Luminé turned to Oxana, his eyes wild like fire, and announced, "One more day of fighting, and we will have our victory."

Oxana smiled, "And what will we do with that victory, Luminé? Live here?"

She could see the tone of her words disturbed him, and she intended it that way. He did not know she had seen his letter to Splendora. He also did not know that if Oxana got her way, Splendora would never be at his side, nor anyone else's, for that matter.

She placed her hand on the maroon cloth that covered the Golden Sword handle she had concealed in her sheath early that morning. She would wait for the opportunity, and as she had always done, to seize control of her own destiny. If Luminé did not want to rule with her, she would rule without him, even if that meant ruling alongside Legion.

"There is something wrong," Luminé said, snapping Oxana out of her thinking.

"What is is it?" she replied nervously.

"There were too many of them," Luminé said, his eyes fixed on the mass of Angels headed their way. "They have not split their forces as I anticipated." He thought for a moment and said, "Oxana, quickly, send a messenger to Antonio. Tell him to come at once with all of his forces."

Oxana looked out onto the horizon filled with Angels on their way and suddenly panicked. She looked around and saw someone she could use as a messenger. She called out, "Sparkis!"

Sparkis raced over, "Yes, Oxana."

"Go at once to the 6th Realm. Tell Antonio the attack is here! He is to come here!"

"At once!" he said as he flew off.

Oxana watched him, then turned to get ready to fight. She needed to stay out of the fray until she found her chance.

~ ~ ~ ~

Luminé and Oxana retreated inland, hoping to get a better view of the battle about to unfold. They kept looking to the east, wondering when Antonio and his 120,000 Angels would arrive from the 6th Heavenly Realm.

Splendora and her commanders were the first to swoop in and engage Luminé's forces. Luminé's heart dropped. He had not wanted Splendora to see any of this and had somehow in his mind, imagined he would not see her.

"Well, look who's here," Oxana said to Luminé. "Don't worry, I'll take care of her myself."

"Stay away from her, Oxana. She is too strong… and too fast for you."

Oxana looked away, kept her eye on Splendora's whereabouts, so she could ascertain when she would have the chance to engage her.

Luminé watched Yuki's army absorb the blows of the incoming line of Angels. There was a crush all along the Northern coast of the 7the Heavenly Realm. Angels from Heaven rushed in on a wide front, swords, and spears drawn. Yuki's Angels bravely met them, fending off as much as they could, but it was too much. Heaven was breaking through.

Luminé realized they were losing. He turned to Oxana and snapped, "Where is Antonio?"

Oxana looked east, shaking her head. Luminé realized his mistake in not being prepared for this move by Heaven's army. He had wrongly assumed they would split their forces. Now, he was paying the price. He needed to do something to inspire his forces. He scoured the battlefield and caught sight of Michael the Archangel. "Wait here, Oxana, I am going to engage Michael myself."

Luminé flew across the vast terrain and landed at the top of a small hill so as to be visible to his fighting Angels. "Great Michael!" he yelled.

Michael heard him, turned for a moment, then swung his sword in a fierce move, cutting off the arm of one of Luminé's Angels. He then flew toward the hill and landed 10 feet from Luminé. He began marching forward, and Luminé let out loud warriors cry, drawing the attention of hundreds of surrounding Angels, and got into his fighting stance.

~ ~ ~ ~

Sparkis reached the 6th Heavenly Realm in a panic, asking any Angel he could find, "Where is Antonio? Where is Antonio?"

"Over there," someone said.

Sparkis bolted over, exhausted from flying so fast, "Antonio."

"What is it?"

"Oxana.... She wants you at the 7th Realm at once."

"Now!"

"Yes, right now!"

Sparkis turned and flew off, heading back to the 7th Realm.

Antonio didn't understand why he would be called away at such a crucial time. He turned to Thaddus. "Thaddus, take charge here. I will be right back."

~ ~ ~ ~

On a muddied, bloodied hillside in view of thousands, Michael and Luminé began their personal battle. The two Archangels fought furiously, with their clanging swords echoing loudly in the surrounding landscape and sky. Luminé was swifter, attacking, slashing. Michael, though, was stronger, blocking every advance, tiring Luminé.

All around them, the battle raged, but no one dared interfere with these two most celebrated of Archangels. Finally, Luminé found the needed burst of energy, and he delivered a decisive blow knocking Michael's sword from his hands. Luminé followed with a deep, slashing cut across Michael's midsection. Michael fell to his knees, agonizing in pain, trying to hold his wound as blood spewed out of it.

He was too far to reach his sword.

Luminé stepped forward, his face determined, sword in hand, knowing the eyes of hundreds were upon him. He was supposed to drive his sword into Michael. Luminé would expect no less of those fighting for him. It was no time for letting up. He lifted his sword, then froze momentarily, second-guessing his decision.

Suddenly he felt a strong force collide into his back, knocking him forward off his feet. He landed on the ground next to Michael and quickly turned. It was Splendora standing 10 feet away, her face chiseled in stone, holding her drawn sword in fighting position.

"Get up, Luminé. You will deal with me today." She said as she kicked Michael's sword back over to Michael, saying, "Michael, go and direct your forces. Now!"

Though wounded, Michael jumped up, holding his bleeding midsection. He grabbed his sword, gave Luminé an angry glance, and flew off.

"Splendora," Luminé said, not willing to engage her. "You received my letter, did you not?"

"I received nothing." She said in a tone that meant one thing, business. She demanded, "Pick up your sword and get ready to defend yourself."

"There is nothing to say. When you attack the Heavens, you attack me. Now pick up your sword."

"I will not." Before the words left his mouth, Splendora lunged at him ferociously, slashing left, then right, wielding her sword faster and in a way he had never seen before. All he could do was block her blows, badly cutting his forearm as he did. He backpedaled across the rocky seaside terrain. Finally, he tripped over a wounded Angel, falling backward. Splendora picked up his sword and threw it on the ground next to him, but Luminé only glared at her, saying, "I will not fight you!"

~ ~ ~ ~

Antonio flew in haste toward the 7th Heavenly Realm. As he got closer, he saw the epic battle unfolding. Yuki's forces were greatly outnumbered. He flew farther inland as fast as he could until he spotted Oxana, standing at the far side of the hill where Luminé and Michael had just battled. Oxana saw him coming and flew up to meet him, shouting her command, "Antonio, you are to attack at once."

"Attack? My army is back there!" he cried, his face aghast.

"What!" Oxana exclaimed. She gritted her teeth and screamed, "Go get them, and bring them back here! Hurry!"

She turned and ran to the top of the hill to assess the battle. That is when she saw her. Splendora had her back to her and was dueling with Luminé. Luminé was on the ground, seemingly pleading with her. Oxana closed her eyes, thinking it all through. If Antonio got back soon, there was still time. Perhaps even, his delay had helped them. Heaven's Angels would not expect his last-minute counterattack. She swallowed hard, feeling the darkness in her mind she only felt when Legion was near. Somehow, he was near, somehow he was with her at this moment, in her mind, egging her on. A wicked smile came over her, and she pulled out the Golden Sword. She pointed it straight ahead, then charged through the air, leveling her body in flight, flying as fast as she had ever flown, right toward Splendora's back.

The voices in her head screamed, *Splendora must die! She is the real enemy! Kill her!*

She used all her strength to make up the ground between them as quickly as she could.

Splendora, her back to Oxana, walked toward Luminé, her sword drawn, ready to impale him.

Oxana bore down, extending the lethal Golden Sword, only two more seconds to impact. She pulled the sword back like a bow and readied herself to plunge it forward between Splendora's shoulder blades and end her life forever.

Luminé saw Oxana, and his eyes widened, and he shouted, "Splendora, look out."

Splendora instinctively wheeled and leaned aside, thrusting her sword upwards in a defensive gesture, sinking it directly into Oxana's charging midsection. Oxana's mouth sprung open in horror as the long steel blade ripped a wide gash all along her chest and midsection.

For a moment, Oxana stopped, and lurched, hung in the air, impaled on Splendora's upheld sword, shaking. She screamed in agony, like a wounded animal, but the shrieking sound was quickly muffled by blood coming out of her mouth like a fountain. Splendora pulled out the blade, and Oxana fell to her knees, looking up at Splendora in shock. "You… I… uhh."

Splendora turned around to see a shocked Luminé still lying where he had warned her. She turned back to Oxana. Oxana fell back, then somehow, forced herself into the air, sword in hand, flying straight up, then erratically through the sky. She had never been wounded, and the excruciating pain scared her into a panic. She shot through the sky, trying to escape the pain. She rolled and bolted even higher in the air, darting far out over the sea. Her body twisted in a painful, writhing frenzy, grasping at her severely torn open chest and midsection with one hand and dangling the Golden Sword in the other.

Splendora turned back to charge Luminé, but he was gone.

Legion

Legion took one more glance at the Golden Dagger then quietly stepped into the cliffside door. He found himself inside a large long dark cave. The air was stale, old as if it had been in there for ages. The floor was damp, too, with periodic sounds of dripping water falling from the ceiling.

Adon had not heard him. He was busy some 30 feet away, staring up at the portal. Legion glanced at the horse standing nearby, then waited another moment, evaluating the conditions for his plan. When he was certain of his course, he said, "Lord Adon, what are you doing here today?"

Adon turned quickly, "Legion, well, I should ask the same of you." Adon instantly knew he was boxed in. His back was to the portal, and Legion blocked his way to the cliffside exit. Adon reached for his sword, but he realized he had left it tied to the horse. He saw Legion was holding a dagger, so he grasped his own dagger and stepped closer, preparing for battle.

Trying to keep Legion off-balance, Adon asked, "Where is the Golden Sword, Legion?"

Legion smiled politely and coolly responded, "I have the Golden Sword."

Adon half-smiled, measuring how long it might take him to charge Legion, as he casually remarked, "Oh, you do, do you?"

Legion started forward, brandishing his dagger. Adon, too, started forward, knowing to be on the offensive in a dagger fight was important. They took opening swipes at each other, then began to circle in the dark cave, illuminated only by the light coming from the open cliffside door. The horse began to nervously neigh, heightening the tense moment. Adon lunged forward, but Legion darted sideways, then dropped low and leaped forward. With one forceful thrust upward, he rammed the Golden Dagger into Adon's heart.

Adon felt the jolt in his mind. It was strong, and ancient, not bound by time or place, but a jolt, like lightning. He suddenly labored to breathe and clutched at his chest, taking hold of the dagger handle, too weak to pull it out. *What is happening to me?* He cried in his mind.

He looked at his hands, filled with blood, then fell to his knees, then fell onto the side. The last thing he heard was Legion laughing.

Suddenly an earth-shattering loud crack of thunder was heard, sending fear through Legion's veins. He turned and saw lightning race through the sky. A massive storm erupted out of nowhere.

Legion turned back to get the dagger, but as he reached for the handle, hooves of the horse beat down violently and forcefully on his back and head, knocking him to the ground. Legion shielded his face, but the horse kept neighing, wheeling its hooves. All Legion could do was try to block them, painfully absorbing those he could not fend off. He rolled and tried to crawl to the door, but the horse followed him, pummeling down on his backside.

Legion fell out the doorway into the shallow water. The horse followed him out, pummeling him further in the shallow water as he tried to stand, unable to. Finally, Legion got away, running to his own horse. He pulled his sword off the saddle and when the horse reared up again, Legion rammed the sword deep into its belly. The horse neighed wildly, then fell over into the surf.

Legion turned to look at the cave door. He would retrieve the dagger and go. That was when Juniper attacked, swooping down with outstretched claws, ripping at Legion's head. "Ahhh!" Legion screamed, as his arms flailed wildly. Jumiper rose up, and darted back down, ferociously screeching, flapping its massive wings to position itself to do the most damage. Legion reached for his other dagger, and grabbed the leg of Juniper with his free hand. He pulled the massive bird downward with a heave, and thrust the dagger into its side, twisting it. Juniper rose up erratically, screeching in pain. Legion jumped on his horse and galloped away, heading into the nearby woods.

Once he reached the cover of the woods, he looked back. The winds had kicked up fiercely, and the rain began to teem as it had during the storm on the day Adam and Eve ate from the forbidden tree.

Legion realized that something epic had just happened. He lifted his head into the driving rain, letting the rushing water drench his face. He laughed loudly and shouted to the Heavens, "I have done it! I have killed Adon!"

~ ~ ~ ~

Luminé could not find her. He quickly circled back, only to see Sparkis flying along the coastline carrying Oxana's lifeless body toward him. Sparkis shouted, "Luminé, I found her."

Luminé took her from his arms and held her. Her eyes were closed, and she could not talk. Her cut was massive, and she was almost unconscious from the pain. Her entire uniform was soaked in blood. Luminé asked, "Where did you find her?"

"Floating out in the sea, almost a mile from the shore."

Luminé held her face, "Oxana, I will take you away from here. I will help you." He looked around at the raging battle, regretting ever having conceived such a plan, then raced down to an area where there was no fighting. He laid Oxana down and took off his shirt, tearing a piece of it off, bandaging her wound.

Splendora watched from the hillside. She raced over and silently landed behind Luminé, walking forward, her sword ready in her hand. All she had to do was thrust it into his back, and the war would be over. She knew full well he would not die. She would only be incapacitating him. Her mind screamed at her to act. *I can end this right now. Do it! Do it!*

Luminé did not notice her. He was busily trying to revive Oxana, trying to stop the profuse bleeding from the gaping wound. Splendora slowly raised her sword, pointed the tip of it squarely between Luminé's shoulders, and momentarily froze.

In the distance, she could hear Michael shouting, "Splendora! What are you waiting for?" She looked over at Michael, hoping to find the courage she needed to drive her sword into Luminé's back.

Luminé, hearing Michael, glanced over his shoulder and saw his predicament. He placed his hands on the ground and spun around, swinging his legs into Splendora, knocking her off her feet. He lifted Oxana, threw her bloody body over his shoulder, and flew off.

The End

Antonio's 120,000 Angels drove through the epic rain and swept into the plains of the battle with a vengeance. Gabriel's and Raphael's armies were waiting for them, knowing they would abandon the 6th Realm once they knew they would not be attacked. All across a three-mile front, Angels were engaged in sword fights, slogging it out through the slippery terrain, as the ground turned to mud and blood.

Antonio looked along the vast battlefield, wondering how he had allowed Luminé to talk him into this attack. The fierce lightning, thunder, and driving wind only reminded him of the power of the Lords. They should have known it could never succeed.

He spotted Luminé high in the sky over the sea, fleeing, holding Oxana in his arms, and he suddenly realized he too should consider fleeing. He hated to leave his Angels, but he could plainly see all was lost, and he did not want to end up in a Dark Cage. He turned to leave when suddenly his leg exploded in pain, as a spear lodged itself deep in his thigh. He winced, then screamed in pain as he pulled it, tearing with it a chunk of flesh. He limped to the top of a nearby hill, then collapsed.

All around him in every direction, Angels were engaged in violent struggles. Looking down at his own grisly wound, he realized it was over. In the distance, near the beach, he could see the Angels of Heaven dragging countless Angels from Luminés forces into the very Dark Cages Luminé had constructed for their adversaries. The Angels, many of them severely wounded, were screaming and struggling to resist as they were shoved inside. Antonio shuddered and, with all his strength, flew up into the sky, dragging his bloodied throbbing leg behind him.

Suddenly he felt another sharp blow, this time in his back. He screamed as he looked down and saw the point of a bloody sword burst through the front of his chest. The pain was too great to bear, and all went black.

~ ~ ~ ~

The cage door opened, and Rana fell out, shuddering uncontrollably. She had been put into the Dark Cage the day before. Two of her Angels helped her up, "Archangel Rana, are you alright?"

"No… no… I am not," she said as she collapsed back onto her knees. The pain Angels endured inside the Dark Cages was as much psychological as it was physical. The darkness bore into every aspect of their being, including their muscle fibers.

"We have won the war, Rana," one of her Angels said. She looked up at her, "Thank God, oh… thank God."

"The other Archangels are assembling at Cirianna's headquarters. The Lords have called a council."

Rana exhaled loudly, "Help me up," she said. She stood and looked around at the thousands of cages sitting on the shore. Some were being opened, and Angels, her Angels, were being taken out. Other cages were also being opened, and Luminé's Angels were being shoved inside, imprisoned in the darkness. "I have to go to my home. Come with me, both of you. We will come back shortly."

"Yes, at once."

~ ~ ~ ~

Antonio opened his eyes and saw nothing but darkness. All at once, his mind exploded in panic as his hands felt along the inside of the Dark Cage. He tried to kick open the door, but his legs, bent at the knees, were already too weak. "No! Please! No! Don't leave me here!"

He stopped, listening for any response, but there was no sound. All at once, the reality that he was trapped inside hit him. He began to weep, overwhelmed at being trapped inside the dark, confined place, perhaps forever.

Then he heard the screams of others, probably his friends, frantically begging to be let out. Putting his hands over his ears, he cursed Luminé and Oxana. Then he did something he had not done in a long time. He began to pray.

~ ~ ~ ~

Sadie landed in front of her home after spending the last two days helping Eve care for her children. She walked up the lawn, looking around. Something was wrong. She stopped, turning in all directions, and realized what it was. No one was around. She flew to the Headquarters, where an empty courtyard greeted her. *Where are my guards?* she exclaimed to herself. She went inside, and it, too, was empty. She came out confused, wondering what had happened. Then, in the distance, she saw them.

Flying slowly in the sky toward the Headquarters were smatterings of scattered Angels, some in small groups, some alone, most injured. It was all of Gabriel's Angels, remnants of his entire army landing in the compound and along the sandy beach of the coast, many wounded, many desperate to lay down. Those not wounded immediately set to the task of caring for the injured.

Sadie ran up to one, asking, "What happened?"

"What happened? Where have you been? There's been a war!"

"I was helping Adam and… a war! What are you talking about?"

"Luminé attacked the Heavens!" exclaimed the Angel.

Sadie stood with her mouth open, in shock, trying to understand. "When?" she asked, adding, "Did he succeed?"

"It started yesterday, and no, he did not." The Angel sighed, looking around at the myriad of bloodied Angels, and said, "It was very hard, but… we won."

Lightning shot across the sky, and an enormous explosion of thunder rang out, sending fear through all, adding great fear onto what was already a horrific day. Then the heavy rain started. Sadie bolted into the sky, headed toward the Earth. Her first duty was to Adam and Eve. She had left there two hours earlier and went swimming to end her day. She needed to make sure they were safe and put her guards on high alert. She needed to do the same with her guards at the Garden of Eden.

The High Council

Toward evening, Splendora, Gabriel, and Raphael flew over the 7th Heavenly Realm, surveying the carnage and devastation. The war was over. The attack had been repelled. All of the traitors were now being held in Dark Cages, awaiting their fate.

"It's time," Gabriel said.

They turned and flew to the headquarters of Cirianna, where Rana, Cirianna, and Marcellus were waiting inside Cirianna's office. All felt a sense of accomplishment as they had repelled the attack handily. "Where is Michael?" asked Raphael.

"He has been taken to the Healing Springs. His wound was very deep," Splendora said, grimly. She was glad he was not there to attest to the fact she had hesitated and lost the chance to subdue Luminé. Gabriel glanced out the window, "They're here!"

Outside, Yeshua and Calla landed their horses near the gate and rode up to the entrance of the Headquarters. They dismounted and came up the steps, Calla first, with a serious look on her face, followed by Yeshua, who seemed concerned for all the wounded around the compound.

They walked into the office, and Calla said, "Where are they?"

"Who?" asked Splendora

"Luminé and Oxana. Have they been found?"

"Not yet," Splendora replied. "We are looking for them. Oxana is badly hurt, so I don't think Luminé is free to travel at will. She will need to rest."

Calla said, "I want every able-bodied Angel scouring the Heavens and the Earth. We also need to find Adon."

"Where is Lord Adon?" asked Gabriel.

Calla turned to look out the window with a worried look on her face, and Yeshua replied for her. "That's just it, Gabriel. We can't find him."

The Hunt

The hunt for Luminé and Oxana began, with almost 300,000 Angels scouring the Heavens and the Earth for them, but after five days, Luminé and Oxana still had not been found. Rana and Michael were searching the Olympus Islands area, with 100 Angels accompanying them. The lack of progress was frustrating everyone.

~ ~ ~ ~

Sadie walked the perimeter of the Garden of Eden, as she did every time she arrived there, inspecting her guard's positioning and assessing the gate built around it. No one knew why, but the Lords had decided that the Garden was to be kept closed and sealed off. No one was to ever live there again.

As she was walking, something struck her. An orange tree she passed many times before without any notice suddenly came to her attention. Something was different. There was fruit missing off one of the branches. She wondered perhaps if one of her guards had taken it, but decided to investigate further. She climbed up the fence and landed softly on the other side. She drew her sword and began creeping in toward the center of the Garden. She reached the clearing where Adam and Eve's abandoned hut was. It was a sad scene, one which she hated beholding every time. A place that had been designed with so much hope, promise, and life in mind, was now desolate, run-down, and void of all life.

She walked up and peered inside the hut. Everything was the same as the last time she was there.

She was about the leave when she heard a sound coming from deeper in the Garden. She crept out along the path toward the center of the Garden, where the river ran next to the Tree of the Knowledge of Good and Evil. There was no one in sight. She looked over at the tree. It had been at the heart of the fall of everything in Heaven and on Earth, and she wondered why it still stood there. If it were her tree, she would have cut it down to rid herself of the reminder. In fact, she would have leveled the entire Garden and let it grow wild, expunged from everyone's memory for good. But the Lords wanted it preserved. She bent down by the edge of the river and scooped up some water to put on her forehead. Then she saw it. A leaf floated by. It had drops of blood on its leaves. Sadie froze and slowly peered up over the brush. In the distance, about a quarter-mile down the stream, Luminé was bent over, scooping water into a small dish which he probably got from Adam and Eve's hut.

Sadie stooped back down, watching through the brush as Luminé washed out a piece of cloth that was covered with blood. He got up and turned and walked back into the forest. Sadie got up, and backed down the path, then ran to the entrance. She told the guard, "Go at once to the Throne Room. Tell the Lords that Luminé and Oxana are hiding in the Garden. Go in all haste."

The guard's eyes widened, and she took off. Sadie went around the perimeter of the Garden and informed all of her guards of what was happening, that they should be on high alert to guard their sections to be sure Luminé nor Oxana got out.

~ ~ ~ ~

Luminé carefully replaced the bandages on Oxana's long wound and hung the ones he had washed in the river up to dry. He had made her a bed of large leaves and spread it with an old blanket he had gotten from Adam and Eve's abandoned hut. Oxana opened her eyes for the first time all day. With very little strength, she lifted her head and asked, "Luminé… what is going to happen to us?"

"We will live here, somewhere on the Earth."

"What about our Angels?"

Luminé said nothing.

"What… what happened to… them?" she asked with great strain in her voice.

"They are all in Dark Cages. I don't know what will happen to them."

Oxana's eyes widened, and she began to weep.

"What's wrong?" asked Luminé.

"I can't go inside a cage, Luminé. I will lose my mind."

"Don't worry. I won't let that happen."

The sound of her crying broke Luminé 's heart. She never cried, but now, her vulnerability shined through, and it saddened him that he had not been more careful.

He laid down next to her, and for the first time since the day he was created a tear rolled down his cheek. He couldn't keep his eyes open any longer and succumbed to exhaustion.

Suddenly a noise woke him. He sat up, just in time to see a large, heavy net dropped from the sky, trapping him and Oxana.

"No! No!" he screamed, as Gabriel, Raphael, and Marcellus along with 20 other Angels pulled on the ropes scooping Luminé and Oxana up into the air. Their bodies knocked together as they tumbled upside down in the net, squeezed together. Oxana let out a horrific scream, startling all, as her wound tore open because of the jerking movements of the net.

"Please, let us down," Luminé pleaded, "Can't you see she's hurt?"

Marcellus shot back. "You only have yourself to blame for her suffering."

"No!" Sadie said, stepping forward, "Luminé is right. Let her down."

Marcellus looked at Gabriel and Raphael, who nodded. The net was lowered to the ground, and Sadie went over and helped Oxana out. She laid her on the ground and turned to her guards, "Guards! Bring me some water and cloth."

At once, six of her guards left and quickly returned. Sadie knelt down and poured water on the open wound, then put the cloth back on it, wrapping strands around Oxana to reaffix her bandage. She said to the six guards, "Carry her away, gently."

Luminé was put in chains, and he and Oxana were carried off to Holy Mountain to learn their fate.

~ ~ ~ ~

Yeshua walked into the Throne Room, where Calla was busy pacing back and forth. She was worried about Adon. He was supposed to come to her home three days ago. He would not have simply not shown up.

"Calla, all of the prisoners are assembled on the beach in the Southern Realm."

She turned, "We can't wait any longer, Yeshua. Justice must be swift."

"But is this too much of a punishment?"

"Yeshua, don't you see. Legion is behind everything. He controls them somehow. What if they had defeated us?"

Just then, Luminé and Oxana were brought in. Calla turned to look at them, then looked away, "Put them into Dark Cages immediately and take them to join the others on the shore of the Southern Realm."

Yeshua watched them leave and said, "I just wish Adon were here."

"I do too. But he's not," she said. "And we must act. It's time."

Deliverance

The Southern Realm was now rumored to be turned into a terrible prison, holding the fallen Angels for all time.

At the Southern Realm border, Splendora's second in command, the Angel Arcano, waited with 10,000 of Heaven's Angels, guarding the chained prisoners on the beach, making sure no one escaped before Oxana and Luminé arrived. Everyone was anxious, with rumors abounding at what terrible fate awaited them.

Arcano watched the skies, and soon Oxana's cage came into view. "Here she is," he said as the four Angels set her cage down on the shore of Luminare and opened the door. Oxana rolled out onto the sand gasping for air. She rolled over once and collapsed nearly unconscious.

Arcano watched her and was moved with pity. He flew down to her side and knelt in the sand next to her. He lifted her head, pulled out his canteen, and offered her a drink. Oxana looked up with her eyes barely open, "Arcano… is that you?"

"Yes, Oxana, I see you remember me."

She half-smiled, "Yes… I do… you know… I used to have a crush on you… " she stopped, wincing in pain.

"Take it easy, Oxana. Just drink this, and rest."

She clutched his arm, "Listen… please. I need you to… you need to tell the Lords."

"Tell them what?"

"Luminé… he… he never told us… he lied about not being able to come back… he lied about everything."

Arcano's eyes grew upset. He had always disliked Luminé, but to hear he had lied to them all enraged him. "Oxana, I will try to talk to them. I don't know if they'll listen."

"No, listen… please listen… to me." She grabbed his shirt with her hands, pulling him down closer to her face, "Arcano… you have to promise me… please. I can't be stuck here... not forever, please."

Tears started to fall from her eyes as the reality of her own words set in.

Arcano felt her sorrow, and it moved him. "Oxana, I promise you, I will try." She closed her eyes, exhausted, as Arcano lifted her up, carried her off the beach, and laid her on the soft grass. He tucked his canteen into her arms and went back to his post.

~ ~ ~ ~

Luminé's cage was the last one to be transported. Splendora's commanders were carrying it through the sky. Splendora raced up and stopped them in mid-air, "Wait, I need to speak to Luminé."

"But Splendora, our orders are from Calla herself."

"I don't care. I will not open the door. I just have to speak to him. Back away, some."

The guard reluctantly nodded and allowed her to approach alone.

She put her face close to the door, asking, "Luminé, are you alright?"

"It is very frightening in here. What is going to happen?"

"I don't know."

"Splendora, I sent you a letter right before we attacked."

"I told you I received no such letter."

"I sent it to you. My plan was to show strength and then ask to come back again."

"No, Luminé!" she yelled, "No more lies!"

"They are not lies! You have to believe me. I was only planning on showing strength. I was going to then tell the Lords that we wanted to come back peacefully." He thought about mentioning the sword, but he realized it might be the only leverage he had left. He would wait and see what his fate would be.

The guards flew back and said, "We have to go."

"Goodbye, Luminé," she said and backed into the sky.

~ ~ ~ ~

Arcano had tens of thousands of Angels under his command, hovering in the skies. Below them, hundreds of thousands of Luminé's

Angels sat anxiously on the beach waiting to see their fate. Only one more prisoner was to be delivered, but he was the most prominent of all, the leader of the rebellion, Luminé.

Suddenly everyone turned. Luminé's Dark Cage approached, and the anxiety began to mount. Despite the attack, and despite him having taken so many followers only one year earlier, Luminé was still well-liked. So were all those Angels who were sitting on the beach, chained together, awaiting some rumored terrible event to befall them. They were all former friends and lovers of the Angels of Heaven. Everyone in Heaven knew they could easily have followed Luminé and been one of those now condemned and about to be punished in a terrible way.

The four Angels flew past the crowd, and past the line of guards, and set Luminé's cage down on the beach. Arcano flew down too and opened the cage door. Luminé rolled out of the cage, with his arms and legs still shackled in chains.

"Take these off of me!" he snapped.

"You will have to wait," replied Arcano.

With that, Arcano raised his hand, and all those who were with him on the shore slowly ascended to rejoin the guards who had encircled the Realm in the sky. Whatever was going to happen was going to happen now.

The Dark Day

Arcano was the first to see it. In the distance, a large, ominous cloud formed and began to drift toward the Southern Realm. It was as immense as a continent itself, and as it neared, it appeared to be dropping lower and lower, like some sort of terrible darkness.

Arcano grew fearful, and he ordered everyone to pull back further and go higher in the sky. They could see condemned Angels on the ground beginning to point to the sky, trying to hide. The cloud grew ominous and larger, drawing closer and closer. The fear of those not only on the ground but also of those in the sky began to mount. Screams were heard, only a few at first, but then more, and more, louder and louder, until the piercing cries of the Angels on the beach drove despair into the hearts and minds of Heaven's Angels looking at them.

Only Luminé seemed to not be afraid. He stood resolute, in his chains, staring up bravely, as if to defy the Heavens once again. Around him, Angels began lamenting they ever followed him. They cursed his name and Oxana's as they fearfully awaited whatever was coming toward them.

But Luminé raised his fist, shouting, "You have betrayed us!"

The Angel Sagas is continued in Book 4, Empire.

Part Two of Judgment begins below.

Part Two
James

A Mob Lawyer Pushes Too Far

After Life Journeys Book 3

THE AFTER LIFE JOURNEYS dramatically tell individual tales of 15 modern-day people's lives and journeys to the After Life. There is an autistic young man, a mob lawyer, a girl with Rett's disease, a middle-aged divorcee, a rigid Baptist preacher, a U.S. Senator, a Muslim American soldier, a woman who suffers abuse as a child, and even an avowed atheist who survived the shark-infested waters after the sinking of the U.S.S. Indianapolis.

Each person lives life the best they can, but suddenly, and often unexpectedly, death crashes into their plans. Many never get to say goodbye or attain the hopes and dreams they often desperately desired.

Some are cautionary tales, like the mob lawyer's story. Even the 9/11 hijackers are addressed in book 12, because the series is not only about Heaven but also about Hell, and about a place in between, for those who don't quite fit into Heaven or Hell. The series is about second chances, and life on the other side, a life we all someday want.

All 15 human stories converge in the last three books of the series, as the Angels, the Heavens, and the Earth race toward their destiny, and all are hurled toward the final showdown between good and evil.

Chapter 1

New York mob boss Bobby Massiano proudly burst through the courtroom doors surrounded by his bodyguards and strode down the long, marble, hallway floor of the Federal Courthouse in New York City. He paused for a moment to allow his lawyer, James, a few moments to get up next to him. Bobby turned and slapped James on the back, and put his arm around his neck, roaring, "This here's the best-goddamned lawyer in Manhattan!"

The whole crowd laughed, everyone smiling, sharing in the joyous moment.

It didn't phase James. In his mind, he *was* 'the best-goddamned lawyer' in Manhattan, certainly the most famous. He was a wildly successful trial attorney in the epicenter of the world of mafia crime: New York City, and he had just delivered another one of his client's family members from the clutches of justice.

Bobby, James, and the entourage continued exuberantly down the hall and out through the courthouse doors into the warm sun of a brisk October morning in downtown Manhattan. The media and the microphones were already set up and waiting. James stepped up to the microphone, putting his arm around Bobby, then paused for effect, staring down at the ravenous media on the steps below, waiting for the moment he would give them the soundbite they would all be leading with this day.

He began, "Today, a jury of ordinary men and women, peers and fellow citizens of my client, Bobby Massiano, spoke loud and clear, sending a message that my client is innocent. Their verdict was what we all expected. Bobby was always innocent of these charges, and we hope this will send a message to the government to stop the harassment of my client."

Immediately the media began the relentless shouting to get their questions answered, but James signaled, and the bodyguards immediately hustled the two men down the courthouse stairs to the waiting limosine.

Once inside, Bobby said, "Get my father on the phone. Now!" He turned to James, "You sure you wanna keep laying it on those Feds. You're taunting them. A little humility might be useful right now."

"Don't worry about that, Bobby. I know what I'm doing."

"I sure hope so. You practically threw down the gauntlet at them back there."

"Hey, Bobby, that's what I do."

Bobby smiled, shaking his head, "You sure as hell got me off. I gotta hand it to you, James." But then Bobby glared, "I mean it, though, James. Back off the bragging right now. We won."

James lifted his hands, "Bobby, winning is my job."

"Yeah, I know. Listen, you come over to the club tonight. I got this dame coming from Long Island, and she has your name written all over her."

"I can't tonight, Bobby. I gotta date."

"Oh yeah, anyone special?"

"Yes, she is."

~ ~ ~ ~

James sat against the headboard of his king-size bed in the luxurious penthouse overlooking downtown Manhattan. He was staring out at the night skyline, quietly thinking, periodically glancing down at the blonde-haired woman resting her head on his lap. Her name was Tanya, and she was his favorite escort, the only one he ever confided in. He brushed her hair to the side so he could see her dark brown eyes.

She glanced up at him, smiling, and said, "You did it again, James. You beat the Feds."

"Yes," James said in a proud tone, glancing out at the Manhattan skyline, "I knew their case was weak from the start."

"How do you always know these things?"

James ran his hand down her back and under the sheets, feeling the warmth of her backside. "It's what I do, Tanya. It's why I get paid the big bucks. It's how I can afford you."

She said, "I'm crazy about you, James. You know that. Right?"

'Yes, yes, I do. Stay the night tonight," he said.

"Yes, I will."

Chapter 2

The next morning James felt the warm morning sun hitting his face. He glanced over at the time and then at the picture of his mother he kept on his dresser. He had vowed many times to put the picture away, partly because it made him feel guilty.

James Boulton had been born the oldest of two children, both boys, in Brooklyn, New York. His father was an alcoholic who was very brutal in the disciplining of his sons. As the oldest, James got the worst of it, being treated much harsher than his younger brother. There was no pleasing his father, and he grew up feeling certain his father did not want him or love him. His mother loved him, and that was his small saving grace.

She did her best to intervene to stop the brutality, both emotional and physical. Still, on many occasions, she, too, caught the back of her husband's hand.

James' father was more than brutal. He was highly critical. This perhaps left the deepest emotional wounds. Many nights were spent cowering under the dining room table, watching his father's feet tapping as he sat drinking and watching TV in the living room. James' favorite spot was because he could just barely see the TV, but his father could not see him, and most of the time did not even know James was there.

There were some happy days, but the dark ones greatly overshadowed them. His father's mood, dictated by whether or not he was drinking, set the tone in every way, and the rest of the family had to go along and get by as best they could.

His father died of cirrhosis of the liver when James was 15 years old. This gave James the desperate relief he needed, but the die had already been cast in many respects. Just like his father had exercised absolute power over him, James vowed in his heart to become a man with absolute power.

This quest for power led him to law school and ultimately to his career as a mob lawyer. James' mother warned him about his involvement with the mob. When she found out he was working for the notorious Massiano family, she frequently called James, begging him to stop working for them. James always told her it was difficult to extricate himself, but that he had thought of a way and worked on it.

He was lying to her. He would never let anything pull him away from the feeling that working for the powerful Massianos gave him.

James glanced up at the time again. It was 7:15 am, and he was already late for his day. He nudged Tanya. "Hey beautiful, it's time to go."

"James, do I have to?"

"Yes, I have a busy day."

James got out of bed and jumped into the shower. When he came out, Tanya was standing by the bedside, stepping into her dress. James walked over and hugged her from behind. "Will I see you tonight?"

"That depends on you?" she said.

"Yes, I want to. Come at 9."

"All right."

James walked over to his dresser and pulled five $100 bills out of his wallet. He started to reach for a sixth, then stopped and put his wallet back down. He turned and handed it to her. "See you later tonight beautiful."

Chapter 3

The Manhattan traffic was at a stand-still as James sat in the back seat of his Limousine reading over the newspaper. The phone rang.

"Hello?"

"James, it's Ernest."

"I was wondering when you were going to call." Ernest was James' publicist, and James hoped he was calling with good news.

"Are you reading the Times?"

"Yes, what else do I do every morning sitting in this god forsaken traffic?"

"Well, you better make sure you read it on Friday."

"Really, why?"

"They're doing an article about you, and about the book."

"No, shit!"

"Yes. You're press conference yesterday put us in the win column with their editor."

"How are we doing with the sales, Ernest?"

"We're doing great, and we're about to explode. They've got us at number 28 right now, but they said the article would pull us way up, probably into the top ten."

"No, shit!"

"Yes, and who knows? Maybe, we will go all the way to the top."

"All right, Ernest. That's great news. I gotta go."

"Prove it, James! Prove it!"

"Very funny. Good work."

James hung up the phone feeling a sense of satisfaction he had never known. There was something unique about this accomplishment. Perhaps it was one even his mother could be proud of. He had written a book detailing his cases, along with all the strategies he had used to get his clients off. He titled the book, "Prove It!"

Though his clients, and even most of his fellow lawyers, would never dream of writing such a book, especially while they were practicing, James knew better. He understood that to win in front of juries had a lot to do with charisma and reputation. James had charisma, and he also had a reputation. This book served as a monument to both, a monument for all to see.

It was not only for them, though. It was for himself too. James needed to be reminded of his greatness, his feelings of well-being depended on it. He would never get away from the deep feelings of inferiority his father's searing criticism had scarred him with. It was ever-present, like a guarded grizzly bear, locked away in a cage, who could escape, and kill him if James let his guard down. He was at the top of his world, and no one was going to change that.

Chapter 4

At 8:45, James walked into his private law firm offices on the 7th floor of the luxurious Metzger Building on Prospect Avenue. He thrust through the wide glass doors, barking out orders to his receptionist, "Debbie, get me some coffee and a few donuts."

"Yes, sir, Mr. Boulton."

James walked further down the hall, getting updates from the junior lawyers and paralegals working under him. When he reached his office, he said to his secretary, "Teddi, get Bobby's secretary on the phone. I want to talk to Bobby at 10:30 sharp."

"Yes, sir."

"I don't want to be disturbed until then."

Teddi got up, picked up a copy of the New York Post, and then extended it toward him. "You may want to see this first."

James looked up, wide-eyed, "What is it?"

"Just an article about the dark side."

James rolled his eyes and took the paper from her. He looked at the headline. "Another victory for the dark side, courtesy of James Boulton."

James laughed and turned, already reading down the page as he turned and went into his office. He was a little nervous. The article about his book would be out tomorrow, and while he loved the limelight, he suddenly began to fear too much of it would anger the Massianos. They were his only client. But he could not help but soak up the article.

"Dark Side! I like it. Darth Vader? James Vader? Darth James? James the Darth Lawyer! Yes, it all has a good ring to it."

He plopped down and swiveled in his chair, reflecting back to how it all began. The idea to join the dark side came to him one night during his second year of law school while he was watching the Godfather. He knew the crime activity in New York was much more sophisticated than in the movie. He instinctively knew they would pay better than anyone else.

James went to work as a junior lawyer for a known mob lawyer. He got his break when he was asked to sit in 3rd chair on a high profile case. James' work in uncovering dirt on the government witness turned the tide of the trial, and from that time forward, James quickly rose in the ranks. Five years later, his boss retired, and James became the lead attorney for the family.

All this served to make James a very rich man, not just in money, but in knowledge: mob knowledge. He knew everything about his clients' wanton guilt, and he knew where most of the bodies were buried.

The phone intercom rang, snapping James out of his reflection.

"James, Bobby is on the line."

James glanced up at the time. It was only 9:30. "I thought I said I want to talk to him at 10:30?"

"He said he needs you now. Right now!"

James worried for a moment. Bobby did not usually talk in such a demanding tone. He picked up. "What's up, Bobby?"

"I just got a call from one of my contacts down at the Feds. They're coming to arrest me. That's what's up! Now, what the hell are you going to do about it, Mr. Hotshot?"

"For what?"

"For the murder of Larry Baxter."

"Don't say another word, Bobby. I'll be right over. We'll have you out on bail before the end of the day."

Chapter 5

James had his limo driver waiting downstairs, and they left immediately for Bobby's mansion across town. On the way, James felt nervous. Perhaps he had taunted the Feds, pushing them too far this time. Larry Baxter was a prominent member of a rival mob family. The Massianos and the Baxters were embroiled in a turf war over the crack trade in New York. The Massiano Family had long controlled this trade, but the Baxters were making a push to break in, and they were making progress.

James already knew that Bobby himself ordered the hit on Larry Baxter, the heir apparent to the Baxter family. He was brutally murdered, gunned down on a dark street outside a nightclub in Queens. Bobby didn't pull the trigger, but he was there. He witnessed the murder. It had taken place over seven months ago, and both James and Bobby felt that all risk of his being caught had passed.

By the time he arrived at the mansion, the FBI had already pulled up right behind him. James hustled in made sure Bobby was treated with dignity as they cuffed him and threw him in the back of their black SUV. James followed them down to the Federal Courthouse where Bobby was to be held pending a bail hearing.

Within hours James and the opposing prosecutor were inside a Federal Judge's chambers arguing whether or not Bobby would be released on bail. "Your honor, Mr. Stephens portrays my client as a flight risk, but as you know, he has deep family and business ties to the community. Besides that, your honor, despite Mr. Stephens claims, the fact is, we have nothing more than circumstantial evidence present. Can we deny Mr. Massiano bail based on that?"

The judge nodded and raised his hand as Mr. Stephens tried to protest. "I'm sorry, he is right. Bail is set at 2,000,000. You may both leave."

~ ~ ~ ~

The next few weeks were the most worrisome of James' career. There was no doubt in his mind that this would be his toughest case to date. The evidence pointing to Bobby was indeed strong enough to convict him. But James had an idea.

He knew that Larry Baxter had prior dealings with a low-level drug dealer recently used by the Massianos. The dealer's name was Richard Matte. Matte was on Bobby's blacklist for nearly blowing a deal. James decided to use this to his advantage. He called up Bobby and drove over for a meeting.

As soon as James arrived back at Bobby's home, they went into his study with a couple of his most trusted men. James first set the stage, "Bobby, we've got a tough case here. The evidence, though not yet convincing, points only one way."

Bobby replied, "Look, James, this is why we pay you. Now, are you gonna do your job, or aren't you?"

James stood up and put his hands behind his back, walking away from the group toward the window. "Yes, I'll do my job, but this could go either way." James already knew which way it would go. He was posturing.

Bobby fell for it. "I'll tell you what. You just make damn sure I get off, and you can plan on a cool million being delivered to you."

James did not flinch, staying at the window, looking out. He said, "Give me a minute to think."

The room grew silent for several minutes. When the silence grew uncomfortable, James asked, "What was the name of that low-life dealer who almost screwed up the drug deal back in April?"

"Matte," said one of the men.

"Ah, yes, Matte, Richard Matte. He's been working for the Baxter's now, hasn't he?"

Bobby replied, "Yes, and come to think of it, we should wack that son of a bitch."

None of this was news to James. He just needed to look brilliant.

James kept staring out the window, with his back to them, and put his finger into the air, signaling for all to wait, because he was thinking. Then he turned around. "We're going to turn this on Larry Baxter."

Bobby asked, "How the hell we gonna do that. He's the fucking victim!"

Everyone chuckled for a moment. But James kept nodding, with a look of serious contemplation on his face, "Yes, that's it. We'll turn it all on, Larry Baxter. We'll, of course, need to use Matte… to be the one who killed him."

Bobby looked confused, "I don't follow."

"It's easy. We will implicate Larry in a recent drug deal that we know he was involved in. We will manufacture proof that it was Matte who killed him over not getting paid. We got witnesses who owe us. And you get to wack Matte as a bonus, as soon as we finger him."

There was silence in the room.

Bobby broke it. "I like it. And why not? The son of a bitch, Larry Baxter is dead anyway. Who's gonna' defend him? His brothers?"

They all had a good laugh.

Bobby turned to his men. "All of you listen. Until James works out the details, this stays in this room. Everyone got it?"

They all agreed.

Chapter 6

Two weeks later, on the first day of the trial, James proudly led Bobby and his entourage up the courthouse steps. It was the first day of the trial. James smiled broadly for the cameras, completely confident of his plan. But he was under no illusions as to what this case meant. The stakes could not be any higher. Bobby was *the* boss. If he went down, James' career would go down too, but it could be much more serious than that. Bobby might smile at him while they were riding out victories in the courtroom, but losing now would unleash the true character of his boss, who James knew was responsible for the deaths of no less than 30 people.

Despite the pressure, James was ready. The judge walked in, made some opening remarks, then asked James if he was ready with his opening statement. Dressed in his finest navy blue suit and bright yellow tie, James rose slowly, then stepped from behind the table like Fred Astaire about to begin a dance. He turned to the jury and lightly stepped toward them, "Your honor, ladies and gentlemen of the jury, as you know from my best-selling book, 'Prove It,' the government has a duty to prove their case. But the government has a big problem today. They can't prove their case, and what you might not know is that they already know this."

He turned, holding his chin in his hand, letting them see his thoughtful pondering, then faced them squarely. His face was set, his smile partial, to help show how serious he was. His eyes were confident and piercing as he looked into the eyes of each juror before speaking his next words. "Ladies and gentlemen of the jury, I will not only show Bobby Massiano to be innocent, but I will also provide compelling evidence that Larry Baxter's own drug-dealing associate, Richard Matte, was the one who killed him."

Immediately the entire courtroom and the prosecuting team were buzzing with everyone asking who Richard Matte was. The prosecution rose, objecting loudly and adamantly, as the judge banged his gavel incessantly, calling for order.

At the back of the courtroom, a man stepped outside and made a phone call. The mention of Matte's name was the signal to make the call to the three men waiting outside Matte's apartment. James had planned everything down to the last detail. Matte would be killed, and the evidence would be planted within the next 10 minutes.

~ ~ ~ ~

James used his glib tongue to flip the Federal Prosecutor's case completely on its head during the trial. James built his case not on defending Bobby, but on planting compelling seeds to his fabricated story that Larry Baxter got greedy, and his underling Matte got fed up. Witnesses were brought forth to corroborate little pieces of James' story. The fact that neither Larry Baxter nor Richard Matte was alive to defend themselves gave James all the doubt he needed to plant in the jury's mind. When the trial ended, it took the jury only three hours to acquit Bobby.

It was, without a doubt, a brilliant move and the latest gem in the long line of James' victories.

~ ~ ~ ~

Getting Bobby off for the murder of Larry Baxter was a huge feather in James' cap. He collected on the million dollars promised by Bobby. He also spent the week taking congratulatory phone calls and granting several interviews. All of it helped promote his book, which was now number five on the New York Times Bestseller List.

In book stores throughout New York City, James' book, with his picture prominently adorning the front cover, was on display everywhere.

A week after the trial, on a Tuesday night, James dialed his favorite escort, Tanya.

"Hello?" she said.

"Tanya, it's James."

"Hi, James."

"Can you come over tonight?"

There was silence. James' brow lowered. She had been acting very peculiar lately. James feared she might be abandoning him.

After an uncomfortable hesitation, she replied, "Yes, I can. But James, don't pay me. I just want to spend time with you."

James was silent for a moment. Her words rattled him, as if someone had suddenly demanded something from him, he was unwilling to give. "Look, uhh, someone just walked in. Let me call you back. I might be tied up for a while."

He hung up, feeling extremely uncomfortable. The memories of his father striking his mother raced through his mind. His fear of being close to anyone surfaced, and he closed his eyes.

Just then, his intercom rang. It was Teddi, his secretary. "James, are we done for the day? I've got somewhere to go."

"Uhh, yes, go. I will lock up."

~ ~ ~ ~

An hour later, James left the office and walked out onto the main street. A car screeched to a stop at the curb, and two men jumped out and ran at him, grabbing him by the arms. James cried out, "Wait, what are you doing! Wait!" But it was already too late. They quickly dragged him to the car and forced him into the backseat, leaving his briefcase on the sidewalk as they sped off.

Inside the large limo were three men. They punched James in the face repeatedly to soften him up, then tied his hands and placed a black hood over his head. James screamed from under the hood, "Please let me go. Look, you've got the wrong person."

One of them laughed, "No, lawyer boy, we got the right person."

From under the black hood, James' eyes widened. He heard the serious tone in their voices, and he realized he was probably dealing with Baxter's men. James had never considered they would take revenge on him. He was only the lawyer, not a real member of the warring crime families.

"Stop, please let me go. Please!"

"Shut up!" one of the men shouted, punching James in the side of the head. Under his hood, James cringed. "Please... I didn't... " James felt a horrendous thud this time, and everything went black.

Now, James barely conscious mind watched as hundreds of lights flickered by. Finally, he felt the motion slow and the car come to a stop. James began to wake, but another jarring thud to the head knocked him out again.

Chapter 7

James shivered and felt the wind on his body as he came to. It was dark, and he was naked. He looked around, seeing nothing but the dark shimmer of the moonlight on the surface of the water. He was standing on the deck of a yacht and it was moving slowly, already far away from the distant lights of the shore. He turned his face away from the cold sea air and instinctively put his hands around his body to warm himself. He looked down at his shriveled penis and shaking knees. His feet fell funny, and it only took one more second for him to realize what was happening. "Holy shit! *Holy Shit!!*"

His vision adjusted, and his eyes could now see what he felt. He had been fitted with a block of cement halfway up his shins that locked both his feet in solid. He panicked and tried to wriggle out, but he could not even fall down. The cement was too far up his shins. Suddenly the boat slowed to a stop, and six men came up from below deck. One of them was Steve Baxter, head of the Baxter crime family and the brother of Larry Baxter. They surrounded him, laughing.

James knew what this meant. He personally knew of at least seven men whose skeletons were probably still sticking out of cement blocks at the bottom of the sea not far from the Long Island Shoreline.

He immediately begged for his life. "Mr. Baxter, please don't!"

Steve Baxter didn't reply but only stared at James, smiling, sizing him up. "Thought you could get away with all your lies, did you?" Baxter said, grimacing, with a tone that shook James. "You're gonna pay for the death of my brother. And so is that little shit Bobby Massiano!"

"Wait," James cried, "Please, wait! Please. I have information… it… it… will help you to take down Bobby… and… I know where his money is… I can get it for you… over a million dollars… by tomorrow!" James knew about more money than that, but a million was all he was willing to part with.

Steve Baxter stood silently pondering what to do with the request of the sniveling man in front of him. After a long while of everyone on deck in complete and utter silence, Baxter turned to his men and asked, "What do you think, boys? Should we give Mr. Lawyer here a chance to redeem himself?"

As soon as he heard it, James breathed a heavy sigh of relief. *They bought it. Thank God.*

There were several more moments of 'all at stake' silence. Baxter's men looked back and forth at each other. James was already plotting, working out in his mind, how to recover the money he was going to have to hand over to Baxter, as well as how to get the hell out of town. He had wisely played his only ace and he was feeling the old thrill of victory.

But then one of Baxter's men ended the silence and shouted, "Fuck him!"

One of the others followed suit, "Yea, I say kill him. Massiano got away with killing Larry! Throw the bastard over."

James' eyes widened as he thought. *Oh, my God! He'll never pass on a million dollars. No, Baxter won't... he won't.*

All eyes now turned to Baxter. He stared at James, stone-faced, not allowing his expression to reveal his thoughts. He had the final say and everyone, including James, knew it.

"Well now, Mr. Fancy Lawyer," Baxter said, pausing, then nodding his head up and down. "I guess you have your answer."

He stepped forward, glared into James's eyes, and shouted, "Do it!"

"No, please," James screamed in a loud of quivering voice as he could manage.

Baxter's men grabbed him as he desperately tried to wriggle free of the cement. "No, no, please!!!" he screamed at the top of his lungs.

James went over the side and hit the water headfirst. Instantly, his cement-laden feet swung violently around, yanking him downward in the pitch-black water. James' mind exploded in panic as he plummeted deeper and deeper, too fast for his mind to fathom what to do. He frantically reached downward, attempting to pull his feet loose from the cement as he continued his rapid descent.

Unable to wait any longer, he gasped for his first breath of air. A horrible jolt of reality shocked his psyche as nothing, but the cold dark ocean water poured in to fill his panic-stricken lungs. He instinctively opened his mouth again, hoping for air, but only more water poured in. Then, as quickly as it had begun, the dark ocean water stopped flowing in. His lungs were already full.

James now closed his eyes in horror as he plummeted further to the bottom of the sea. After several short minutes, his mind-wrenching struggle ended, and he felt his mind go black for the third time tonight.

~ ~ ~ ~

The yacht overhead turned and headed back to the dock as James' lifeless body floated like an underwater buoy on the bottom of the ocean. Suddenly James' mind awakened, and his eyes opened. He felt himself rising out of the now illuminated water. He could see below him what looked like his body with lifeless arms extended, willowing back and forth in the ocean current, anchored in the cement block on the floor of the ocean. He felt strange in a way he had never before felt, and he wondered where he was. He broke through the surface of the water and immediately heard the roar of an engine, and even though it was dark, he could see Baxter's boat speeding away in the distance.

Suddenly a hand grabbed his elbow and continued to pull him up into the air. Something, someone was saving him. James looked up at his savior and saw the face of an Angel.

"Who are you?" James said as they flew higher into the sky.

The Angel looked at him for a long moment, then looked away, shaking his head. James could clearly see that he wore a disappointed look on his face, and he was bothered by the affront he perceived he had just received from the Angel.

James yelled, "Hey, stop. I demand an answer! Who are you?"

The Angel stopped in midair and held James out in front of him, so they were face to face. "James, your life on Earth is over. You have wasted many gifts in the pursuit of power, pleasure, and riches. Your soul is greatly damaged. I am taking you to your judgment. It may not go well for you, James."

The Angel was surprised not to see the customary look of dismay such an announcement would bring to a person. He shook his head slightly and continued, "But on the other hand, the Lords have been known to be merciful. We shall see." The Angel now took him by the arm and continued to fly. James felt immensely relieved.

So, there is an afterlife. It looks like I made it. He snickered to himself, thinking about his mother's old parish priest, who was always after him to get back to Church. For James, this was old thinking, the thinking that belonged to poor immigrants, not too educated, not powerful men like himself.

The Angel interrupted his thought, "James, do not think so smugly about yourself or your 'instincts.' Your sins in life were very serious. You hurt many people. It is only God's mercy that can save you from what you deserve. And it may not. I can see you clearly on the borderline."

"The borderline?" James asked in a bothered tone.

The Angel stopped again and pulled James in front of him again, "James, a lot of people in your situation don't make it." He paused and continued. "I had hoped I would have more time with you. Unfortunately, I did not."

James heard the opening he needed. He was used to listening for them and pouncing on them. "Oh, so it's your fault... well, I am not..."

The Angel raised his hand, and James was suddenly unable to speak. James' eyes widened. For the first time since coming out of the water, he felt powerless.

The Angel said, "There is a special judgment session in progress concerning you. You will find out your fate after they are finished. If you are lucky, you will be taken to a place of reform. If not, you will be taken to a place you will not want to go to. Trust me."

James raised his hand, pointing to his mouth, nodding, trying to convey he needed to say one more thing. The Angel lowered his hand, and James exhaled, then exclaimed, "Place of reform! Why would I need that?"

The Angel looked sternly into his face. "James, don't you get it? It may be over for you. Does Hell ring any bells?"

For the first time since being pulled out of the water, James now felt fear. Baxter's final words to him, *'Do it'* and their certainty, when he thought he was off the hook, came rushing back to his mind. He now realized the Angel might be doing the same thing, telling him something that was inevitable.

The Angel could see his mind turning. He was glad that normal fear had taken its rightful place. Perhaps it would yield some remorse, remorse he knew James desperately needed right now.

"Take your sleep now, James. I will wake you when the judgment is completed."

The Angel waved his hand in front of James' eyes. James tried to speak, but his eyes grew heavy and closed as he drifted off for a long sleep.

Chapter 8

James blinked, then squinted, trying to see through the darkness. He could feel that he was sitting on a cold, damp, wooden surface. He reached out his hands in front of him. He felt nothing, saw nothing, and heard nothing. The air smelled stale as if he were in a musty cellar. He suddenly remembered being on the seafloor, with water-filled lungs. Then he remembered the Angel, then the special judgment session. He began to panic, suddenly realizing he might be in Hell.

"Help!" he yelled as his voice echoed in the darkness.

A voice replied from somewhere nearby, "James Boulton?"

James turned toward the voice, "Yes, I am James Boulton."

"James, I am Mercio. I am an Angel in the 1st Heavenly Realm under the command of the Archangel Splendora."

"You're who? Never mind. Where am I?" James asked, adding, "And what did you say your name was?"

"My name is Mercio. You are at the place of judgment."

"I already told the other guy. I don't need any judgment or reform for that matter." James was quickly becoming his old cocky self.

Mercio was a tall, broad-shouldered Angel with long black hair held back by a golden band across his forehead. He stepped closer and put his hand on James' shoulder, then picked James up with one hand and stood him on his feet.

"James, you wasted your life on Earth. But the Lords have shown you mercy. I am to take you to the place where you will begin your time of repentance and reform. We are going to the 4th Land of Reform.

As his eyes adjusted, James could now vaguely see in the darkness. His hands touched his own body, and he realized he was still naked. Knowing he had avoided Hell, just as he had anticipated, he began to take control of the situation. "Eventually, you say? How long exactly do I have to stay there?"

"I'm afraid it will seem like a very long time to you," replied Mercio. "But be grateful, James. You are being given a great second chance."

A creaking door suddenly swung open, letting light into the room. James could see a small table on which were some clothes and shoes piled. Mercio pointed and nodded, signaling for James to get dressed.

James put on the clothes and laced up the shoes. The clothes felt stiff and scratchy, not like the smooth silk suits he was used to wearing. Mercio then pointed to the door and signaled for James to walk through.

James stuck his neck out and peered through the doorway. Outside he saw a gray landscape covered in a fog of misty, cloudy air. It was chilly. James saw people milling about in the distance. Mercio nudged him forward as James stepped out of the waiting room and onto the cold, wet pavement.

"Follow me," Mercio said. They walked for a ways, with others a short distance in front of them, and others a short distance behind them. A small wooden sign, crookedly staked in the ground and painted with crooked white letters read, "1st Land of Reform Dock." Underneath the words was an arrow pointing to the right, where an adjoining path trailed off into the mist. As James passed the adjoining path, he could hear the sound of waves, or water, lapping against something. He and Mercio kept walking straight ahead. A while later, James saw a few people in front of him turn off onto another path. Soon he saw the sign, just as small and unofficial looking as the first one. It read, "2nd Land of Reform Dock." An arrow was drawn underneath, also pointing to the right.

Further on, as they continued walking, they approached a third sign, which read, "3rd Land of Reform Dock." James started to turn onto this path, but Mercio grabbed him by the arm and shook his head, pulling him back and pointing ahead, signaling they needed to keep going. James watched a few people disappear into the mist down this path, and for some reason, he did not understand, he wished he was going with them.

Now the number of people on the pathway thinned and slowed, as it seemed any enthusiasm amongst the remaining path goers for the journey was all but gone. Ahead of him, James saw a woman bolt to the right down a path. Immediately several Angels ran after her, grabbing her. She screamed, begging them to let her go, but they dragged her off the path and continued with her, dragging her writhing body straight down the pathway, passing the turn off she had tried to go down.

Now James saw the sign at the turnoff. It read, "4th Land of Reform Dock."

James' voice quivered with trepidation as he asked, "Where... where did they take that woman?"

Mercio frowned and lowered his eyes. "Never mind, James. Her life and her destiny are none of your business. We turn off here. Let's go."

James shuddered as he turned onto the path, looking over his shoulder at the faint image of the woman in the distant mist, being dragged to a place she did not want to go. The sound of her voice, desperately pleading, begging for mercy, rattled him to the core. Mercio took him by the arm and pulled him along, saying, "Forget about her. She is in God's hands now."

James thought it strange Mercio would say that, as if going to Hell put her in God's hands, but it was all too much to bear, and he closed his mind to it. They continued walking down the adjacent path. As they walked, they were surrounded by mist for a long time, and James began to hear the sound of waves. Finally, the mist cleared, and James saw an immense ship filled with people.

"You will board that ship, James, and I will see you at the 4th Land of Reform. I have some other clients to attend to."

"How... how long is the trip?"

"It's about three hours, and I am sorry to say it will not pass quickly."

"Look, I am not... " Suddenly James' eyes widened, and his mouth kept moving, with no sound coming out.

Mercio smiled, "James, for reasons we have deemed important with people going to the 4th Land of Reform, you will be unable to speak until you arrive. Go now, and I will see you before long."

James gritted his teeth, and looked up into the cloudy sky, then turned, and went up the gangplank. A friendly looking female Angel greeted him at the top and pointed to a spot on the deck where James was to sit. There were hundreds of people on board, men and women, but more men than women. The men were all wearing plain clothing as James was, jeans, plain shirts, and simple tennis shoes. The women mostly wore longer tunics of differing shades of gray with tennis shoes. Some had on jeans, like the men, but only a few.

James sat next down where he was assigned, and a woman looked over at him with a sad look on her face. James gave her a half-smile, then looked to the other side, where an older man sat. His face was resolute, staring into the distance, but James could see a tear forming in the corner of his eye.

Suddenly, the shipped lurched ahead, and they were off.

Chapter 9

The ship approached an immense tract of land, and everyone on board got up and crowded along the rails to see. It was only mid-afternoon, and the land looked gloomy. Clouds of various shades of gray covered the entire sky, and the wind began blowing, causing the waters below to begin kicking up the murky waters of the sea.

The ship sailed toward a large structure that looked like an ocean-going gate. As they neared, a horn sounded, and the gate parted in the middle, swinging open to each side, allowing the ship to pass through into a large harbor. There was another ship docked, but no sooner had James ship entered than the other ship pulled out and passed them, heading out through the gates, obviously returning to pick up another batch of "passengers."

Jame's ship pulled up to a dock, and the gangplank was lowered. One by one, they entered a line and disembarked. As James walked down, he saw Mercio standing at the dock waiting for him.

James smiled, and Mercio turned, signaling for him to follow. They walked up a hill leading away from the dock. They were soon on a winding pathway that seemed to cut through the countryside of grayish tinted green fields. They walked in silence for a very long time, neither saying a word. As they walked, James saw numerous large houses dotting the landscape. They looked like motels or inns you might see in an old black and white English horror movie. The strange thing, though, as they were the only type of house. All were the same.

They passed by many people, but no one spoke, and only a few looked up to make eye contact. After an hour on the road, Mercio stopped and pointed to a large house some 100 feet from the road with a long sidewalk leading to a large white porch. Mercio said, "This is the place where you will stay while you are in the 4th Land of Reform. Go up the pathway. They will help you."

James looked up at the house. It had gray shutters and a long winding walkway. It looked like a grand old Victorian house with balconies and enormous windows. Suddenly, James saw something that made him shudder. In every window, he saw the faces of men and women sitting quietly, staring out at the sky. They all just seemed to be looking out at nothing.

It spooked him, so he turned and started to walk away. Mercio raised his hand to stop him, and James suddenly felt his legs stop churning.

Mercio called out, "James, stop. Consider now that if you want to have any chance of seeing Heaven, you must submit your time to the Lands of Reform. If you don't submit you will forfeit your second chance."

James was scared. A feeling he was not used to. He felt his heart shaking. He looked at Mercio with desperation in his eyes, saying, "Listen, Mercio. I don't want to go up there!" He looked up at the house then back again. "Isn't there another option?"

Mercio shook his head, "James, ever hear the old saying, 'beggars can't be choosers?'"

James nodded, not getting it.

"Well, it applies here, James. You need to trust me right now. Your time here will not be as bad as you think. Go up the hill now, and the caregivers will get you situated."

James knew about cutting deals, and he knew there was none to cut here. He had rarely trusted others in life, but he had the feeling this Angel was his only hope at the moment. Reluctantly, he turned and walked up the path to the big house on the hill.

~ ~ ~ ~

As he neared the front door, a striking woman came out onto the porch step and greeted him from the top of the steps. "James Boulton?"

"Yes, that's me," he replied.

"Welcome, James," she said. "My name is Cindy. I am in charge of this house. We have much work ahead, and it will not be easy. But try to remember that you and all these people are here for one reason only. It is because of the mercy of the Lords. Now follow me, and I will show you to your room."

James found himself speechless, so he nodded.

Cindy led him down a long wide hallway. The place reminded James of an inner-city nursing home with its narrow halls and institutionally clean feeling. As they reached the end of the hall, Cindy opened a door and stepped aside to allow James to enter.

The first thing he noticed was the room was not very spacious. There was a bed, a lounge chair, and a light brown carpet. At the far wall, there was a patio door leading out to the balcony. To the left of the patio door was a bay window with a plain wooden chair and table. On the table was a large book that James somehow knew was the Bible. He thought, *Oh great, the Bible. I can't wait.*

He walked into the room with a cocky stride and sat down on the rickety bed. "So that's it? I'm stuck here?"

"Actually, James, you are not stuck. Being here is a privilege. If you don't want to stay, you may take that up with your Angel Counselor. But I have to tell you, the alternative to being here is not very good."

James did not ask about the alternative. He had already gathered where that was. Hell.

Cindy waited for him to reply. When he did not, she said, "Well then, we have supper together at 5. The final event of the day is the evening prayer at 6. I'll give you some other details later this evening. We have a full day tomorrow, including Church service at 9 in the morning. The big event each day here in the 4th Land of Reform is at 3 in the afternoon. It will be your first time to experience the Hour of Contemplation of Past Sins. That is what all the people were doing when you arrived. Here in the 4th Land of Reform, our guests have some serious reflecting to do."

James replied, "Oh, great. I can't wait."

Cindy half-smiled and started for the door.

"Uh, Cindy, may I ask you a question?"

She stopped, "Sure, James."

"How many people are here?"

"Here in the Land of Reform or here in this house?" Cindy asked.

"Both. If you don't mind."

"Were you this good as a lawyer, James?"

He did not answer but merely smiled and waited for her reply.

"Well, I will tell you. Here in this house, there are 244 men and women. But here in the 4th Land of Reform, there are untold millions."

"Untold millions?" James said, as his face registered the shock he felt at the very existence of this unseen world.

"James, you must realize, millions of people threw away their lives in all sorts of ways. The Lords could not simply let everyone suffer in Hell forever. I mean, would you let your child go to Hell just because he didn't follow the rules?"

"Well, I… don't know. I don't have kids."

Cindy frowned, disappointed he could not even imagine her example. "C'mon James, think about it. Forever is a long time. It is like, well, forever. I mean, don't get me wrong, James. There are plenty of people in Hell… who were… well… beyond repair. The Lords have been very selective about who truly deserves that place."

"I will get out of here then?"

"James, there are four separate Lands of Reform."

"Am I in the lowest?"

"James, that's really not important right now."

"No, tell me, please, I want to know." He was becoming extremely nervous.

"James, you were assigned to begin here, and yes, it is the lowest level."

His face froze, "Does that mean I have a long way to go?"

"Yes, it will be long. We take one step at a time around here. I am here to help you progress through this. Eventually you will pass up to the 3rd Land of Reform, and then continue upwards. and someday, you will be ready to live forever with the Lords and the people you love."

Her words did not excite James entirely. He could not really think of any people he loved unless he counted his mother. Being with the Lords did not exactly excite him either. But more than anything, he needed information. He had to make sense of his predicament.

"Cindy, what is below the 4th Land of Reform?"

"The underworld is below here. Some call it Hell. The devil, his followers, and people who hated the Lords during their lives are there. At night, you can hear cries of anguish. It serves as a reminder of how great and merciful the Lords are for giving the people here another chance.

James was stunned. He asked, "Can people from here fail... and end up there?"

"Yes, it happens, more often than I would like. Every person has to make choices, James. You see, people are not sent to Hell. They choose it."

He snapped, "Who would *choose* to go to Hell?"

"People choose it by their lives on Earth, and even if they get here, some end up being deceived by the devil and his helpers. They don't put in the effort here." Cindy herself had some people under her care sent down. It haunted her that they would never see Heaven.

James was silent. "Cindy, one more thing. You said the Lords want us to get to know who they are. Do you know them? Are they open to negotiation?"

"James, you are good! I must admit. I wish I had a lawyer like you in my days on Earth. Oh, and please don't worry, that old joke about no lawyers in Heaven is not really true. However, I must admit, many begin their journey here in the 4th Land of Reform." Cindy laughed.

James just rolled his eyes.

She then said, "But to answer your question, yes, I have met the Lords. They are wonderful. But no, they don't negotiate."

"What are *they* like?"

"James, when the Lords are near you feel the deepest sense of love and well-being that you could imagine, and you also feel the sense of eternity, the realization that love and life will last forever. I am going to let you find that out for yourself. Trust me, you will not be disappointed."

James acted interested, but he was already thinking of finding a way out.

Chapter 10

Cindy left, closing the door, and James was left standing in his room. He glanced out the window and then turned around slowly, scanning all four walls of his tiny room. It felt like a prison, perhaps one of the less barbaric Federal ones, but a prison nonetheless. Then, he remembered sinking into the ocean. He had died. His life was over. His book fame, his times with Tanya, his meetings with the Massianos, his ordering his staff about, all of this was gone, and it was gone forever.

His mind began spinning out of control, and he felt dizzy for the first time in his adult life. He sat down on the bed, but the feeling quickly escalated into a full-blown panic attack.

James grabbed his chest as it suddenly tightened, and his breathing became strained. A feeling of suffocation gripped his body. He fell onto the floor, rolling and writhing in pain, then got up and ran to the window, looking out in desperation at the dismal, cloudy, evening sky, hoping to calm the panic. It wasn't working. He needed air.

He ran to the door, thrust it open, and ran out into the hallway, hastily nodding to the few people he passed. His heart was racing. He felt like he did as a little boy when his father had once lost track of him in an old-fashioned carnival fun-house.

He found the stairs and hustled down, almost tripping half way. He stumbled across the lobby and out the front door. He continued past several people on the porch, down the front steps, and collapsed, face down, on the grass in front of the house.

Several people from the front porch raced down and gathered around. A woman knelt beside him and put her head close to his face, trying to hear if he was breathing. She looked up at the others, "He's having a panic attack. Quick, get a bag from the kitchen."

One of the men raced into the house. The woman rubbed James' forehead and back, saying, "Breathe, breathe… " She looked back to the house, "Hurry up with that bag!"

She pressed her forehead close to his, gently rubbing his hair. "It's okay, just breathe. You're going to be okay."

James closed his eyes tightly, his body quivering and shuddering, tears streamed down his face, as he labored to breathe.

The man returned with the bag and handed it to the woman, and she held it over James' mouth. He tried to shake her off, feeling the same panic he felt when his lungs filled with the dark, cold, ocean water. She held it firm, saying calmly, "Breathe into the bag. Breathe... that's it. Keep going!"

Within a few moments, James' breathing slowed, and his panic-stricken clenched eyes finally relaxed. The woman brushed his hair out of his face. She looked up at the others, "All right, everyone. Let's give him some room. I'll take it from here."

They all nodded and walked back to the porch.

She helped James sit upon the grass, "You had quite a scare. Are you all right?"

Inside, James still shuddered. He replied, "Yes… I am… I don't know what came over me. I… I just panicked." He looked at the woman, surprised she had been willing to help him. No one had ever helped him unless he had paid them to. She had kind-looking, green-colored eyes and auburn hair. Her skin was fair, with just the right amount of freckles. James closed his eyes again, his breathing laboring again. He said, "I'm sorry."

"Oh, don't be sorry. You're not the first person who had a panic attack here. It happens a lot. Although I must admit, you're one of the first we had to revive on the front lawn."

James looked at her, his eyes wide, his mind still reeling, and exhaled loudly, letting out one last shudder as the panic left his body.

The woman smiled and said, "My name is Ellen."

James nodded, "My name is James."

Just then, a bell rang. Ellen stood up and helped James to his feet. "It's time for us to go to supper. Are you going to be okay?"

"Yes, I am."

"Well, I am meeting some friends inside. I have to go. Go up one flight of stairs to your room and change your shirt. You have about five minutes before supper."

"Thank you," said James.

James watched her turn and walked up the steps. Her beauty struck him, but more than anything, by her kindness. He did not remember anyone doing a kind deed for him, except his mother, and that was long, long ago.

For the first time, it occurred to him that he had no life outside of the mob and his work defending them. Partaking in the fruits of the pleasures afforded him by the upscale stripper clubs they controlled held little opportunities for genuine human kindness. He felt strange that he had never realized this before now.

He walked back up the steps, across the porch, and into the house. Everyone was coming down the steps or walking in from the first-floor hall, crossing the large lobby, heading toward the main dining room. James ignored them and trudged up the center steps to his floor, then down the hall to his room.

He reached his room, then stopped. *Think James. Think. You're dreaming. That's it.* He slapped his face trying to wake himself from the dream. He racked his brain to quickly figure a way to prove he was still alive and only dreaming. *Where is my phone?* He quickly padded his pockets, no phone, no keys, nothing. *In my room! They're in my room!* He opened the door and went in, scanning every corner. He dropped to his knees, scouring the entire floor, then went onto his stomach, peering carefully under the bed. But there was nothing.

Wait a minute. This is a dream. I have to wake up first. He jumped up and carefully laid down on the bed. He situated himself, folded his hands across his chest, and closed his eyes, smiling now, convinced he had found his way out of the rabbit hole. He tried to nod off, but it was not working. Every time he pretended to wake up, he was still in the room.

He buried his head in his pillow. *What the Hell is happening to me?* Then it hit him again, but this time harder. He wasted his life, and now he was going to have to pay the price. For the first time in memory, he cried, and after a half-hour of sobbing into his pillow, he turned his head and whimpered out something he had not said since he was a boy. "Mother Mary, please help me!"

~ ~ ~ ~

As he laid on the floor, trying to sleep, and his mind drifted back. Long ago, when he was a boy, his mother, a devout Catholic, taught him to say the Hail Mary prayer. She always told him, "James, if you ever need anything, say Ten Hail Mary's, because Mary will talk to her son Jesus for you, and he does not like to say 'no' to his mother."

This nightly devotion stayed with him when he was young. The years of turmoil living with his alcoholic and abusive father made it one of his only ways of coping. Whenever his father began arguing with his mother, it was a signal to James to be ready. If things got heated, he knew the anger could easily turn toward him. When it did, he would run to his room and hide under the bed. He would inevitably pray, "Please, Mother Mary, help my dad to stop yelling." He would then repeat the Hail Mary prayer as many times as he could, hiding under his bed, afraid, until he fell asleep.

James thought back to his mother. She never stopped praying for him and frequently reminded him that she was doing so. He had thought her foolish and old-school. Now, he understood perfectly well; she had been right about everything. He had been the foolish one.

~ ~ ~ ~

James felt the sun on his face. He opened his eyes and realized it was morning. He had fallen asleep on the floor. He stretched, gave out a loud yawn, and got up off the floor. He looked out the window to the horizon. As far as he could see there were rolling green hills, speckled with large houses just like the one he was in. The houses seemed to be arranged in larger clusters. Nestled in the middle of the area of every group of 15 or so houses sat an old-looking stone church with a tall steeple. James could make out at least three of them in the distance.

Strange, these churches look ancient and yet modern at the same time.

He declared aloud, "There's got to be a way out of here. I am going to find it."

Suddenly a bell rang, followed by an announcement that breakfast would be served. James looked up at the time. It was 7:50 a.m. He looked in the dresser drawer and found three neatly folded shirts along with a couple of pairs of jeans. He took out fresh clothes and changed into them. They did not fit as well as he was used to, but they worked. He then put on the tennis shoes he had been given by Mercio the day before and left the room, heading to the dining room for his first meal.

The dining hall was just off the main lobby. It was spacious but very plain, and it reminded James of his inner-city high school cafeteria. Nevertheless, it had a buffet line, and that was all that mattered to James. He was starving.

Several kitchen workers in white uniforms manned the other side of the buffet line. He recognized one of them from the porch and realized they must be inmates. The lineup of food was short and simple. There were scrambled eggs, toast, oatmeal, and dry cereal that looked like Cheerios. There was also a drink station with pitchers of milk, coffee, tea, or orange juice. James took a tray and started down, loading up his plate with some of everything, pouring himself a bowl of cereal, and pouring a cup of coffee as well as juice.

He went over to an empty table and sat down. The room was full. James remembered Cindy, the administrator, had told him 244 people were living there, and James surprised they were all present and accounted for. He scanned the room. *Who are all these people? I wonder what they did to end up here?*

James noticed someone walking toward him out of the corner of his eye. He turned. It was the woman who helped him yesterday. She was holding a tray of food. She said, "Hi, James. Remember me? Ellen."

"Oh, hi. Yes, I remember you."

"Do you mind if I join you?"

"Sure, go ahead." James motioned for her to join him.

She sat down, smiled briefly, then bowed her head, silently whispering a short prayer. When she finished, she began to eat her breakfast. After chewing for a moment, she swallowed and asked, "So, James, where are you from?"

"Uhh, well, I'm from New York. Born and raised… and died, I guess."

Ellen laughed. "I've never heard it put quite like that. Forgive me for laughing, but it sounds very funny."

James was amused by his guest, though he rarely had any interest, much less time, to talk to people during his hectic days as a selfish mob lawyer. She intrigued him, though. He asked, "Where are you from?"

"I am from Montreal. Born in Quebec, raised in Montreal, and unfortunately, died in Montreal." She lowered her head, obviously saddened at her death.

"I am sorry," said James. "What happened to you? I mean, if you don't mind me asking."

Ellen wiped a small tear from the side of her cheek. "I umm… was killed in a car accident when I was 47 years old."

"I'm sorry to hear that. Hey, look on the bright side, you're alive again." James was doing his best. He was surprised that his conversation was lasting so long. It was way longer than any of the short, impersonal ones he was used to on Earth.

Ellen said, "Yes, I am glad for that. And I am glad for the mercy of the Lords in giving me a chance to amend my life. I really am."

"Well, why are you here?"

"James, umm, perhaps I will share that with you someday but not right now. Let's just say there are some good reasons, some very good reasons."

"Oh, sure, I understand."

They talked for a little while longer and quietly ate their meals. A bell rang, and everyone immediately rose to their feet and brought their trays and dishes to the return area. Then they all headed out the front door.

"Hey, where's everyone going?" he asked.

"They are going to the morning church service."

"What?" James said as he watched everyone filing out past him, "Is this mandatory?"

Ellen replied, "Well, technically you don't have to go, but as the guidelines say, 'it helps.'"

The corners of James' lips turned down as he looked again at everyone filing out. "Ellen, I have not been to church in ages. I would probably prefer not to go."

"Well, that is up to you, James. But if you like, you can sit with me. It's very nice."

He looked at her kind eyes and considered her request. He looked again to the people, almost all out of the room. He said, "All right, I'll go."

Chapter 11

James followed Ellen out the front door and down the pathway to the main path that led beyond the church's nearby hills. The slightly misty morning air gave him an eerie feeling about the whole thing.

As they crested a nearby hill, James now had a clear view of the church. It sat on top of a large hill. Its steeple rose high into the air and was brilliantly illuminated by a sliver of the morning sun breaking through the clouds. James and Ellen strolled down the path, bringing up the rear of the thousands of people from the surrounding houses. The morning air was brisk, and it reminded James of a morning in late October, furthering the eerie feeling he had.

As they drew near the entrance, James took notice of the ancient-looking, stone architecture. He instantly imagined an old, dull-looking interior. Still, as he walked through the door, the ancient exterior gave way to a stunning, colorful, and sunlit interior. Two thousand people were sitting in pews, waiting quietly. It was the most immense gathering of churchgoers James had ever seen. He was amazed that the building did not look that large on the outside, but it was very spacious on the inside.

Ellen grabbed James by the arm and led him up the center aisle all the way to the front. She asked some people in the pew to move down and make some room. They sat down.

James had not imagined sitting all the way in the front, but he was glad they did. The altar was spectacular. At the back, a large cross was affixed to the wall. As he gazed at the impressive cross, James saw his life flash before his eyes. Memories of childhood flooded back to him. He remembered attending Mass with his mother and grandmother. He remembered the pipe organ's sound and the choir's melodic voices he so loved as a boy. His grandmother had always sat proudly in the first pew with James by her side. Now here, he sat in the first pew, but he was "dead."

A bell rang, and a man and a woman, clothed in priestly garb, came out of the sanctuary door. As they entered, everyone rose to their feet and broke out in a resounding song, and then the service began. It felt very much like the services he had attended as a child. There were a few readings from the Bible, then there was offertory, and finally, the priest blessed bread and wine for distribution. James was amazed. It all felt like the old days. Days and times he had not thought important, and yet here they were, being conducted much the same, on the other side.

Many times during the service, he found himself tearing up. His Angel, Mercio, had been right. He had wasted his life on Earth. As they walked home from the service, James began to understand that the idea of a second chance, the idea of a being in the Land of Reform, was not such a bad thing. It was all suddenly starting to appeal to him.

~ ~ ~ ~

Later that night, James sat on the edge of his bed, thinking. He used to sit on his bed, thinking like this the night before trial appearances, but tonight was different. There was no trial. There was only his newfound imprisonment. He thought about the day, the people, the church, and Ellen. He was trying to piece it all together, to understand his predicament. A little voice in his head still tried to tell him he might be dreaming, but the odds of that seemed to be vanishing.

He opened the patio door and stepped out onto the balcony. Before him lay a darkened land with no lights. It was vastly different than the Manhattan skyline and busy New York streets he was used to. The never-ending view into darkness was quiet and still, devoid of any life other than the life his fellow inmates were all participating in. He wondered why they were all going along with everything. He wondered why there were no revolts, no uprisings, no defiance. Perhaps there were, and he just had not seen it yet.

He looked up into the sky, the only place where there was anything to see. The stars were there, and while he was not used to watching them in his days on Earth, now it was all he had. Suddenly he stopped. *Wait! Is that?* He realized the stars looked familiar. He was no expert, but he remembered and made out many of the constellations he knew from Earth. He began to murmur aloud with excitement. "Yes, it is true. There is the Big Dipper… and over there is the Little Dipper." He went on, seeing and naming more constellations.

Then, his lawyer's mind kicked in. He pondered, *How can I possibly see these from here if Earth is somewhere else? Earth must be near. Maybe there is a way out of here after all.*

His thoughts were abruptly interrupted. In the distance he heard noises, no, voices. He tuned his vision in more keenly. The noises were faint, but they were human. They were screams, and ones filled with terror. James focused his hearing, straining, and they became clearer still. *What the Hell is that?*

When he realized what it might be, his blood curdled right where he stood, and his heart sank as he felt the hair on the back of his neck raise up.

The sounds were coming from the south. He quickly went back inside, put his shoes on, and took off down the hall, down the stairs, and out the front door. At a quickened pace, he jogged alone in the dark, cold night, his heart pounding loudly. He stopped to listen, and then he heard them again. This time they were louder. James ran, but then he stopped for a moment, thinking, suddenly afraid to find out what they were. He considered turning around. Fear tried to dominate his will, but he decided he had to see what it was.

He kept going, following the cries in the night. Within 20 minutes, he found himself running up an incline. He was on a hill. He stopped halfway up to rest for a moment and again contemplated turning back. His breathing was heavy. The screams were coming from the other side of the hill.

With a fearful look on his face, he looked up to the top of the hill and saw a glow as if from a large forest fire. The hill was too steep to run anymore. He walked, slipping and falling several times. He then half walked, half crawled toward the top of the hill. As he neared the top, he saw hundreds of people lined up. All of them were looking over the edge of what looked like a cliff. It was as if they were at a tourist attraction. Only the distant screams signaled this was no place for tourists.

A few more labored, frightful steps, and he was at the top, where a startling scene greeted him. The onlookers were indeed standing at the edge of a cliff. There was no other side to the hill. They were all looking at a fiery desolate plateau of land in the distance. When he looked down, all he could see was a great chasm between where he stood and the fiery land beyond. He had never seen a landscape like this on Earth. It seemed to be several miles away but was illuminated by the glowing flames.

Then they started again. The moans, cries, and shrieks of people, sending shivers through his entire body. *Are these the cries of the damned?* The sound of men and women crying out in despair was too much to bear. He closed his eyes and shook his head. *Why am I not over there with them? I deserve to be over there with them.*

When he opened his eyes and looked down to the plateau, he could make out the fuzzy outlines of crowds of men and women, all in agony, all being tormented and herded by crude-looking Angels holding spears and what looked like pitchforks. Again, he had to look away, unable to handle the sight of people who were forever damned.

James turned to the woman standing next to him and asked, "Is that Hell?"

She slowly turned her head, looked at him somberly, and said, "Yes, that it is Hell."

Chapter 12

James stumbled back home from the chasm in stunned disbelief. The shrill cries of the men and women condemned to Hell haunted his every step. He feared he would never be able to forget what he had heard and seen. He wondered about people like Bobby Massiano and wondered if he had already been killed like Baxter said they were going to do? For a moment, James wondered if Bobby was over there in Hell? *Of course, Bobby is in Hell. He was a lot worse than me.* And suddenly James stopped walking and shuddered, picturing Bobby's tortured face, screaming in despair, like the people he had just seen.

James vowed he would never return to the chasm. It was too horrifying, but he also vowed he would never forget what he saw. He made his mind up to take advantage of the second chance he had been given.

~ ~ ~ ~

The years in the 4th Land of Reform passed ever so slowly for James. He spent countless hours at night watching the stars trying to figure out how they could be so close to Earth. During his free time during the day, he would venture as far from the house as he could, hoping to find clues as to their location. Because of his nearly life-long dealing with the mob, James was used to feeling like the smartest guy in the room, and he was confident he would crack the code and find a way back to his old life.

Despite his determination to find a way out, James kept his backup plan in full gear, and that was to cooperate with Mercio, his Angel Counselor, and with the rules and guidelines set forth by the powers that be.

He was progressing well, as evidenced by the frequent compliments from his house Administrator, Cindy. In accordance with his good behavior, James was given an important job. He had been placed on the team of people overseeing the docks where the new arrivals came in each night of the week.

New arrivals to the 4th Land of Reform arrived on a boats. These boats were massive old wooden ships, the kind used in the 14th to 19th Centuries throughout the world. The docks were a massive structure at the southern tip of each of the four Lands of Reform. Harbors had been carved out to allow ships ample room to sail in, dock, unload their passengers, and sail back out onto the open waters of the Heavenly Sea.

Massive steel gates guarded the harbors and could only be opened from this inside of the dock. When ships arrived outside, they would be verified, then the gates would open, and they would sail through.

The workers were told this was to protect the Lands of Reform from the forces of Hell, the Dark Angels, who many feared might someday try to attack or take over the Lands of Reform. Not only were the dock gates a deterrent, but in the skies above all the Lands of Reform, Angels regularly patrolled, always ready to not only defend, but also sound the alarm for any intrusion.

Upon death, people who would not be going directly to Heaven were taken to a particular place of judgment. Once judged, they were loaded onto the ships and taken to whichever place they needed to go. Some ships sailed to one of the four Lands of Reform, the worst cases going to the 4th Land, the ones needed only modest reform going to the 1st Land, and the others somewhere in between. Those whose lives determined they truly deserved to be in Hell were loaded, or rather, forcibly dragged onto those ships, and sent there.

The docks were one of the most interesting places to work. The myriad of new women and men arriving nightly, with aghast and fearful looks on their faces yielded constant intrigue from the workers. While dock workers were not supposed to talk with them, it was inevitable for the workers to strike up brief conversations with the new arrivals. People from all over the world, disembarking the ships, pleading their cases to dock workers who pretended to listen as if their listening could make a difference, when in fact, the fates of all had already been decided, else they would not be coming into the dock aboard the ship in the first place.

Chapter 13

James was getting bored. Being a model citizen in a place that was no fun had zero appeal to him. His hope of finding a way out was slowly diminishing. With their passing, James' reason for living was also passing. It was only his friendship and admiration for Ellen that kept him going. If it were not for her, he might have given up long ago.

During his sixth year, the monthly meetings with his Angel Counselor, Mercio, were also losing their effectiveness. James had missed three of the last five meetings, making excuses each time, but Mercio knew it was more than this. He knew James was struggling, and he made a point to visit James at the house.

Early in the morning, he arrived and made his way up the stairs and knocked on James' door. There was no reply. Mercio knocked again, then put his ear to the door, listening. Nothing. He knocked a third time. This time he heard the ruffling of coverings, and James said in a voice full of lament, "Whaaatt?"

"James, it's Mercio."

Mercio listened and heard a loud sigh. He heard movement, and finally, the door opened.

James half-smiled and said, "Mercio, good morning."

"Hello James," Mercio said cheerfully. "Did I wake you?"

James paused momentarily, then said, "No, I had to get up to answer the door anyway."

Mercio began nodding, then realized James had made a joke. He laughed, "That's a good one, James. I'm going to have to remember to use it."

James nodded, "I got it from an old uncle of mine, Uncle Coy. He used to say it all the time."

"Well, it's a good one."

James finally said, "What can I do for you, Mercio? Would you like to come in?"

"No, no, James. I just wanted to make sure you're okay. You've missed our last few meetings, and I just... well... wanted to touch base."

James took a deep breath, trying to find an excuse. He rubbed his hand across his forehead and said, "Yeah, I don't have a good reason, old friend."

Mercio said nothing and only nodded, keeping the ball in James' court. James felt it and said, "We are scheduled for tomorrow, aren't we?"

Mercio nodded, "Yes, we are. Can you make it?"

"I will," said James.

"That's great, James. Have a great day. We have lots to talk about tomorrow. I'll see you then." Mercio turned and walked down the hall, happy he had stopped. Sometimes clients needed a little bit of encouragement, and James, while one of his more peculiar cases, apparently did.

~ ~ ~ ~

From the moment Mercio left, James did very little except brood over the fact that he had been in the 4th Level of the Land of Reform for far too long. All day, his mind rehearsed the reasons he was going to give to Mercio as to why he should be promoted up and transferred to the 3rd Land of Reform.

The only thing that saddened him about the whole idea was Ellen. He loved her. He was sure of it. But he trusted she would be moving up too, either soon, before, or soon after him. Her life and the reason she was in the Land of Reform were still a mystery to him. He simply could not imagine a woman committing worse sins than he had.

The next morning James woke up and seriously contemplated skipping his meeting again. He went downstairs and sat with Ellen during breakfast. The faint sun was shining through the dining hall window onto the side of her face, making her look especially radiant this morning. While they were eating, she asked, "So James, what are you doing before work tonight?"

"I have a counseling appointment."

"Oh. That's great. Do you think your time to move up is drawing near?" As she finished saying it, she lowered her head slightly, signaling non-verbally that the answer for her might not be hopeful.

James did answer right away. He watched her eyes looking down at her food. He saw her humility, and her gentle, sorrowful soul. It was something he never saw before in a woman, or in anyone for that matter. He never took the time to see people. In his busy world of being a lawyer, people were merely pawns to move his life forward.

Ellen looked up and caught him gazing at her. She smiled and asked again, "Do you think your time is drawing near, James?"

"What?" he asked, caught off guard.

"Do you think your time is drawing near?"

"Oh, I don't know, Ellen. It seems the more I do. The more dismal I feel my prospects are. I am not sure I am even going to go to the appointment."

"No, James. You have to go. You cannot give up. You have to get out of here." She paused for a moment, lowered her head slightly again, and said somberly, "We both do. We both have to get out of here."

James nodded, smiling, but the despair in her last sentence did not get past him. He asked, "Can I walk to church with you this morning?"

Ellen shook her head, "I'm sorry. I need to be by myself today." She looked up and smiled as a small tear rolled down the side of her cheek. "But I'll see you here tomorrow for breakfast."

James nodded and turned away. Now he felt more determined than ever. He was going to his meeting, and he was going to demand some action, not only for himself but for Ellen.

~ ~ ~ ~

James sat alone in his room, staring out the window as expected, enduring another day's 3 p.m. hour-long requirement of past contemplation of sins. This time had been an almost unbearable requirement from the very first day because James had no regret for any past sins. He was doing business in his mind, and if it hurt others, that was a casualty of modern life, well-lived. They were not sins. They were maneuvers.

After the daily hour ended, James set off for his meeting with Mercio. He walked for a mile or so to the building where Mercio had his office and went inside. He went up the stairs and turned right down the long corridor where the Angels in this region of the 4th Land of Reform had their offices. As he passed office after office, he marveled at all of the Angels working quietly at their desks. It reminded him of some of the big law firms he had traversed in his day, filled with the office after office of busy attorneys.

Finally, near the end of the hall, he reached Mercio's office. James approached quietly and peaked his head around the corner. Mercio was reviewing a file carefully. James watched him for a moment until Mercio finally looked up.

"Well, look who's here. Come in, James." Mercio stood up and made his way around to the other side of the desk to greet James.

"Hello Mercio, I told you I would be here."

Mercio sat down next to James and pulled out his report, scanning the first-page summary section. "James, you are doing well, except, of course, for missing meetings of late."

"Thank you, Mercio… but I have… "

Mercio interrupted him. "However, James, I am concerned about one thing. You seem to be bothered lately. I do not know why you are worried. What is troubling you?"

James drew in a breath, preparing his words. But then he realized he needed to let Mercio finish first. His case could only be made stronger if he understood where he stood with the system. So, he shrugged and said, "I don't know what's troubling me, Mercio."

Mercio thumbed through the pages looking for James's most recent report. "Okay, here it is. Your House Administrator reported you are an exceptional member of the household. She said… let me see… I have it here somewhere… " He flipped through a few more pages and zeroed in on his findings. "Oh, yes, here it is. It says here that you have been outstanding around the house and grounds. She also says that you are well-liked, and she has observed that you often help the new people get adjusted."

"Well, I'm glad she noticed. I hope that my good behavior will soon pay off. After all, it is not that hard to follow the rules here. I guess helping people comes easily to me, at least for now."

Mercio was not exactly thrilled to hear James' response. He was starting to sound cocky like he did in his old lawyer days. "James, that's fine, but I do want to come back to what is upsetting you. First, though, tell me, why, all of a sudden, is it easy for you to help people. I mean, altruism was never your strong suit on Earth."

James puckered his lips and glanced at the ceiling, the way people do when they are searching for an acceptable answer. He said, "Well, I guess the difference is that back then, I was only interested in myself. I wanted to succeed, get rich, and have powerful friends in high places."

James sighed and continued, "You know, sometimes I really do miss those days. I mean, my life was exhilarating."

"So, what has changed?" asked Mercio. "Why do you want to help people now?"

"Well, there is no motivation to succeed here. There is no 'getting ahead' here. You know what I mean. I may as well help people. I've got nothing else to do."

Mercio shook his head with a disappointed look on his face. "Uhh… James, you are talking yourself right out of a good report."

James shot back with a tinge of anger in his voice. "Look, Mercio, I am just trying to be upfront with you. I thought we are supposed to be honest."

"Yes, we are, James. But I must admit, I was hoping you might have a different reason for helping others."

"Well, does it really matter why? I am doing it, aren't I? And… honestly… it feels good."

Mercio laughed. "Okay, James, your answer is not textbook, but I guess I'll take what I can get right now. After all, this is why we're here. You are learning that helping people can help you as well. That's a positive step."

James nodded.

"Well, James, that's about all I have. The big thing now is to make sure you keep going and make your appointments. Is that okay with you?"

James smiled and laughed. "Yes, it is." James needed to say more, but it was the most positive meeting he had with Mercio in a long time. He wondered if he should take a small victory and plan to present his case at the next meeting. He sat still, thinking. *Mercio is in a good mood today, now is as good a time as any to ask him.*

James asked, "Mercio, can I ask you a couple of questions?"

"Shoot."

"Number one, when will I graduate to the 3rd Land of Reform? And number two, I met this woman. Her name is Ellen. I want to ask about her getting out of here too. She deserves to graduate, too, more than I do. Lastly, Mercio, I really like her, like a lot… I was wondering if there is any way… I mean, if there is any way… if we can spend some… well, you know… some alone time together?"

Mercio took a deep breath, sighed, and leaned back in his chair. Without saying a word, he glanced over at the window and shook his head again.

"James, let's handle the third matter first. I have seen Ellen. I know who she is. In fact, I am friends with her Angel Counselor. She is a beautiful woman, and I am glad the two of you have hit it off. While that is all fine and dandy, there is a problem, James. The rules are very clear. There is no sexual activity here in the Land of Reform. Sexual pleasure is a reward of Heaven. James, this is not Heaven. So, the answer is no."

"But is it really a big deal?" asked James, "You know, would I really get in trouble?"

"Yes, it really is, and yes, you would get in trouble."

James anticipated this reply. He jumped out of his chair and raised his hand protesting, as if he was addressing a key witness, trying to manipulate the jury. "You know that I know the rules, Mercio. I was just hoping… Couldn't you find a little way to make an exception? It's not like the old days, Mercio. Look, I really like her. I have never met anyone like her. Hell, we even go to church together almost every day! Sorry for the language!"

Mercio answered in a firm voice. "James, I know what you want and why. However, the answer is no. I am sorry. That is the rule, and if you ask me, it is a damn-oops!... It's a good rule!"

Mercio continued, "Now, for the other matters. James, you are doing well. Nevertheless, I am sorry. You are not ready to graduate yet. And as for Ellen: You don't know her situation. Only her Angel does." He paused and said, "But I have to tell you. Your concern for her and your love for her shows you are opening yourself up to others, and that is a good thing."

Mercio made a quick note in the file.

James rolled his eyes. He was tired of getting stonewalled. "Mercio. I have to protest. I have been here for over five years! How long does it take? This is ridiculous!"

James sat back down, thoroughly discouraged, but not ready to throw in the towel on getting his way.

"It is not for you to know how long it takes, James. By the way, it has just barely been five years yet. To answer your question, I do not know the time. I just know if you are nearing being ready. When I see that, I will apply. You are getting closer, but you are not ready."

James started to speak, then stopped.

Mercio said, "James, you must trust that it will work out. Keep up your friendship with Ellen and keep following the program."

James put his head in his hands. "I am frustrated Mercio, I don't know how much longer I can do this."

Mercio put his hand on James' shoulder. "James, take courage. You are going to make it. Ellen is too. I have a feeling that you two will be going to the next level very close to each other. Who knows, maybe you will go all the way up the line. Your friendship is helping you both. True love is capable of wondrous things."

James could only reply with a faint smile. He did not come here to be rebuffed. He got up to leave, but Mercio stopped him.

"James, I almost forgot. Before you go, there is one more thing I need to talk to you about and please listen carefully. My supervisor has advised me that there may be trouble brewing in the various Lands of Reform. We are urging everyone to keep an eye out for anything unfamiliar or suspicious. If you do see anything come to me immediately. Do you understand?"

"I haven't seen anything yet; everything is always the same around here," James replied.

With a serious look on his face, Mercio said, "Okay, but please remember to come to me if you do."

"Will do, boss," James said, looking over his shoulder as he walked out the door, dejected.

Chapter 14

The springtime of his sixth year in the 4th Land of Reform found James hitting his stride. His love for Ellen was deepening, and his appointments with Mercio were back on track. He had even turned the corner with his respect for Mercio. He now looked forward to his monthly meetings. Besides Ellen, James realized that Mercio was the only person who understood him. James would often find himself telling Ellen, "Mercio gets me."

But that was before James found out about an attorney at a nearby house. One morning James overheard some people talking about a lawyer who had punched his Angel Counselor square in the face. The word was that the lawyer had been in the 4th Land of Reform for over 16 years. He apparently demanded to be promoted, and when he was told no, he hauled off and punched his counselor. What alarmed James more than anything was that he heard that this lawyer had been a model citizen.

After hearing the story, James went straight up to his room and collapsed on the floor in despair. He had already been there six years, and he had resigned himself to the fact that he would have to be there a while longer, but James was thinking months, not years. He could never stand being there 10 more years. He stayed on the floor, curled up in a fetal position for hours, grieving at his sudden revelation.

The following morning, he had recovered some. He met Ellen at breakfast, and his despair began to leave him. Her beauty, her presence, her smile always lifted him. He realized this day that for the first time in his adult life, he actually loved someone. And more, for the first time in his life, he suddenly knew what it felt like to be in love. His desire to have her sexually did not matter anymore. He just wanted to be with her all the time.

Ellen ate her breakfast slowly. She could tell something was on James' mind. "James, are you all right this morning? You seem quiet."

"I'm okay. I was just shaken up hearing about that lawyer."

"Oh, yes, I heard."

"What's going to happen to him?" James asked.

"I heard there is going to be a trial. They say hitting your Angel Counselor is very serious. It might land him in Hell. But I heard too, that he has some legitimate grievances."

"Yes!" James replied, scoffing, "Don't we all."

Ellen did not answer. After she finished, she asked, "James, are you ready to go to church?"

"Sure," he said. They put their trays away and walked out to the pathway leading over the hills to the church. Ellen was unusually quiet during their walk. James did not press her to talk. He had plenty on his mind knowing it would be another nine years before he reached the number of years that attorney had reached.

After church, they strolled up to the inland lake and sat on one of the benches watching four white swans sail around the water. James held Ellen's soft hands, watching her stare out at the swans. He could feel that she was burdened this morning. He tried to clasp her hands as lovingly as he could, hoping to give her comfort somehow. After a long while, she said, "James, long ago, I told you that I was not ready to share with you how I arrived here. Do you remember?"

"Yes, I do. I have always wondered, but it doesn't matter. I love you." He put his arm around her and pulled her closer. She rested her head on his shoulder, taking in the tender moment.

"I love you too, James, but I've been thinking about it. I want you to know… to know everything about me." She raised her head from his shoulder and moved away slightly so she could face him.

"James, when I was alive, I mean, on Earth, I was not a very nice person."

He started to interrupt, to tell her it wasn't important for him to know, but she stopped him. "No, please, James, I have to get this off my chest." She continued, "I was very selfish. I had a husband once, but we divorced. I had a lot of girlfriends, and we spent most of our time at night clubs drinking. I had lots of men and lots of lovers over the years. But the main thing was that I lived only for myself. I had no thought of God or anyone else. I thought I didn't have time for God and other people, family, and such."

James tried to help by saying, "Ellen, I'm sorry. I've told you about me, you know I was an even worse person. It's okay."

"I know it is okay, now, but I need to tell you the rest." She wiped a tear from her cheek, paused, and continued. "People were trying to warn me, James. Family, even our old Parish priest, even some of my friends. But I rebuffed them all. I thought they were all stupid and prudish. I was smarter than them, and they had no right to judge me. James, they were trying to help me."

James said nothing, letting her go on. "This went on for years. Finally, near the end, there was a time I was getting wild, partying and getting drunk, even sometimes high, four or five nights a week. I had two different lovers, and I was out of control. Anyway, one night I was driving home and was very drunk. I passed out at the wheel and got into a head-on collision… I killed a man, his wife, and their three young children. They all died. So, did I, and I have to live with that every day, James. That is my dark secret."

James lowered his head and waited a few moments. He took her by the hand and said, "I'm sorry, Ellen. That must be difficult."

She was trying to stop the tears that were escaping from her eyes, "It is, James. My Angel has assured me that that family I killed are all happy in Heaven. Still, I destroyed a family and lost my chance to ever reconcile with my own family. I miss my sisters and parents. They are all still there... on the Earth. I never got to say goodbye."

James sat still with her for a long while, neither of them saying a word. His desire to be close to Ellen was growing. Her words, "I never got to say goodbye," and her broken heart at the tragedy, stayed with him.

It was about a week later that he studied the stars again. There it was, again, plain as day, the Big Dipper and the Little Dipper. He was sure of it. James picked up his old quest, reasoning again that if he could see them, then Earth and his old life, could not be too far away. He thought to himself: *There must be a way to get back. The Angels obviously go back and forth. Ellen would be so happy. We could start a new life together.*

James' impatience was fighting to get the best of him, and it was not a difficult fight. Parts of the old James were creeping back. One day, after feeling particularly low, he again found himself thinking about an exit strategy. *I shouldn't be thinking these things,* he thought. *But what if I can find a way out?*

Chapter 15

James was walking out of church when he first noticed them. There were three unfamiliar people, a man and two women he had never seen before. James did not bother to speak with them, but they caught his eye because the two women were extremely attractive.

A few days later while sitting in church James noticed one of the women sitting on the other side of the aisle right across from him. James admired her long dark hair and striking features. She noticed

James looking at her, turned toward him, smiled, and discreetly waved. James, feeling a little foolish at having been caught staring at her, smiled and waved back. He did not think much more of it.

After services that day, Ellen left right away to meet with her counselor. So, James began the walk home by himself. He was about halfway home, at the bend in the road near the top of the hill, when he heard a woman's voice.

"Hey, wait up."

He turned to see the woman from church, running to catch up with him. When she got close, she smiled, "Hi, I am new here. I wanted to introduce myself."

He extended his hand to meet hers, "Oh hi. My name is James."

"I am Marian. It is nice to meet you, James."

James felt flattered that she stopped him. She was a real beauty. He asked, "I haven't seen you before. How long have you been here?"

"Longer than I want to be and hopefully not for much longer." She was baiting him.

"What do you mean by that?" asked James, lowering his voice and looking around to see if anyone was near.

"Well, I heard there is a way out of here. Some friends of mine say they have found it."

James quickly looked around again, seeing if anyone was within earshot. He grabbed her by the arm and said, "Hey, let's step over here. It's a little more private."

Ignoring his better instincts, James heard himself continue, "It's funny you should mention that because I want to get out of here too, and I want to bring one of my friends. Can you help us?"

The woman paused and said quietly, "I can if you join with us. The thing is, we need a few helpers to make it work. Maybe this meeting is more than a chance."

"Helpers? What do you need helpers for?"

"Well, we actually could get by with one. We need someone who has been here for a few years, someone who has access to the infrastructure, someone who works at the docks so that they can open the old portal. Once we do that, we can get back to our old lives on Earth."

"Are you kidding me? Is that possible?" James' mind was racing. As long as he could bring Ellen, getting back to his old life would be the sweetest thing he could think of.

"Oh, it's possible, James. No one remembers that when the Land of Reform was created, a doorway to the other side was built. Only a few people knew about it. The great Archangel Luminé was in charge of the entire original infrastructure plan, and only he and a few Archangels know about the portal."

"You mean it has been here the whole time? Where is this portal, and who is this Luminé?"

"James, you're joking, right. Everyone has heard of Luminé. He is the greatest of the Archangels. In fact, of all the Angels ever created, it is said that at one time, Luminé was the favorite of the Lords of Heaven."

Mercio's warning about keeping an eye out for anything out of the ordinary flashed through James' mind, but he quickly dismissed it. The thought of escaping was too much. He was already all-in. *My old life. The best lawyer the mob ever saw! But this time with Ellen by my side.*

The woman looked around, pretending to be worried someone might hear them. "I have said enough. I will meet you here tomorrow, a half-hour after church gets out. Tell no one. If you do, you will not be able to join us. Is that clear?"

"Yes, it is clear, but wait, I want… "

She turned and hurried away without letting him finish.

~ ~ ~ ~

James raced home as excited as he had ever been. He desperately wanted to tell Ellen and almost did. Still, ultimately, the woman's warning not to tell anyone kept him from doing so. The following day he had breakfast with Ellen and accompanied her to church. After church, he walked her home and pretended to go to his room. He immediately left and doubled back to the place halfway between the church. The woman, Marian, was there on the hilltop waiting for him.

As he approached, he could see her nervously looking around to make sure no one watched them.

"James, you are late."

"Sorry. I got here as fast as I could."

"Have you decided?"

James had decided, but he needed to know more, and he knew he held the leverage at this moment. "I have a couple of final questions. So, let's say I decide to help, exactly where is this… this portal?"

Marian's facial expression did not flinch, "I can't tell you unless you agree to help. Then, I have to run it by my associates. That does not matter now, James. The question I have for you is, do you want to join us?"

James nodded and raised his finger, signaling he needed a moment. He began to reason in his mind. *It will take a least another 5 to 10 more years to get out of the 4th Land of Reform. After that, I still have three more Lands of Reform to go through. It could be another 30 to 50 years before Ellen and I finally make it out.*

Marian interrupted his pondering. "Look, James, I'll get someone else. Forget it." She turned and started to walk down the hill.

James' eyes widened, "Wait, wait… hold on a second. I want to do this. I'm in."

Marian paused, keeping her back to him. A wicked smile came across her face, accompanied by a look of immense satisfaction. She took a deep breath, softened her smile, and stepped closer, searching his eyes as if to validate his commitment. "Are you sure? We do not have time to waste. You have to be in or out. I need your final answer now. What is it?"

"I'm in!"

"All right. There is one more thing. I need to get the final approval of my associates. I will meet you here tomorrow afternoon at 2. Again, tell no one, or you are out. Is that clear?"

"Yes, it is clear. Thank you." James smiled and started back for his home.

Marian stopped him. "James, wait."

James stopped, fearing she was changing her mind. He turned. "Yes?"

"Remember, tell no one. Do you understand? No one! Not even your pretty friend. If you do, the deal is off."

James nodded and said in a dead-serious tone, "Don't worry. I understand completely."

~ ~ ~ ~

When James arrived at the house, he went straight to his room. He had never been so excited in his life, not even since he received his first big payoff from a mob trial victory, complete with a weekend at Bobby's Catskill's resort house accompanied by one of the sexiest strippers Bobby's mob money could buy.

James closed the door behind him and began to laugh. He dropped to his knees, exclaiming, "Thank you, God! Thank you, God! I have found the way. I knew I would!"

He stayed still for a few minutes letting the feeling of victory that had so long eluded him resonate with his soul. He wanted to run and tell Ellen, but he knew how to keep a secret, and this was a time to do just that. He could tell her when it was time. It would have to wait until then.

James got up and went over to the window. He looked out into the distance in the direction of the administrative offices for his region. He thought of Mercio for a moment. He wondered what he might say if he suddenly found out James had escaped. He reasoned with Ellen by his side he could make a new start, even as a mob attorney, but this time a kinder, gentler one, who was in love with a beautiful woman and didn't need the sordid lifestyle that came along with mob work.

At 3 p.m. that afternoon, James could think of nothing except going home during the hour of contemplation of past sins. Near the end of the hour, he began to worry. He said aloud, "What if this costs me more years? What if I have to start over? I won't be able to handle it!"

He was quiet for a few moments. Then a new worry hit him. He clenched his fist and exclaimed aloud, "What if Ellen won't come? Then what?"

He threw his Bible down and walked across the room, talking to himself outloud. "Calm down, James. Ellen will come. And you're going to do it differently this time. Mercio will see. And Marian's associates are going to approve of you. Now relax, because you are going home!" He dropped to his knees again, this time weeping tears of happiness. He had weighed all the risks and exhausted all possibilities, and he was willing to move forward.

~ ~ ~ ~

The following day James went purposefully late to breakfast. He was hoping to avoid Ellen entirely, but she waved him down. He sat quietly and made an excuse he was not feeling well. He hardly spoke with her, except for a little small talk, and when they were finished, he made an excuse to miss church services.

He went straight to his room and nervously watched the clock tick by painfully slow until finally, it was 1:45 in the afternoon. He planned to meet Marian at 2 p.m. and find out whatever she needed to tell him, then get home in time for the Hour of Contemplation of Past Sins, then leave for work at the docks right after supper.

At 1:45 p.m., he put on a cap and went downstairs, careful not to speak with anyone. He headed out the door and onto the pathway toward the church, which would lead him to the rendezvous point with Marian.

When he reached the hilltop, Marian was not there. James checked his watch. He was on time. He walked over to some nearby boulders just off the path and sat down. Over an hour later, he knew they had decided against him joining, so he went home, dejected, but at the same time encouraged. He had been right. There was a way out. Now, he was sure he would find it.

Chapter 16

That evening, after supper, James went alone out onto the grounds in a panic. "I've been set up," he said aloud as he began walking faster. "Mercio did this to test me, and I failed. This is trouble. I am in big trouble."

He began walking toward Mercio's office, anxiously thinking of how he would explain his way out of it. *I'll tell him I was trying to flesh them out. I'll tell him it was my training as a mob lawyer to flesh out the opposition that gave me the idea, and… that I was going to… make a citizens arrest.*

He looked at his watch. It was now 5:45. He hoped Mercio would still be there and began to pray as he walked, "I'm sorry, God. I messed up. I am going to really change. Just get me off the hook this… "

Suddenly a voice, "James?"

James stopped in his tracks. He turned to see who was calling him. It was from Marian. He closed his eyes momentarily, as every thought of being set up and repenting for participating in this scheme suddenly vanished. "What are you doing here?"

"I was looking for you."

"But you were not there at 2."

"James, we were supposed to meet at 1." Marian was lying. She had purposefully not shown up and had been spying on him all day. Of course, James failed the test, as he was clearly on his way to see his Angel Counselor, but Marian needed to know how weak he was. They were stuck with him, and she knew it. His job at the dock made him the absolute best candidate.

"You said, 2! I am sure."

"James, sorry. I know what I said. Anyway, are you still interested?"

"Yes, yes, I am."

She smiled, "Good because I have some news." She paused again for effect and said, "You're in. My associates have accepted you and your friend."

"Yes!" he said aloud, clenching his fist. Instantly, the old adrenalin began coursing through his veins. The victory was near, very near, and he could already taste his freedom.

Marian looked around and said, "Walk with me. Let's head back to the rendezvous point. It will be safer there."

They headed back to the top of the hill halfway from the church and his home, with neither saying a word. When they reached the top, Marian led the way off the path over to nearby boulders. She sat and waited for James to sit. "Now listen carefully, James. Here is the deal. You will be opening the ancient portal in advance on the night we are escaping. The portal is inside a cave, six feet below the water's surface behind the dock where the transport boats arrive. There is an underwater tunnel in the face of the cliff which ascends to a chamber. Once you crawl inside, you will be able to stand up, walk, and breathe.

This chamber leads directly to the portal, which is currently locked and has been locked for thousands of years. *Do you have all that*?"

James began to show some signs of concern. Marian quickly took control. "James, I asked, do you have all that?"

"Yes, Yes!" James said. He was going to have to hear it again to be sure, but he dared not feign even the slightest hint of weakness or stupidity.

Marian glared at him, "James, my freedom, as well as yours and Ellen's, depends on you getting this right."

"Yes, I understand. Go on."

"Fine," Marian said, cautiously sitting back slightly to size him up. She then looked around again to make sure no one was near, and leaned forward. "All right, next month, on one of the nights when you work the transport dock, as soon as your shift ends, you will slip behind the guardhouse, go under the dock, and swim along the surface of the water until you find the place marking the opening. You will swim down into the opening in the cliff wall and swim through the short section of cave into the chamber. You will only have to be under water for 30 seconds or so until you reach the inside of the chamber. Then you will climb out of the water onto the chamber surface. You will be able to breathe and stand up. You will then follow the path for about 40 feet to the back of the chamber. At the back is a wide crevice, big enough to walk in. This crevice is the short passage that leads to the portal."

Marian stopped, "Do you have all that?"

"Yes."

"Good, now, once you are there, James, you will use this key to unlock the portal." She pulled a large golden key out from under her shirt and slipped the string it was on from around her neck. James went to grab it, but she pulled it away. "Not now, James, later, on the day. You will have it on the day."

"You've got to be kidding me," James said, flabbergasted, but also nervous and slightly in doubt of her motives. He stood up and said, "It can't be that simple. How am I going to get into a cave wall under the water?"

Marian quickly looked around to make sure he was not drawing attention. "Sit down, James, quickly!"

After he sat, she said, "James, there is an ancient marking in the cliff several feet below the waterline. You will be able to feel it. The opening is several feet below the marking. The docks were built over it. No one even remembers it."

James took a deep breath. "Okay, so let's say that all works. What is the catch? Wait, forget the catch. Why don't you unlock it yourselves?"

Marian looked around, then turned to him, and coolly said, "James, we have been watching you. We did not pick you by accident. Our helper has to work down at the docks. You just drew the luck of the draw because you lock up at night. Don't you get it, James? You got lucky."

Marian paused. "There are several other people we can use James, but as I said, it is now too late to back out."

James thought for a moment, weighing his options. He calmed his nerves and asked, "How long will it take to open the portal?"

Marian replied, "It will take exactly ten minutes to slip through the back of the dock into the water, swim into the chamber, climb out and unlock the portal, and then come back out."

"I really don't know what to say. How long do I have to think about this?"

"James, my associates will not be happy to hear about these games you are playing. You have *zero* time. There is no backing out now, James. Unless you want to invite serious trouble."

"What kind of trouble?" James asked in a defiant tone.

"James, do you remember the bad men from the mafia you used to work for. My associates are much worse men than that. One, in particular, is a man who would make your mafia buddies look like girl scouts. He has already told me to warn you it will not go well for you or Ellen if you try to back out now. He mentioned the words 'painful and pieces'."

James was quiet for a moment. He believed her threat, and he did not know why. He decided he was already too far in. He asked, "Wait, what happens after I open the portal?"

Marian stood up, smiling. "After you open the portal, you simply return to your post. You then lock up at night like normal. You then go home and wait. We have planned a diversion several miles away from the dock at 2 a.m.. As soon as the diversion begins, you will bring Ellen to the dock. We will meet at the hillside behind it. We will all walk into the docks, with your help, open the gates, and go under the water into the cave and out through the portal, to *freedom*!"

"Wait, what is on the other side of the portal?"

"None of us know exactly where it comes out. But the rumor is it opens into the Ancient Garden of Eden."

"The Garden of Eden!" James exclaimed. "That's not real. This is a hoax!"

Marian grabbed him by the shirt. "It is not a hoax, James. I was there when my associate discovered all of this. The Garden of Eden is real. It is hidden and nearly covered with sand in modern-day Iraq. But the portal supposedly opens in another cliff cave that used to overlook the Garden. It was at the back of a waterfall that flowed right past the ancient Tree of the Knowledge of Good and Evil. We were shown a map. Trust me it is still there."

"Where is the water then?"

"It was all covered by sand and desert. But the cliff where the waterfall fell from is still there. And the opening in the cliff is there, and it leads to a nearly identical chamber that leads to the other side of the ancient portal."

James was satisfied now. No one could make up such an outlandish story. "Modern-day Iraq, huh. I guess that will do. All right, I am ready."

"I will contact you several days in advance. Remember. If you speak a word to anyone, including Ellen, you will not be coming with us, and you will face the consequences. Is that understood?"

"Yes," James said.

"I will be in touch… don't try to contact me." She smiled at him, nodded, observing the expression on his face for any hint of doubt, then turned and left.

Chapter 17

As the days and weeks passed, James desperately wished there was not so much time in between his agreeing to the plan and the actual execution of the plan. With each passing day, seeds of doubt were pouring into his mind. It was Mercio, more than anything, causing his doubts. James had come to respect him, and he began imagining what Mercio would think of him and how much he would disappoint him.

In his mind, he rationalized that Ellen was his reason for escaping, concluding whatever disappointment he caused Mercio would be worth it, and even perhaps understood by Mercio, once they got through to the other side. He would be free to love her and live a new life with her. He imagined the excitement on her face when he would finally tell her of the plan!

Soon, the day was fast approaching, and his anxiousness was beginning to show. While exiting church one morning, Ellen stopped outside the doors and pulled him aside onto the grass near the entryway. "James, what is going with you? You seem nervous and distracted lately."

"Who? Me? Nothing is going on."

"James, something is wrong. What is it?"

"I guess… I guess I'm just happy."

Ellen looked confused, "James, just the other day, you were telling me how sick of this place you are."

James felt trapped in his lie, but only for a moment. "Well, actually Ellen, I have decided, just today, not to worry about being here anymore." As he said it, he scanned over her head quickly to see if Marian was there today. He had not seen her in a while, and it was beginning to worry him.

Ellen replied, "Well, at least you have hope!"

Her tone caught him off guard and brought his attention back to her. "What?"

"Darn it, James, aren't you paying attention to me?"

"I am… I didn't hear what you said?"

"I said at least you have hope!" She turned, but not before James noticed the tears starting to fall from her eyes.

He ran up and tried to grasp her arm, but she shook him off, storming along the path toward their house.

"Ellen, wait! Please! I'm sorry!"

She turned her head slightly, her face now red with tears, "You only care about yourself, James!"

James stopped and looked back to see if Marian was at church. He could not see her, so he turned and ran ahead of Ellen. "Ellen, please. What's wrong."

"I'm going to be here for a long time. That's what's wrong."

"Why? I don't understand. I thought things were going well."

"Well, apparently, my counselor doesn't think so. He said my answers in our latest meetings show that I am just going through the motions, that I am not really sorry for my past life."

"That's bullshit!" said James loudly.

Ellen did not reply. Angry or not, she was fully aware there was no swearing in the Land of Reform. To do so was a big offense. She quickly looked around and saw two people looking at them, but they quickly looked away. She turned and looked behind her and saw an Angel not far away talking with someone. The person he was talking to looked over, staring momentarily. Still, he turned back to the Angel and resumed his conversation. Ellen breathed a sigh of relief and grabbed James by the arm.

"James, you can't say that."

"I don't care!" James exclaimed loudly. "It is… " He stopped. In the distance he saw Marian walking slowly toward them along the path. He immediately realized he was drawing undue attention.

James said to Ellen, "Ellen, hold on to hope. I will… I will talk to my counselor. He may have some pull. I am going to take a walk and blow off some steam. I'll see you back at the house."

He hugged her tightly, hoping to convey hope to her, the hope he knew was genuine, and now that he had seen Marian, imminent.

James began walking back toward the church. He periodically looked back to make sure Ellen was heading home. Within moments she was over the hilltop and out of sight. He turned his attention ahead to Marian, now only 500 feet away.

As he approached, she turned and nodded to two individuals another several hundred yards behind her. She motioned to James and walked off the path. "James, what were you and Ellen arguing about?"

"That's none of your business," said James.

"James, you forget, you're with us now, and she will be. Everything is our business. Now, unless you want trouble, tell me what you were arguing about."

James grimaced and told Marian of their conversation. She listened intently and nodded, showing she was satisfied. "All right, James. But remember, you cannot say anything to her. Not until we all meet on the hillside that night. Is that understood?"

"Yes, fine. When are we going?"

"A week from tonight."

James' eyes lit up. A wide sinister smile came over his face. He had not smiled like this since the day he got Bobby off, arguably the best day of his life.

Marian asked, "Are you ready?"

"Yes, I've been over it a hundred times in my mind. I'm ready. Do you have the key?"

"Yes, you will get it on the day. I will meet you after church. You cannot walk with Ellen that day. Make an excuse and wait until everyone is almost gone. Then meet me right here."

Chapter 18

Two days later, James had his scheduled monthly meeting with Mercio. He thought long and hard about not attending. Only his promise to speak to him about Ellen compelled him to go. He knew it did not matter, but he hoped an encouraging word from Mercio could be shared with Ellen to give her a small bit of hope, just in case things backfired, or in case she would not go.

James walked anxiously to the appointment. Going, he risked Mercio discovering something. Not going would bring Mercio knocking on his door. He walked up the steps and down the hall, and to the office. Mercio was sitting at his desk, pouring over James' file.

"Hello, Mercio."

"James, you're on time. That is nearly a first."

James put on a fake smile. The last thing he wanted to do was act unusual, and he was not off to a good start.

Mercio held up the file, "Okay, James, give me a moment. I have a few more things to review."

James watched Mercio's eyes dart back and forth as he made his way down the report from James' new house administrator. When he reached the bottom, he paused. He put the file down flat on the desk. "So, James, can you explain this report? Can you tell me what is really going on?"

James' eyes widened. *Does he know? He can't. It's impossible.* "What do you mean? Did I do something?"

"No, that's just it. It's a perfect report." Mercio paused, then said, "It seems a little too perfect. What has changed James? It says you haven't missed church since we spoke. It says you've been at all prayer services. Need I go on?"

James chuckled nervously, "No, you... no. You don't have to go on. Look, Mercio, what do you want? You said you wanted me to improve. I'm improving."

Mercio sat back, "Sorry to have upset you, James. I guess you're right. I did ask you to improve, and it looks like you've really applied yourself."

"Thank you, Mercio." As soon as he said it, he felt like a crumb knowing that Mercio would be recalling this conversation in a few days.

"Well, James, is there anything you'd like to discuss or request?"

James thought about asking for Ellen but decided against it. "No, everything is just fine, actually. I'll... see you next... meeting... next month."

"Okay," said Mercio.

James stood and turned to leave.

"Oh James, there is one more thing. Don't forget about my warning."

"Warning?"

"Remember to be on the lookout for suspicious activity or people. The warnings are very strong that the forces of darkness are up to something."

"Oh yes," James exclaimed. "I remember now. Don't worry, Mercio. I am keeping my eyes peeled."

~ ~ ~ ~

As James left the meeting, Mercio smiled, thinking how pleasant their meeting had been. James had not made any requests. He had no complaints, and he did not ask for any special favors. Mercio stood up, smiling, folded up the file, and said aloud, "James is doing well. He has really turned things around quickly."

Mercio resumed his duties and got busy, but within five minutes, he dropped what he was doing and stood up, exclaiming aloud, "James is up to something!"

The rest of the day and all the way home, he could not shake the feeling about what might be behind James' strange behavior.

Later that night, the Angel Alexia arrived at Mercio's home in the 1st Heavenly Realm. She was a petite Angel, thin, with short blonde hair and dark green eyes. She was small compared to the towering Mercio. They had met over 20 years earlier and had been in a Season of Love together ever since. She knocked at the door, and Mercio opened. "Alexia, I didn't expect you. Come in."

"I told you I was coming over. Did you forget?"

"Oh, yes. I did forget. I'm sorry."

She stepped inside, "Are you, All right? I can feel the stress coming from you."

"It's probably nothing. I just have some difficult clients that worry me."

"Well, that's what happens when you spend the day counseling in the 4th Land of Reform. It's not exactly paradise."

"We'll talk about it after dinner. Come in."

During a joint training exercise between Splendora's and Gabriel's armies long ago, they had met by chance. It was love at first sight. Their work in their Realms kept them busy. Still, they made it a point to have dinner together twice a week, as well as spending most weekends together at one of their homes, either in the 1st Heavenly Realm or the 5th Heavenly Realm.

All through dinner, Alexia could tell Mercio was preoccupied. After finishing, she poured them both a glass of wine and led him over to sit in front of the fireplace. Mercio lit a small fire, and they sat back, sipping their wine and watching the flames.

She could feel his mind turning. He was far away. Finally, she said, "Mercio, you know we have been warned to keep watch for anything unusual going on. If your gut is telling you something, you may not want to ignore it. Could this client be involved?"

He exhaled, "You know, I'm not sure, Alexia. I kind of doubt it. He… he respects me. I like him. He's a lawyer."

"Oh, great. A lawyer. Sound like you know him pretty well."

"I do, and I care about him. I have been working with him for a long time and he has come a long way. Of all the lawyers I have met here in the Land of Reform, he is definitely the brightest. I know we are not supposed to develop close relationships with lower-level candidates, but I really like him. He is kind of my friend now."

"Mercio, we are not supposed to make friends with our clients. When you get too close, you can lose your perspective. I hate to tell you this, but it sounds to me like you've already crossed that line."

Mercio paused and put his wine down. "I have to get some air and clear my head." He stood up and walked out onto the patio. She followed him out. They stood by the balcony looking out at the stars in the night sky. He continued, "I'm all of a sudden worried James could be in trouble, or even worse, be involved in the trouble itself."

"You better not ignore your instincts. The Lords gave them to us for a reason."

"You're right. I'm going to put an Angelic guard on him for the next month or so. Thank you."

"You're welcome. I think it is wise. Better safe than sorry in times like these."

~ ~ ~ ~

First thing in the morning, Mercio assigned a covert guard to keep an eye on James. The surveillance began within a few hours. After several days, the guard reported to Mercio that James had been carrying on with his usual routine. He had not spoken to any strangers. They asked if they should continue, and Mercio told them yes.

Chapter 19

On the morning of the big day, James woke from his most peaceful night of sleep ever. He was ecstatic. He jumped up and looked around his room, "I'm kissing this joint goodbye!" The next time he woke up, he would be back on Earth, back to his old life and this time with Ellen.

He sat down on his chair and got dressed, glancing out the window at the typical, mostly cloudy day. The morning dragged on as it would never end. James went to church and told Ellen he was busy and would see her later. After everyone left the church, he lingered for a while, then went to the spot to meet Marian. She was waiting.

"Are you ready, James?"

"Yes, I am."

"All right, here is the key. Tell me the plan again."

James relayed the entire plan to her. Marian smiled, "We will see you tonight."

The rest of the day proved to be the longest of James' life. He purposefully stayed away from Ellen, not wanting to arouse any suspicions. Waiting until his shift was going to begin at 6 p.m. was more than he could bear. All he could think about was going home and starting a new life with Ellen.

Near 4:30, just before dinner, he heard someone knock at his door. James froze. He already knew who it was. *Mercio! What is he doing here!* He waited, considering pretending he was not in. Again, came another knock. James grimaced and walked over to open the door. "Who is it?"

There was another knock.

James asked louder, "Who is it?"

"Delivery for you, sir."

James shook his head. He opened the door a crack. It was not Mercio. It was Marian, disguised as a delivery person. "James, it's Marian. Open up."

James opened the door a little wider. He suddenly feared the worse. They were calling it off. He whispered excitedly, "What are you doing here?"

"I had to come and make sure you knew exactly what to do. Are you all set?"

"Yes. I start work at 6 p.m. and get off at 10 p.m. I am planning to go down to open the portal right after the 9:30 transport leaves. That will give me 20 minutes before the last transport arrives at 9:50. Then I will lock up the gates at 10:15."

"That will work," Marian said, smiling.

"James, one more thing, make sure you don't say anything to Ellen. Not until we gather at 2 a.m.. It's very important. Do you understand?"

"Yes! Yes! That's the plan. I got it. We will all meet at the hillside at 2. I will tell her then."

"Okay, James. This is it. I have to go." Marian adjusted her hat and walked back down the hall.

~ ~ ~ ~

Getting ready for work that night, James was as excited as he was nervous. Slipping on his work boots, he could not stop thinking this might be his last night ever in the Land of Reform.

He arrived at work and tended to the incoming ships. The first few hours of work passed uneventfully. After the 9:30 transport ship unloaded, and then set sail back to the judgment intake area, the dock was empty. James now had 20 minutes before the arrival of the final transport.

He checked his watch. He tied the key and flashed a light on a small rope, and put it around his neck. He took off his pants and shirt and squeezed himself through the opening at the back of the dock. He lowered himself into the water and began looking for the ancient marking along the waterline's stone face. After a couple of minutes, he found it. *It's here. I have it!*

He could directly see the dock floor and the lights shining through the cracks in the boards onto the water surface.

His mind was now racing. Putting his hands carefully on the stone cliff, he drew in a deep breath and pushed himself straight down under the water, feeling for the opening with his feet. *There… it's an opening.* He quickly pushed down further and grasped the upper part of the entrance ceiling with his hands. He panicked that he was running out of breath and went back up. Again, he surfaced and tried to calm his racing nerves. He took one more breath and went under. He found the entrance again and put his hands on the ceiling of the underwater cavern. He pushed in and began pulling himself along, half swimming, half crawling, with his hands along the underwater tunnel.

He was beginning to remember the sickening feeling from the day he died, when his lungs filled with black water. He was starting to panic and about to turn away when all of a sudden, his head broke through the water. He was in the chamber. *She was right! I'm in.*

He quickly fumbled to take the flashlight and key off his neck. He shined the flashlight and scoured the cave. He could see the floor ahead, and he swam for ten more yards. He climbed out of the water onto the cave floor. Everything was musty, wet, and old. An ancient, eerie feeling suddenly came over him. James took a deep breath and shined the light across the chamber. At the very end, he could make out a narrow passage. *That's it, the narrow passage! It's not very wide.* James thought *I would have to squeeze in sideways.*

As he turned sideways and inched his way in, he brushed aside a tangle of cobwebs with his flashlight. He was feeling extremely closed in, and with every step, he thought of turning back. He managed to go almost 10 feet into the narrow passage when he spotted the portal. At the end of the passageway, the passage widened enough to allow the door to open.

The portal door was magnificent and ancient-looking. Emblazoned on the bronze façade was the image of three people. James did not recognize them. They looked like gods or something. There were two males and one female. Above their image, a phrase of ancient-looking letters stared down at him. It was in some language or letters he did not recognize.

He pulled the key out of his pocket but fumbled and dropped it. The tunnel was too narrow to bend over, so he tried to lower himself to pick it up. It was extremely difficult. He could not get low enough because it was too tight of a squeeze. He looked at his watch.

Damn! I only have nine minutes left, think, think! He was starting to panic. *I got it!*

He backed up two feet and reached out with his foot to pull the key closer. He kept doing this until he finally got out of the tunnel. Then he went back in, this time being careful not to drop it again.

At last, he inserted the key into the portal door. *Perfect*, he thought, as the key clicked, and the latch dropped down. One push and the door would open, allowing for escape. James was curious and began to swing open the ancient door, but then he decided it could wait. He was almost out of time.

He backed out of the passage and lowered himself into the water. He swam out, squeezed himself back up through the dock floorboards, quickly dried off, and dressed. He was back at his dock post before the last transport arrived at 9:50 p.m. He quickly went to his post and blew the loud horn, then ran over and unlocked the large harbor gates and used the pulley to swing them gradually open. As they opened, he went back over to the dock while the ship entered and swung around to dock. James set the gangplank and watched all the new arrivals come ashore. He then raised the plank and waited for the ship to turn and head back out into the sea through the enormous gates. He used the pulley to pull the immense gates shut, locked them, and went home. He needed to find Ellen.

Chapter 20

James ran home and went straight to Ellen's room and knocked on her door.

"Who is it?"

"Ellen, it's James. Can you let me in? I have something important to tell you."

"James, it's already after 10. Can't it wait until tomorrow?"

"No, it can't. Sorry."

Ellen opened the door with a frown on her face, wearing her nightgown, "What is it, James?"

"Ellen, I have some fantastic news. I could not tell you earlier. You will never believe it. I have a way out of here… for us… You don't have to worry about being stuck here."

"Out of here? To where?"

"Ellen, it's fantastic. We are not just leaving. We are going back to our old life. Tonight!"

Ellen looked shocked. "What are you talking about, James? We already died! Are you crazy?" She started to close the door.

James put his hand on the door. "Ellen, please."

"No, James."

She closed the door.

James took a deep breath. He gently knocked. From inside, he heard, "What?"

He looked up and down the hall, then pressed his face close to the door. "Ellen, I met some people. They know the way out, the way back to the Earth."

Ellen opened again and stood with her arms crossed. "James, you are making no sense."

"Look," he said as he nervously glanced up and down the hall. "Let me come in. I'll tell you."

Ellen stepped aside with a guarded look on her face. James walked past her, then turned with an excited look on his face. "Close the door."

Ellen closed the door and crossed her arms again, "What do you have to tell me?"

"Ellen, this lady approached me about a month ago. She said they had a way out."

"A way out? Of here? There is no way out."

"No, there is. She knows this Angel named Luminé, and he told her about an ancient portal… and… "

Ellen interrupted him, "James, what have you done?"

He pulled out the key, brandishing it in front of her. "I opened it. I opened the portal, and tonight, we are going home."

"James, wait. *Who* did you say?"

"I opened it for us."

"No, *who* did… ?" Ellen was fumbling for the words, finally, she exclaimed in a panicked tone. "Did you say Luminé?"

"Yes, he is one of the favorite Angels of the Lords. I don't know why he's helping these people, but he is. Look, never mind that, listen. I need you to get dressed and make it quick. We have to go!"

"Oh, my God! What did you do?"

"That is what I am trying to tell you, Ellen. I helped them open the ancient portal, which is the old entranceway back to Earth, back to our old lives. We are meeting them in a couple of hours."

Ellen put her hands over her mouth. "James, please tell me you did not help them."

"Yes, what's wrong?"

"James, they tricked you!" she cried out, her voice trembling, "James, *Luminé is the devil!*"

"The what?"

Ellen yelled, "He is the Devil!"

James froze for several painful seconds. Then he pushed past Ellen and ran down the hall and the steps to the lobby. He grabbed the phone and feverishly dialed Mercio's home number.

Mercio answered. "Hello?"

"Mercio… Mercio, this is James… I… did… something really wrong… please you have to help me, like right now."

"James, slow down! What are you talking about?"

James could not think of any way to sugar-coat it, so he blurted it out. "I unlocked the ancient portal under the transport dock for Luminé."

Mercio's eyes widened, and his mouth froze.

He turned to Alexia and let the phone drop from his ear to his side. She looked at him strangely, wondering why he suddenly had a petrified look on his face.

Mercio put the phone back to his ear and asked, "Where are you?"

"I'm at the house. Please. You have to stop them. There is still time!"

"What portal? What are you talking about? Where?"

"Under the docks. I had to use a key to open it."

"A key! Stay there!" Mercio said, only because he did not know what else to say.

He put down the phone and stared dumbfounded at Alexia. "What happened?" she asked.

Hanging up the phone, he said to her, "We've got big trouble. Hurry, we have to alert the Lords and the Archangels."

"What happened?"

"It's James." He stared at her, blankly, "He opened the ancient portal for Luminé."

"The what?"

"I don't know what it means either, but it sounds like we have a major trouble."

To be continued…

James' journey is continued in the final books of the After Life Series.

His story is also published separately. It is called James: A Mob Lawyer Goes Too Far.

The Angel Sagas are continued in Book 4 of the series, Empire.

Click Here to View on Amazon.

Thank you for Reading

Help this sad Wittle puppy smile
by posting a Weview.

Review on Amazon

Follow me on Amazon

Join my Newsletter & Get Starry Night Free

Here or at **dpconway.com**

A Magical Short Story You'll Never Forget

Also by D. P. Conway

And much more to come

Acknowledgments

Mary and Colleen, thank you for your excellent ideas and first-class editing. Having both of you carefully and tirelessly team up to shape and refine this book has made it as much yours as it is mine.

For Elizabeth Dawson, aka Megan Franciscus. Megan you were there at the beginning to help me craft the foundational ideas and stories that became the heart of this book series. Thank you.

For Marisa, your love and encouragement, made it possible for me to write this series. Thanks for letting me spend all these years refining this series. I love you more than these words can say… *Cara Mia, Io ti amo. Solo tu femmina.*

For Carla Reid, who with her strength and flare inspired the Archangel Splendora. Carla, the joy I receive from your wonderful friendship can never be measured.

For Sadie Sutton, who inspired the Angel Sadie. Sadie, you really must be an Angel, because meeting you changed me forever. Always… my friend.

For Ed Markovich, King Edward, thank you for the years of your edits, ideas, and counsel.

For Reda Nelson, our long-time associate, who helped keep the ball rolling, and moving through seven long, difficult years.

Also, thanks to Jocelyn Caradang, Rosie Queen, Mary Greene, Angela Rabbitts, Annette Joseph, Bridget Mae Conway, Patrick Conway, and Christopher Conway (who thought of Legion), and all 50 or so test readers over the last five years.

And to Caroline Knecht, who really brought this story to its final form by doing some awesome developmental editing. Wow.

Special Thanks to Beta Readers Katie Schantz, Peggy Stewart, Collette Murray, Courtney McKirgan, and Sara Cornwell. Thanks also to Larry, Tanja, AJ, and the wonderful team at Books Go Social

Copyright & Publication

Daylights Publishing
5498 Dorothy Drive Suite 3:16
Cleveland, OH 44070

www.dpconway.com
www.daylightspublishing.com

Photo sources and credits are listed at www.dpconway.com

Cover: Nate Myers, Colleen Conway Cooper
Contributing Story Editor: Elizabeth Dawson
Developmental Editor: Mary Egan, Colleen Conway Cooper
Editor: Connie Swenson
Final Developmental Editor: Caroline Knecht

Made in the USA
Monee, IL
20 December 2020

54945710R00152